CHRISTMAS
IN JULY

CHRISTMAS IN JULY

A NOVEL

ALAN MICHAEL PARKER

DZANC
BOOKS

DZANC BOOKS

5220 Dexter Ann Arbor Rd.
Ann Arbor, MI 48103
www.dzancbooks.org

Library of Congress Cataloging-in-Publication Data

Names: Parker, Alan Michael, 1961- author.
Title: Christmas in July : a novel / Alan Michael Parker.
Description: First edition. | Ann Arbor, MI : Dzanc Books, [2018]
Identifiers: LCCN 2017027310 | ISBN 9781945814464 (softcover)
Subjects: LCSH: Interpersonal relations--Fiction. | Terminally ill
  children--Fiction. | Teenage girls--Fiction.
Classification: LCC PS3566.A674738 C48 2018 | DDC 813/.54--dc23
LC record available at https://lccn.loc.gov/2017027310

First US edition: January 2018
Interior design by Michelle Dotter

Printed in the United States of America

10   9   8   7   6   5   4   3   2   1

CONTENTS

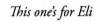

This one's for Eli

HELLO. THIS IS YOUR MOTHER.

Hello. This is your mother. Your father thinks you should hire a different lawyer. We were having breakfast, and you know how he is, I hate when he reads from the paper like I'm not here, he does it all the time, just starts in and I'm supposed to listen, like that's why I married him. As though I don't have my plans for the day, or my birds aren't right out the window, they need me, or I'm not thinking about anything myself. Really. I believe the man waits for my tea to cool—it's just so evil. But no, he didn't read some awful story to me, not this morning, which he did the other day, all about a poor child who was in the war and had to fly to England in a helicopter for treatment, and they gave her a white kitten, a stuffed animal, because she couldn't have a real one in the helicopter and definitely not in the hospital, that poor girl, something about her oxygen. I think they give dogs. But there are a lot of kittens in England—I don't know why I know that, I just do. Must have seen it somewhere.

Your father said he doesn't like your lawyer. He was looking up at me, you know that look—it's those new half-glasses he has, they're just perfect for a judgmental man—and he said, "She needs to fire that horse's ass." That's what your father thinks. And I'm telling you what he said only to help you, Angela.

Call me later. Byyeee.

●

Hello. This is your mother. I know I just called. I can picture your face, you shouldn't make that face, it's not flattering. But I wanted to tell you that your father had some kind of procedure done. I don't know what it was, but I found the bill. I think it's a bill. I'll show it to you next time— I hid it. If it's a bill, they'll send it again, right? So he'll just think he misplaced it. That's what I'm calling to ask, Angela. I'm sure it's nothing. They'll send another one.

I'll be home for an hour or so, and then I'll be out. I know you're at work, so don't worry about it. I know I shouldn't bother you at work, but I love to hear your voice, even on the machine. You have such a pretty voice, you should sing more. Do you still sing when you get dressed? Do the boys sing like you used to when you were a little girl?

If you don't get this message during the day, because you're at work, that's fine. Call me. Byyeee.

●

Hello. This is your mother. Do you remember that Murcherson child who lived on the corner? Well, I guess he's not a child now, and his poor cousin, what was her name, so sad, we met her at the train station that one time, she was a Murcherson, only she had a different last name, she was on the other side, do you remember her? She was in the newspaper, your father sent it to you. I think she went to school with your brother—isn't she older? I know she's not the same age as that Murcherson child—who's a man now, well, by it all goes, doesn't it? That Murcherson man is painting his parents' house again. I think it's nice he cares, that's what I think. Your father says it looks like ditchwater. That someone could just go and drown, that's what. So how am I supposed to step outside, with all those painters right there? Your father says they're stealing.

That's all. I was just calling to tell you what your father said. I think he might be right—the man's got to get something right, much as he talks, you know, the monkey and the nut and all that. The house is an ugly color, that's the truth. But if you don't let them in the house, how could they be stealing? That part he's wrong about. True, Mr. Murcherson never did get on with his grandfather, leastways that's what I heard, he was the one that built that house. I think he built that house, it was before our time. Lots of people don't get on with their people, Angela.

That's all. Oh, I said that. Maybe you can show me how to use the camera on my phone, and I can take a picture of that house and then you can call me, and we'll see what we find in the picture. Sometimes I think I watch too much TV, it makes me so...I don't know. I just watch everything now. Not that I watch what's on, it's just on, so what's the difference, that's what I always say.

Home later. Byyeee.

•

That I ever call my mother back is God's own miracle. As Janet says, "She's like Fox News, your mother, all by herself." Too true—all that worrying about everything, and then when something actually goes wrong, she's just so smug, because she knew, the whole country's wrong and she predicted it, didn't she. What I think: all that blame she's carrying around can bend a person permanently, it's too heavy. It can gather inside and make a person different.

I don't want to live like that—I'm trying not to—because it's not the answer. Because that's what all of this is about, maybe not the answer, the answer, but more about how I want to live, or how anyone does. Deciding how to live: I'm deciding. Lucas and Fremont are at their dad's, and I've got the next three weeks—well, seventeen days, more precisely, since they left on Saturday and it's Tuesday already. But waste no time, Janet says, and she's right. Janet is Financial Services in the office, and she's the best friend a woman could ever have, plus she did two years of Accounting. Janet knows.

I'm not wasting time. Mr. Ramirez from around the corner and I are getting busy every night together, as they say on TV, and the sex's fun, and doesn't he have such a wonderful mustache, Mr. Ramirez. It's all I can do to keep from touching it when he talks, even though that wouldn't be polite. Sometimes during the day, when I close my eyes and touch something just above my upper lip, I can feel Mr. Ramirez's scratchy, stiff mustache. I can believe he's touching me—even if it's just the lip of my own coffee mug. It works better with the end of a paper clip, though.

Not wasting time is easier in the summer. Wouldn't that seem just the opposite of life when you're really young? That it's slower in the summer, and more of a waste? But I think time's easier to understand in July. I can't speak for other people, but my July here in Saxon Hills allows me to unfocus, fuzz out, and time's not wasted, time's part of me. I see what I see, but I'm thinking more. It lets me hear what I'm hearing, too. That might seem an odd statement—to hear what I'm hearing—but it's accurate. It's precise. I'm a precise person. You have to be, to be me.

When I walk to work on a July morning, and it's already hot, I take the little footbridge and then the path along the Green Way that the county built with the last bond when they voted down the School Bond, when the charter school monkey business with the vouchers and everything made people crazy and they put all of the staff on ten-month contracts, so now we only have three of us in the office through the summer. Walking slowly, or trying to remember to walk slowly, I can hear the woods and the bugs and the birds. I can't hear the wind, the air's too close for that, even at seven in the morning, and I'm not hearing the cars on the highway, or the garbage truck with that deep engine sound as the forklift picks up a dumpster, or the seventh-graders by the gym door—the racket the seventh-graders make is the worst—I'm only hearing what I'm hearing, I'm hearing my thoughts. That's usually a good thing first thing in the morning; my thoughts and the world around me come together, and I can hear them without all that riot or interference.

But I'm not quiet all the time, I'm not one of those people, I sure love that noisy noise, too, especially at night, when I want more noise, all the noise, I want to be in the ocean of noise and have it everywhere, every sound. I want the boys chasing each other in the house and out into the backyard, Lucas screaming about this toy or that, he's snotty-faced, and Fremont's laughing, and I've got a bottle of Bud and I'm in my housedress after work, and I follow them a little, and stop, and say, "Time out, time out! You two need to solve this yourselves. Be the jury."—that's a code phrase we have for problem-solving, what I wrote in the "Teen Empowerment Tips" handout I made for the school kids in trouble. Of course, sometimes Lucas just slugs Fremont, but the little one's not strong enough to hurt his big brother, and that's what Fremont wants, too, just to get under his little brother's skin. The look in Fremont's eyes, he's just like me that way—Fremont, who keeps stealing stuff and hiding his loot in a shoebox in his hockey bag, and who thinks I don't know.

Even then, unless it's bloody murder, I'm not watching the boys in a manner that makes them answer me. They're on their own. I turn back a little, I'm only peeking, and listening at the sliding screen door. I'm giving them a chance as brothers, in part because of the noise they make, they fill up the whole yard, it's exactly what I want. They should work out their differences together—which usually happens, but only after Fremont makes Lucas cry, or sits on his chest, or once in a while just gives back whatever toy to keep Lucas from blubbering.

That's when I sip my cold beer, and I listen to the CD, the guitar and the singer cranked, the music sexing up the moment, it's usually R&B and deep, and the whole house is making reverb. I'm in those waves of music, and it's filling all the corners and secrets in me, smoothing me inside, and I'm swimming and breathing in the bass and guitars and the throaty singer, and that's everything I want, all of that family and noise. It's drowning. It's love.

•

Hello. This is your mother. Your machine cut me off. Why don't you get a machine that doesn't cut a person off? I was saying something important, and now I forgot. You should teach me how to call and listen to my own message on your phone, and then I would remember, and I wouldn't have to bother you. I could say what I want. I'm not a bother, am I? Of course I'm not.

This isn't what I meant to say, but your father says that if Tommy thinks he can take you to the cleaners, he's got another think coming. Isn't that a funny thing to say—he's got another think coming. Sometimes, your father's such a card.

I'll be home tonight. Your father gets home at seven, but I'll be home before that. Byyeee.

•

During the summer months, the school's closed but the main doors stay unlocked, and Janet and I work at the front desk rather than back in our offices, in case someone comes. People show up with the kookiest questions, or they try to wriggle out of things—as if this weren't my job, to notice and check. I'm the registrar, after all, and no, your child cannot attend SHMS without your showing me three forms of identification and establishing that you live here. We usually accept some combination of a driver's license, a utility bill with your name on it, a military ID, a lease, a payroll stub, a W-2, a bank statement...think about all of those pieces of paper that say you're you, and be prepared to be you, when I ask, three ways. I don't care, of course, if you're you, but show me.

All of the pertinent information's on the Web, the World Wide Web we call it here, and there are handouts in the rack on the wall, along with the PTA's newsletter and the immunizations form, the emergency dismissal forms, and extra copies of my "Teen Empower-ment Tips"—I make sure that's always stocked—and the new handout on digital literacy, which tells you in English and Spanish how to get a free laptop if you're indigent, basically. There are children coming to school starving, but the District wants to give them a laptop. To eat? "To look up pictures on the World Wide Web of other starving families," says Janet.

I would be nowhere without Janet. She's my rock. A rock keeps you from being nowhere: it's a thing in the ground, and it makes the ground the ground. That's what Janet does for me. Only I wish her Nana weren't so sick in Chicago, because every day, I expect Janet to say that she's quitting, Nana needs her, family first. I would find that reasonable; I'm bracing for it. I'm clutching my heart through my blouse every time I see Janet make a face that will tell me she's leaving tomorrow.

Janet has a couple of kids, too, but they're older, and a husband she likes well enough. I guess that means she still loves him. Me, I don't love Tommy anymore—not that I love Seve, either, which is Mr. Ramirez's first name. Nice enough, Seve, but not much without that mustache. *Mr. Ramirez's mustache* is how I think about it. Of course I know that Seve is a whole person, but he's also *Mr. Ramirez's mustache*.

Our principal, Mr. Charlton, works in his office in the back all summer. He's the busiest man I know, with the most energy of any-one I've ever met, and a good principal, even though he wears those sleeveless sweaters that make him look like a piece of fruit stuffed in a bag that's too small. He can't control his weight, it yo-yos, and he ends up all sweaty and looks over-ripe when he puts on the pounds. He's such a bad dresser. Luckily the A/C wall units work in the front and back offices, or he would have a heart attack for sure. We keep the EST2s set on a higher temp when the classrooms are empty— we have to, or the District would have a conniption, and the stress would kill Mr. Charlton, who wouldn't live to see New Student Open House.

It's not all men in my life—there's Janet, and my mom—but sometimes, especially raising two boys, it seems like it's all men. Mr. Charlton's my boss, my dad bosses around my mom (although if you ask me, she's the one who handles feeding time in their little zoo), and Tommy's going to get whatever he wants in the settlement because of Mr. Ramirez's mustache. I started it, the end. We stopped loving one another pretty much at the same time, Tommy and I, but it was my decision to hook up with Mr. Ramirez, in the way that a decision happens and then you realize that you went and decided, that was the decision you made.

Mom and Dad don't know about Mr. Ramirez's mustache, or they wouldn't be such a pain. Mom wouldn't call me five times a day, every day since the boys went to stay with Tommy, and she wouldn't be crazy and worried about me or what I'll do without the boys these next three weeks, she would just be crazy and worried about something else, and Dad wouldn't notice. Sometimes I think her being crazy works to keep Dad from talking about anything important.

But it's worse. Because Fremont's been stealing things since Tommy left, or maybe even before, I don't know, but now I know. I haven't told anyone, not even Janet: there's a shoebox wrapped in a dress shirt of Tommy's that my screwed-up son keeps in his hockey bag, a box filled with small pieces of jewelry (some of them mine), and a real-looking silver money clip and an old guy's driver's license and a stack of photos I didn't want to see (they're pornos), and then I found a big hunter's knife in a scabbard or a sheath. I took that, even if Fremont notices. We'll deal with the knife issue when he comes back in August. A nine-year-old doesn't need a knife like that.

The split's my fault, although I can't tell Mom and Dad, since I already told them that Tommy had cheated on me and not the other way around. Now the lie has become true, which is what happens when you lie and someone believes you. Just ask the school board. We were on the phone, Mom and I, and I knew what she wanted to hear, so that's what I said, I said Tommy cheated on me, and now it's true, and I don't know how to fix it, because it's too big a lie.

I tell myself it doesn't make a difference, that I'm not going to call her back for a couple of days, no matter how often she calls. I tell myself that when I feel like I'm falling, I'll just grab hold of something.

•

I was about to make two lists at work when the girl arrived with her aunt. The first list was in my head, before I typed it up, because that's how I think:

What I Love About My Job

The nice people; the girls who work in the office; Gina, the new police officer who runs Code of Conduct with Vice Principal Simmons (there we go, both of them are women). The parents and guardians, the foster parents. We had two children register last week who were from Saudi Arabia. They were so interesting, especially in the middle of the summer.

Lunch. My lunch break on my bench on the Green Way with Janet, unless Janet's on the phone to Chicago.

That no one taught me how to be the registrar—the old registrar had been gone for almost three weeks when I transferred in—so it was all mine right away. Plus the software I had to teach myself, which I did.

Order. It's like I get to understand everyone, when they come to me, because of course they have to come to me, I'm the Saxon Hills Middle School registrar, and I get to figure out where they'll go in the system by using different color Post-Its for everyone, in my mind. I get to keep order, to keep everyone where they're supposed to be. Of course, keeping everyone organized isn't the same as being organized, and I know the difference.

Positives. The positive paradigm I have about myself: who I am is who I think I am. (That's from "Teen Empowerment Tips": be who you are.)

My boys know where I am, always, and they always will. Like I tell them, I'm like a cell phone, only I'm a person, but I'm always on. Lucas is about to start SHMS next year, and he'll always know that I'm here, in the office.

I saved the second list, the obvious one, the negatives, for tomorrow. It's the summertime, and there's no hurry to be negative.

•

Hello. This is your mother. I wanted to read to you something I found online, it's a little article. Are you there? Well, your machine can hear me, so here goes.

It's called "My Good Divorce." I think that the girl in it is your age, Angela, she sounds like she must be your age. She's writing on the Internet. One of my ladies gave me the article—she knows I can't read on the Internet, the screen's just so small—which was very nice of her. A little bit nosy and pushy, to give me this article for you, Ange, don't you agree? That's Mrs. Rakinsumar, she's from Pakistan, remember?

"My Good Divorce." Wait, now I think about it, maybe the article was in a magazine, so she's an expert. I'm looking at the pages now, but I can't tell if it was on the Internet. How is a person supposed to tell afterward?

"My Good Divorce." It says, and here, I'll read it to you: "My Good Divorce. In the fall of 2014, my husband left me for another man. I had long suspected that my husband liked men, from the games he liked to play in the bedroom to the way he looked at my cousin one New Year's Eve, when we were very drunk together, my gay cousin who was always the most handsome man in our family..."

Angela, are you there? I don't think I'll read this to you. I didn't know it was about gays. I think you have enough on your mind right now.

Sorry to bother you. Byyeee.

•

Hello. This is your mother. I wanted to tell you that I was looking again at the bill for your father's procedure, and it must be nothing, it looks routine. He had blood work done, I think, because it's from a lab, and it's not even a bill. It says "This Is Not a Bill" in big letters.

Not that he tells me what's bothering him. Sometimes...I know you don't like when I say this, Angela, I can tell, but sometimes, you're just like your father. That's what I'm calling to tell you. I'm sorry if I've hurt your feelings, but the truth between a mother and daughter isn't about feelings, it's about what's good for you. For you and the boys, now that you only have each other, and no one else is there for you, there's no one coming home. Because I'm your mother.

My, I seem to be very upset today. Must be the heat: they say it's going to be hot again tomorrow.

If you want to talk later, you can call me up until seven, when your father gets home. Byyeee.

•

Janet says that a middle school should only have one class, biology, even if they call it all of those other names. Every one of those children becomes hormonal in our building, and then they act so surprised by their changes, and then they get all reckless and stupid, because they don't know what to do, so then they are incorrigible. That's a word my dad would use—*incorrigible*—and it would make a person feel bad, but not forever. Janet says these kids should study biology every day, all day, and then everyone should put on some nice clothes and go to church. Janet approves of church, even if she never goes.

There's something to say about what Janet says, the way a child can be so calm in the hallway outside the media room, when I'm going to use the Fac/Staff facilities, and I come out five minutes later and that same child's crying on the floor, and she has torn up all of her class notes—or maybe someone was sending her mean notes, middle school girls, they're awful—and she's just a big lump of unhappiness, the poor dear. I ask if she's all right, and she looks up at me, and her face looks terrible, streaked and puffy, doughy, like a piece of bread, and she looks older by a couple of years. Or she looks like a younger me, but older than herself. That's when I take it personally: I check to see that no one's around and I sit down right there in the hallway with her, and I gather up those torn pieces of paper and give her a tissue, and we talk a little while. If it's busy in the hallway, I take her to my office.

I'm not her mom. I've got Lucas and Fremont: I know the difference. I'm not her friend, either. I'm just Ms. Angela Macon, the registrar, but I can see that she's such a victim of her body and those feelings, and it happens so quickly to girls, those changes, and how do we expect that she'd understand her womanhood quickly, too?

Some of the girls I see, they could be little dolls, they're so break-able and delicate. They haven't started their cycles yet—although that's pretty rare, these days the girls start early—and they seem like they're wearing Halloween costumes of princesses. Then the next day they're tall and skinny, and then they're young women, and then some of them are fully developed women. It's that fast. There's a lot of sex at SHMS, much more than there used to be. I didn't have sex until I was fifteen, but these girls, they're earlier than me.

The boys are worse off, when they melt down. The boys with their overbites and their noses and feet too big, their voices crack, their eyes look like something's spinning in there, those panicky boys. Some of them are learning to be mean, to compensate. And it's not only the big ones. The girls too—cruelty is easy when you're off bal-ance. That's "Teen Empowerment Tip" #4: "Being mean hurts your-self the most."

•

Here goes my life. I am at the front desk alone, because Janet is down the hall, using the Fac/Staff facilities, and her news from Chicago this morning isn't good, and she's taking more time, I encouraged her to collect herself. It's clear that I'll be lunching alone. It's 10:45 in the morning, early for most people to think about lunch, but in July, I think about lunch earlier.

The aunt comes in first. She has on a sleeveless blouse, dark beige or light tan, and a pretty necklace strung with blue and brown and green wooden beads—I wouldn't wear that, but it works on her—and chocolate slacks and black pumps. Or maybe they're slingbacks, low heels. She works in an office with a lot of men, I think right away. She's carrying a medium-sized purse in the bend of her right elbow, the way some women do to make a point, the arm and the hand up, because there's always a point to be made by certain kinds of women. In her other hand, she's got a big envelope, which I know must be the papers. She's maybe my age, mid-thirties, I can't tell, and she's working hard to make sure I can't tell, it probably takes her an hour a day, maybe more. I'd rather sleep than fuss, but what do I know? She's got someplace else to be. Her hair's too red. I don't like her.

Her smile's better than her body language, though, even if it's too quick. She looks really tired under all of that, like most of the women I meet who have kids.

The aunt takes three steps into the office, then she notices that no one has followed her: that's when her smile stops completely. She turns around, goes back to the door, and opens it again, leaning down toward the handle to hold open the door, bobbing her head with frustration. "Come on," she says. "Now," she stage-whispers.

The girl's in a terrible way: she's tall, hunched over a little to hide how tall, and very skinny. She's wearing a little skirt—a red plaid, thrift-store schoolgirl skirt—over torn tights, a baggy button-down men's shirt, and a cap. She's wearing plaid, up and down, which I've seen our girls do before, what a mistake. She looks like a sick lumberjack. She's got those combat boots, like Doc Martens or some brand I don't know.

She doesn't have any hair under that hat, I think. She might really be sick. She must be hot in all those clothes.

"May I help you?"

"Come on," the aunt says again. "Yes. Hi. We would like to register Beatrice for school. Beatrice Danzig. I'm Nikki Danzig."

"Great," I say. "Nice to meet you. I'm Angela Macon. You've come to the right place, and I'm the person for you. Did you just move here? Are you new?" I ask the last question of Beatrice, who stays a foot or so behind her aunt, eyes askance. "It's a great school," I say. "Everyone wants to go here."

"Well, that's fine," says the aunt. Her phone gives a quick *ting*. She reads as she talks. "Beatrice is my niece. She is living with me for now. Hold on—" She shakes her phone in midair, showing me. "Sorry, but I have to answer this." She waves her purse hand too, but not for any reason. What she hasn't noticed: there's a big sign on the main desk, NO CELL PHONES. But it's okay, it's the summer.

The aunt steps away from the desk and into the main hallway. The door closes with a last shush.

"Hi, Beatrice," I say very slowly, the two words separate. Beatrice doesn't answer. This one's going to be tough, I think. "I'm Mrs. Macon, in the office. I'm the registrar. Welcome to Saxon Hills—you'll love it here. Everyone does."

No reply.

I've told her everything already. There's not a lot to do until the aunt gives me the paperwork. Beatrice and I stand there for a couple of silent moments, me behind the desk and her beneath that awful hat, her illness in rings under her eyes, like ashes.

It's awful when a child is sick.

"I have two kids," I say, which is the first thing I say that makes no sense—why do I say this? Then I say, "I'm getting a divorce."

•

Hello. This is your mother. Your father says that second marriages are happier than first marriages—I think he means when the first marriage isn't happy, don't you? But then, one of my ladies told me that third marriages are the happiest. Like we can just keep trying, and then we get it right.

I don't think that's a good idea, being married a lot. I think the boys wouldn't like it. Of course, I could like anyone you like—maybe not that Tommy, I never liked him—but I could come to like anyone. That's the kind of person I think of myself as.

Your father says most second marriages happen at City Hall, or they elope. Second marriages happen in secret, I think he means. He wanted me to tell you this about second marriages, I know he did, even if he didn't say that. I can tell what your father wants.

It's getting used to someone that I wouldn't like, I think. Is that what you're thinking, Angela?

•

You want to believe you've got it together. You want to believe you can go to work in the morning, take the looping path over the foot-bridge through the yellow woods, through the early light and the thoughts in your head, and there's Janet, and there's work to do. Then there's lunch, then work to do. Then you're done, you leave, you pick up takeout, and Mr. Ramirez brings his mustache over, and that's fun, and then he leaves, and you have a drink or two but not three. Then you do it again the next day, and that is the point, doing it all again, knowing it's happening tomorrow.

Somewhere in there, in the evening, you wait and you wait and then at last your boys call to be tucked in, and you talk with them, and your jealousy makes a vein in your temple go bump—which must be so unattractive—and through all of it, through the beautiful, quiet July evening, you're fine.

I'm not the girl's mother. I have kids. And I have Mom, who makes me the one in charge, with all of her questions, who leans too hard on me whenever I need to lean on her. I know she can't help it, but when I'm in trouble, Mom's worse. It's like, psychologically, Mom is giving me signals to be strong by being worse herself. I think she wants me to rescue her so I keep from drowning myself, or something like that.

Janet comes back into the office the same time as the aunt, Mrs. Danzig, and Beatrice hasn't moved much at all, except to turn her back and look at the Fac/Staff picnic photo from 2013, the one where we've all got SHMS T-shirts on over our dresses and jeans and such, and we could be a football team or in the Olympics or something, if we were good at anything together.

Janet gives me the sad eye, so maybe she's got bad news. She was in the bathroom a long time.

"Well, then," says Mrs. Danzig. "Beatrice."

"We're so happy you're here to join our Saxon Hills family," I say. I'm wondering what Beatrice thinks of me, blurting out my business like that. I'm ashamed, but also kind of giddy—a little high on myself, in a way. It feels like a good secret. "I've got all the forms here," I say.

Janet's been crying, I see now, as she moves around the front desk toward her chair across from mine: she has a tissue clamped tightly in her left hand. She's squeezing the life out of that tissue. She's wearing my favorite shoes of hers today, the little orange ones, they're kind of like sneakers, but they're shoes.

I'm taller than Janet. I reach and touch her shoulder lightly as she walks by, *there, there*, and I mean it, and she knows.

"Well, good," says Mrs. Danzig. "I've brought everything. If you don't mind filling it all out"—she opens her envelope, pulls out a stack of papers, and lays them on the front desk, straightens them for me—"I need to make some calls."

"Mrs. Danzig," I say. "We have some forms here for you to fill out. You'll have to bear with us this morning, we're just so busy, all the paperwork takes a little doing and it must be done right, and there are only the two of us here, as you can see. So. We'll need three forms of identification: a driver's license with a photo ID or a U.S. passport or Green Card..."

She doesn't like me either, I can tell.

I'm on autopilot, the automatic registrar. I do my job by heart, not thinking too much, pulling the registration forms, asking the questions, showing Mrs. Danzig what she needs to do, getting a clip-board and a pen, listing the documents required, the ones we need to copy—and the whole time, it's Beatrice who has me spooked, who looks sicker each time I glance at her, who's the saddest child I've ever seen. Something in me begins to fall, I feel it, something's falling into a hole in me, I'm falling in.

I break protocol. With the aunt assigned all the paperwork, which will take a long while, I turn to look at Janet. She's holding her head, leaning one hand into one cheek, not good. "Jan," I say, "I'm going to give Beatrice a tour. Mrs. Danzig, we'll be back in a few." I'm not being fair to Janet, I know.

Then Beatrice talks, and it's the first time, which I didn't realize until then. She talks, her voice not really her voice, not what I expect from her body, and I know how deep the hole is inside me, how I'll never find the bottom, it's that deep. A person should never have such a hole inside.

"My name's Christmas," Beatrice Danzig says. "Not Beatrice."

"We've been through this—" Nikki Danzig doesn't turn from the counter, but she raises her hand and wags the pen I gave her.

"It's my name," she interrupts. "I'm not Beatrice anymore. I'm Christmas."

"In July," says Janet from behind me. We all turn to look at her, and she gives me a tight smile. I think only I can tell she's been crying.

"That's right," says Christmas. "I'm Christmas in July."

I grab my purse from the bottom drawer in my desk, snag my zipchain keys from the hook, and try not to look at Janet. I hurt everyone. "Let's go," I say to Christmas. "We'll start at the start."

We're in the hallway, and we haven't said anything. I've been leading young Christmas—I like the name, I've decided—down through the A Wing into the B Wing and then across the courtyard near the art room, the one where the fire was on the last half day, those bad art kids, probably stoned, and I lead her into the cafeteria, my least favorite area at SHMS. It's the front, it's World War I, the cafeteria. It's where everyone goes to learn how awful human beings are. Not that I figured this idea out myself: Mr. Binder, the history teacher, said it to me once.

The chairs are up on the tables as though the floor's been flooded, or will be, the ghosts of all those years of children getting ready to sit on the chairs on the tables. Even when it's empty, the cafeteria seems so full to me. I don't turn on the lights. I wonder what the mean ones will do to Christmas here.

"Why'd you tell me that?" Her words hiss a little. She's not looking at me. "About your divorce. Who are you?"

I think about her questions. "I don't know," I say, and realize that I'm answering both questions, why and who. "Why do you want to be called Christmas?"

"Because it pisses her off," she says quickly.

That makes sense. I want to piss off Aunt Nikki too. "I'm Angela," I say.

Christmas takes a few steps into the cafeteria, turns or spins, her arms just too long and awkward. "What are we doing here?" She waves at the room.

"So who are you?" I answer, and again, I don't know what I'm saying. "What am I saying? You're a girl named Christmas."

Christmas stops, focuses on me. She tilts her head, squeezes her eyes a little. We're about the same height, but my god, I must weigh forty pounds more than her, this sick girl, maybe fifty. She's wearing makeup to cover up the worst part, I think, the darkest circles under her eyes. It's not working, anyone can see.

"I want..." I begin to say, but then I don't know what to say. She's just a teenager: she's not supposed to die. "Let's go outside," I suggest. "Let's eat lunch on my bench."

While she goes to the bathroom, I buy snacks from the vending machines: a can of juice, chocolate chip cookies, and chips. I'll share my lunch with her—that's my plan—assuming that she eats. She doesn't look like she eats. I realize I don't know anything about dying teenagers, or even just dying.

We walk, and I think she's surprised by how far, across the soccer practice field to the fence that isn't a fence, just a gate opening into the woods, and then we're walking on the footbridge. I love this footbridge, how it elevates me, keeps me above the leaves and the branches when I walk in the woods, how the little creek never gets me and the bugs and the critters are kept safe. It's humanity at our best, I want to tell Christmas.

The bench was donated in honor of Sergeant Robert C. Finnegan. Christmas runs her finger along the raised words, tracing the plaque.

"Here," I say, sitting to join her.

She slides a few inches away and slumps a bit more, hunches those shoulders, and then pulls her hat down, hard, almost to her jawline. It's an ugly hat, a woven thing she must have gotten at the thrift store, although it's possible the hospital gives cancer kids hats.

"What are we doing here?" she says.

"Lunch," I answer as cheerily as I can, which is not very. "I...I'm sorry," I say.

"She's a bitch," Christmas says, and means Aunt Nikki.

"That's possible," I say, and giggle a little.

"You're weird," Christmas says.

Weird's good. I feel like we're beginning to understand each other. Maybe we can eat. I take out my snap-lid lunch container, which has a leftover piece of pizza that I've cut up, to make it fit. I offer her a piece.

"I'm not hungry," she says.

Of course she's not. What was I thinking? She's probably throwing up everywhere, on her Aunt Nikki and all over the carpet, and on herself. She's losing, leaving her body, emptying herself; that's what dying is like, when you empty out so much that even your outside empties out, and then you're gone.

Or it's nothing like that. "I come here a lot," I say.

Christmas lifts her head. "Same bench."

"Yes," I say. "Do you want to put your name on it?"

"What?"

I'm digging into my purse, feeling for and then finding the knife I took from Fremont, who took it from someone else, who took it from someone else, who took it from a bad dad or grandfather, who left it lying around. I take out the knife, slide it out of its leather holder, a heavily tooled sheath. It's a long knife, maybe five or six inches of the scary part, the handle dark wood, the blade serrated, the teeth like little ridges or something down the blade to the point. It's a very nice knife.

"Whoa," Christmas says.

I jab the knife hard into the wood between us, dig it in. "Right here."

"Whoa," she says, but she reaches for the handle. She wiggles it and then unsticks the knife from the wooden slat, looks at the blade, then begins to poke into the wood, little pokes, but getting into it, then jabbing and then, finally, carving with clear purpose.

We don't speak for a long time. "I'm sorry that you're sick," I say. "Does it hurt?"

Christmas stops for a moment, gives me a funny look. I'm no good at people, I think. She doesn't like me.

"No," she says, and we both know she's lying.

I take a bite of cold pizza, chew. It tastes awful: I think I'll never eat again, and that will show everyone, I'll go on a hunger strike, if Christmas won't eat, if that's how she's going to die, then I won't eat, too. She's so brave.

She's digging the knife into the wood, hard, white-knuckled, then dragging the blade tip through the gouge. She digs again into the same wound she has made. I watch. She's carving an X.

If I have to do it alone, okay, I will fix everything. Even if no one makes me, I will stop making mistakes, stop falling, I will help everyone be happy: Mom, Dad, Fremont, Lucas, Janet. Making other people happy will cure me, I think. So what if no one comes home to me.

The X that Christmas digs feels like my name too, I think.

I will change everything, call Mom back, tell her the truth, insist. Why is Mom the one I need to feel better?

"Make sure to put the date," I tell Christmas in July. "You were here."

"Can I have this?"

She wants to keep the knife. I think of all the reasons it's a bad idea, no. There are too many ways this could go wrong. I think of the other reasons.

It's a moment. The girl has to bear more than any of us. Life's a bad idea for Christmas.

"It's yours," I say.

WAR

A wife, a best friend—they don't die. No one expects to outlive them. I was going first, but now here I am and there's no one to notice. That's the surprising part. Monica's gone, Tony Malone's gone, and I'm seventy-three with the pills and the bad foot, and I'm working the register at Bing's Hardware and Garden Center thirty-six hours a week, as I always have, where they let me sit down. I would like to tell someone I'm still here, but I don't know who.

I outlived all of the dogs. Monica gave the dogs the same name, each Mini Schnauzer named Geraldine to preserve our memory of the very first Geraldine, to keep that sweetheart alive, Monica would say. Geraldine was never a sweetheart the way Monica remembered, but Monica died with those nice memories, so she can keep them, it doesn't matter to anyone but me.

All of those dogs, all four, they were the same breed but unpredictable. They were people, not like our kids but more like adopted kids, never turning out the way you think. All girls, our dogs—that's what Monica wanted.

The second Geraldine wasn't the same; she wouldn't go outside for the longest time, she liked to sneak into the hallway to pee, so she didn't seem much like the first Geraldine, who did everything right, Monica always said. We shortened the second Geraldine's name from

"Geraldine Two" to "Two," and then of course the third one had to be "Three," and then "Four" became a kind of joke, like yelling when you hit a golf ball. "Four!" We'd call the dog for her dinner, and that was kind of funny—or so I thought, and Monica did too, she laughed. But right around that time Monica wasn't laughing at much of anything anymore, and then she got angry, and then it got worse. Two, Three, and Four would never compare to Geraldine, according to Monica. Monica had to be right. Sure, I would say, there will never be another Geraldine.

At the end, Monica talked a lot about the first Geraldine. The memories were better than the feelings, I think.

I liked Two the most—she never stopped being bad. But I outlived them all, which I guess isn't much to brag about. Dogs die a lot, and at some point, even if you'd like to, you can't get another dog, you're too old, you live too long. You're in your efficiency making dinner or you're working thirty-six hours a week, and it wouldn't be fair. My new home care health worker, whose name is Jana—they don't stay on the job either, I make that little joke to myself—says I could get a grown dog, but a puppy's not a good idea. Even then I might have to consider retiring from Bing's, to be fair to the dog. I say working at Bing's is retiring, and she laughs. Well, she sort of laughs: she's too busy to laugh. All these people rushing by me.

I remember where most everything is in the aisles, usually, but with my laminate, I know exactly where everything is. No one seems to mind that I check my chart. Looking up something looks helpful, official. Sometimes, when Hakim forgets, he asks me to check on my chart.

I know the difference between kinds of string, rope, twine, cord, and cable. I'm good at being good. I smile. I like to put on my uniform, black pants and the little red vest, even though it doesn't zip up anymore, and to see my nametag there, Richard, and the big service button that they gave me—Mr. Bing Jr. himself stopped by for the party, the day the three of us got our service buttons, including Julie McLaren, who retired. She was extra nice. I'm not going to retire for a while, I've decided. I like to hear the door shush open, the way the air inside and outside are always different. The customer looks lost and I help, I can help. I'm helpful. Being helpful is being someone for a little while.

A girl walks into the store, which sounds like the start of a joke, but it isn't, and I hear the air but I don't look up right away, I am doing my drawer. My drawer's a mess, I want to say to Sal—who was once married to a Bing, so they say, and always screws up my drawer when I'm at lunch, putting twenties with tens and checks with coupons under the rack, where none of it goes. So I have to redo my drawer every day after lunch, and some days a few times more, if I take a long break, or if I leave the register for any reason. So I'm looking down before I'm looking up, and there's the girl, but even I know that everything's different because of her. She comes into the store like some sort of earthquake in Japan. We don't have earthquakes at Bing's.

Monica worked twenty-plus years for Hutchinson's, at the front desk, taking phone orders and making arrangements at the walk-in according to the FTD book, and helping customers choose which flower and which spray went where in the bouquet, if the book wasn't to their liking. Even though Hutchinson's did more than flowers, Monica only wanted to do flowers, and Hutchinson agreed. Working there, she had her theories: she could tell when a customer was going to let her arrange the baby's breath, she'd say, although there wasn't a lot of difference between the people sending an engagement spray and the people sending condolences, that was the hardest to guess right. She would see how some people screwed up their faces, they were feeling so much when they came into Hutchinson's—and she would guess what they were feeling, and she said she was right a lot. It was like working for a doctor, Monica said, because of who wanted flowers and when, guessing the good news and bad.

It wasn't like working for a doctor, I knew that. But I kept my mouth shut. I'm not much of a talker. I'd just as soon read another military history during my break than talk to anyone ever again.

From my stool at Register One, I say to the girl who walks into Bing's what I say to every customer: "Welcome to Bing's. Can I help you with something?" And I think about my Monica, and what Monica would say, is the girl here for a funeral or a wedding, and how do I tell?

The girl doesn't look at me. She's tall but in the middle of growing up, with pointy elbows and her hands in her pockets even though it's warm inside, the A/C already clunking hard today, and instead of walking she's kind of shuffling, bending over, and she's wearing a hat, and that's funny in July, and she's the skinniest girl I've seen in the longest time. She's so skinny I have a thought: I think I should send her on into light bulbs, she looks like a lamp that's gone out, in her black watch cap. We sell those caps too, but not too many in the summer.

She doesn't answer, a lot of customers don't answer, especially the ones who see their pictures on the security video right next to the registers—they walk in and their faces get big on the screen, they're walking toward their faces getting bigger, and they look different, and then they walk under their faces and that seems to make them get quiet. But since I'm helpful, I say the second thing I always say to customers, "Let me know if you need anything," and no matter it's my job, my voice comes out a little pinched, and then the words seem to end quicker, I know it's because of her, and something's wrong.

She slouches past my register, and I smell her. Teenagers smell bad. Then I realize, it might not be her: I'm smelling myself, my hands, and my Italian hoagie from lunch, which I have every Tuesday, it's the special at Ragazzi's. Oil and vinegar and oregano and salami and American—those are my favorites. The hoagie comes wrapped in waxy paper and you can see the oil and vinegar through the paper, and that's the best. I smell my right hand, the one I waved: I smell like a hoagie. I should probably go wash, but instead I just use the antibacterial. With my arthritis, I try not to do too much.

I pull out my laminate. Light bulbs are on aisle seven.

Saxon Hills was Italian way back, before it was anything. There were farms off Highway 252, big green fields of cabbages, then beans, and then the pumpkin fields, my favorite in the fall, and those farm trucks with the open slats you could hang from in high school, which Tony Malone and I would do, hook an elbow through the slat and swing on his father and Little Uncle Louie's farm truck. We would drink beers, hanging onto the six-pack with the plastic rings, ripping off one beer at a time, shaking it before handing it over, and swing from the truck as someone else drove, maybe Tony's brother, I don't remember, as we bounced in the truck down the rutted farm road. It was the best time a boy could have, the end of a day after working as a picker—that was hard work, but I could do it with my foot, no problem—and the taste of the beer like the sun itself going down, if the sun were cold in your mouth, nothing ever better.

Tony Malone's been in my thoughts a lot since he died. That would be two years this March. I probably think about him more now that he's dead and we're not watching the Steelers every Sunday—which I can't explain, how I think about him, which Monica, who's dead too of course, would have a theory for. He's like someone sitting behind me, now, rather than next to me. Like a guy on the bus to the city who's making a little noise and doing something funny with his hands, using a little penknife to cut up and peel an apple, maybe, or pressing the buttons of his cell phone, which he just bought but doesn't know how to use. Like me, only it's Tony

Malone, who always was called Tony Malone, both names, one of those people who gets both names every time. He got both names his whole life, because his names make a name together, like George Bush. I can't imagine ever calling George Bush just George.

Richie Addabrazzi and Tony Malone, we were a pair. His mom always called me Reechee. She had an accent, she was from Italy, not like these people today who come to the United States. She worked harder than Tony Malone and I did, picking in the pumpkin patch, and then she would cook us dinner—or she had already cooked before we started, I guess I don't really know which. We would eat when it got too dark to work. Every weekend in October, picking. Tony Malone used to tease her about it, because his mom was pretty much a terrible cook, she hated cooking, even Italian dishes. I can't say I noticed, food just tasted good to me. But she was a different kind of person, that Mrs. Malone, which I did notice when I got older and she got really old. Maybe because Tony's father was Irish Catholic and she married him anyway. She's still around—she's in assisted living but doing good, especially for ninety-three. I visit every other Sunday, and last fall we watched a couple of Steelers games together, even if I did have to tell her what was happening. I wore my favorite Bradshaw jersey.

Of course, we are all going to die, some today, tomorrow maybe, that's how it is, which is why I think about better things. But you can't think about Tony Malone without thinking how he died—run over by a little kid on a bicycle, hitting his head like that. A bicycle, for Chrissakes. He was a veteran, he was seventy-one years old, he had survived everything in life, and he was killed by a girl on a bicycle. That poor little kid who killed him, too, what that little girl has to think about the rest of her life, how screwed up is that.

My foot kept me out of the service. I was born this way. The fifth metatarsal's missing from my right foot, that's on the outside;

the pinky toe's gone too, and even though I have always worn orthopedics, since there's an ankle ligament missing, the foot drags, it dragged even after the operations. You can tell by looking at me—that's all it takes, a look. You can tell everything by looking at a person, they don't have to talk. I can't run fast and I have hip problems on the other side, with the wear and tear hard on the muscles that go across my body. But I never complained, I don't like complainers, even if I would have liked to have seen what Tony Malone saw in the service. It's true that I complain about not having been to the Vietnam, but only to myself. I would have liked the war.

People assume I'm not smart because I don't like to talk, and because of my foot. They're backward: I think more, and I have more time to think than any one of them, not like those people who talk forever. Monica would say that she could see me thinking. A lot of the time, that would make her kind of pissed with me, because Monica liked to talk and she thought talking and thinking made for one another. She would say, *If you're thinking something you should say it, Richard.*

If a man doesn't talk, he gets to be right. That's what I would say to Monica, if she were here.

If that girl gives you a thought about what she's doing, and it's bad, you should say so, Richard. That's what Monica would say. *Speak up. If no one can hear you, they'll stop listening. If they stop listening to you, you're not there.*

The tall, strange girl is moving real quiet around the store and there are six of us working: me; Walonda, the part-time accountant, doing the books together with Sal in the office up the little stairs; Frank, the store manager, probably on the phone with his girlfriend; Mark in the Gardening Center; and Hakim in the back somewhere. We're down a couple of people today: Jack has jury duty, and Dee went to the beach this week with her grandkids. Those of us here, we're all in our vests (except for Frank), and we're all proud to be at Bing's. That's how I see it.

I think Hakim's in the back, but he likes to wander the store. He has worked here since he started high school—I'm pretty sure he's nineteen now, so that would be almost three years—and he's planning what to do next, but he doesn't know what that is. He has a year to go in high school, because of when he started. He talks to me a lot, and he doesn't always need me to answer like everyone else does. He's funny because of all he doesn't know. But I know a lot about him, because of him being such a talker: his family, sisters, the war, his coming here, catching up to American ideas, the ones that don't make sense, and his own ideas. He and I are responsible for cleaning the graffiti: if kids paint the walls outside, first thing that happens when we come in, Frank gives us the bucket and the Wipe-Out. We hook up the pressure washer, and we wear our lined latex gloves and rubber boots we keep in the metal shed by the paving stones. It's been happening more—the store's being sprayed more because of the neighborhood changing. Hakim doesn't mind, he's good like that. Hakim's a Muslim from Ethiopia. "I know about neighborhoods changing, Mr. Richard," he says. Hakim calls me "Mr. Richard." He calls Frank by his first name, we all do, but me, Mr. Richard.

Over my divider, I can see the girl shuffle down the center aisle, moving pretty slowly, and no one's here to watch her. The first four aisles on that side, including the front displays, are Seasonal: lawn and weed care, grills, push mowers, weed whackers, and the garbage cans. I don't know why the garbage cans are Seasonal—the red plastic snap lids, the brown leaf cans, the metal "Critter Dome" brand, the blue oversized trash bins, even the gray contractors' buckets—but Frank's right, we sell a lot of garbage cans in July. People cleaning out, in the summer, getting rid of what they don't care about anymore. Maybe it's nice weather to throw out stuff.

I can't see Hakim. I could page him, but the store's small, and Frank likes us to holler, he thinks it's more friendly and it makes the store seem like somebody's house and we're all the dad. I don't like to holler.

The girl worries me. I'm trying to see why.

Some customers like to wander the aisles, up and down one, up and down the other, never reading the signs hanging from the ceiling, the helpful signs, but trying to remember what else they want. If they see it, they'll know. Frank says customers come looking for one thing and then they find everything else they need—"That's a hardware store!" he likes to say. Those customers, the ones who wander, some of them can be in the store a long time, especially when they've wandered the whole store, and then they go back to aisle five (Stains, Paint, Brushes) because they remember what they want, a four-inch Wooster brush with natural bristles for oil-based staining. I'm on my chair, at the register. I'm ready to help them check out, to ask if they have a Bing's Buyer's Card, if they want to give a dollar today to the Kiddie Korps Foundation that runs the after-school musical theater program. I greet those customers when they come in the store, I'm nice, and I see them appear and disappear as they wander the aisles, and I think that my life's been like that, too. Here and gone, turning a corner, heading back, turning another, one aisle and then the next.

Other customers like to ask me right away where something is: they walk into the store, and I'm on my chair at the register, and I ask if I can help them, and they say, "I think so…" or "I hope so…" or "Yes, please…" or they don't say any of those things, they just say, "Do you have a four-inch Wooster brush with natural bristles for oil-based staining?" If I know where in aisle five those brushes are, I tell them, and if not, I look it up on my laminate. My feelings aren't hurt: there are different ways to be nice. My way's my own, because

I don't like to talk. I would have even said that to my Monica, if she had ever stopped talking enough to ask.

Maybe Frank's with a distributor or a sales rep, Hakim's probably hiding in the stock room or actually on a real break, Mark's got a propane tank refill, Sal and Walonda are in the office, and the security monitors are up there in the office, the four TVs they keep that no one sees a reason to watch. We're short a couple of people. It's a quiet Tuesday afternoon in July. There's nothing worth being worried about, I tell myself.

What is a tall, scrawny teenager in a black hat and combat boots, who looks kind of like she's dressed for Halloween, doing at Bing's on a Tuesday afternoon by herself, wandering like a regular person? I scoot up to see, peek over the divider with the Maglite display and the Top Choice Knives case that's padlocked (Frank has the key) that blocks my view of the back left of the store. I think she's in twenty-eight—Shop Vacs, Vacuum Equipment, Mops/Brooms, Squeegees—but I can't see for sure, and she hasn't come out to the main aisle again, and now I've got a customer, and I have to work the register. It's the girl's hat that worries me; the hat doesn't make any sense in July. I'm not a guy who senses stuff, but I know what's peculiar.

"Is that all for you today?"

My customer's a guy not as old as me. He's got a brush mustache, which you can tell right away he's proud of, and bits of spackle shining in his hair. He's changed his T-shirt to come to Bing's, I think. We see a lot of work people in the middle of the workday, on the job, they run out of something.

Like Tony Malone did, I think. He was walking. He was on the job, on a nice day in March, walking along, easy as he goes, easy peasy. Smack in the middle of his life, walking downtown, stepping off a curb, bang, just a little girl on a bike. That's a morbid memory,

I know, but having these kinds of thoughts keeps me from holding onto them too long. I'm trying to think the thing away.

"Will that be all for today? Did you find everything you need? Do you have a Bing's Buyer's Card?"

The transaction goes on, I say what I say, I don't have to think, and the customer takes his jug of Rug Doctor Carpet Cleaner and leaves. He declines to donate a dollar. He doesn't need a bag. I'm glad he's gone.

The customers are okay. But yesterday morning, first thing, Hakim and I had to scrub the brick wall by the parking lot, the graffiti somebody sprayed onto the brick facing of Bing's Hardware and Garden Center a swirly mess of letters no one could read. Sometimes there's been hateful graffiti, not just bragging words. What's the point of that, I wonder.

"Mr. Richard, did you see the Internet last night?"

Hakim's a news addict: he is always on websites, and he keeps up with events. He likes to see the news as it happens, he says. I can't do that; the news is different when you're older, plus I'm happy with my military history. There's always enough history to keep me in books, more news in military history than there is in the news, and that's fine. I don't like what happens, I want it to be history.

Hakim might still aim to be a reporter, he did for a little while last year, but he doesn't think journalists make enough money. Hakim has to make a lot of money, and who can blame him. He hopes to own his own store of some kind, but not a hardware store, he's sure of that, although first he wants to go to business school at night, maybe for accounting, once he finishes high school. I think he could own a hardware store: he has a great memory for all of the doodads, what they all do, which Allen wrench a string trimmer needs.

This morning, we were working on cleaning the graffiti again, which made it easier not to respond to Hakim's blabber. I didn't. I was confident that one bucket of diluted Wipe-Out would be enough to handle the job, and since the arthritis in my hands wasn't so bad, the work was okay. But I get mad at whoever's graffitiing the store—I admit it—even though it's not my store.

"There was a bombing in a market in Pakistan, a suicide bomber, they think a girl. If I was a girl, I wouldn't do that. Not for anyone. Not for Al-lah—" Hakim said the name in two syllables. I say it differently. "Not for my mother and sisters. Maybe for my mother, maybe. A boy's mother is his light, his way in the world, right, Mr. Richard? My mother, she has taken me from the darkness. A boy's mother is his sacred duty, *Alhamdulillah*. If I were a girl, that would be different, but a boy...don't you think?"

Hakim is kind of round, a big young man who will be a really big old man if he's not careful, bigger than Tony Malone was. Hakim likes sweets, stealing Life Savers from my courtesy dish, and chips, and he especially likes his Funyuns. That boy can eat bags and bags of junk food, like he's eating to catch up, which might be true. His eyes do funny things when he eats—he looks to the side, instead of at his food. Nervous, as though I might steal his Funyuns. Like I would ever want Hakim's Funyuns.

Big as he is, Hakim gets sweaty, even at nine in the morning. His hands sweat in the gloves we wear, his forehead sweats, and when he takes off his boots, his socks are soaked through. Early on, Hakim wore sandals to work one day, but Frank didn't approve, and he gave the boy a talking.

I like Hakim. I like how smart he is, and how he's going to be successful. Of course, I wish he would shut up, although I think that's the case with most people. He's living proof of hell, I think, because he's been through it. So I remind myself that he's a good person— even when he's being immature and obnoxious, a little game he plays, let's get Mr. Richard upset, isn't this amusing.

"You would do that for your mother, wouldn't you, Mr. Richard? You would die for her? Now, I know she is dead, may she rest in peace, in God's arms, so you don't have to answer. But if you were a girl, would you do that for your mother? You would be a funny girl, Mr. Richard..."

Hakim's father was killed in the war, and his mother and his three sisters and Hakim were sponsored by a relief organization, and he got out, left Africa for Canada. Then his cousin knew someone in DC who knew someone in Saxon Hills who sponsored him and two of his sisters, one older and one younger, to come live here. His mother stayed in Toronto, for now, with his youngest sister, who must still be very young. His mother and sister are there until Hakim can bring them up, he says. Canada's north of us, so technically he would be bringing them down, but I don't say that, and he'll learn when he reads history eventually. Hakim's not the oldest, but he acts like he is, because he's the boy.

It's a good story, of Hakim and his sisters and his mother being saved. I've heard the best part many times; Hakim likes to tell it. He especially likes the bit about arriving in Toronto and staying there for the winter, and how cold it was, he thought he would die, he thought his nose and lips would freeze and fall off, his blood would freeze before his face hit the ground, that's what happens at the North Pole. Then he loves the part in the story when he came here with his sisters, to Maryland in the springtime, how warm and green it was, and all of the flowers, you wouldn't believe all of the flowers. Even in places no one lives. That's always a funny idea to me, that he would expect flowers only where people live. I think they came here in the middle of his holy month, and that was confusing, but I don't really understand that part. Not much use in that for me.

"Mr. Richard, did you see the Internet..."

"Mr. Richard, do you think there really are other galaxies?"

"Mr. Richard, did you see the Internet, did you see YouTube, the lion and the puppy who are best friends? I am the lion and you are the puppy, Mr. Richard!"

"Mr. Richard, would you cut off your finger or your toe, if you had to choose? A finger, you could still walk okay—oh, I am sorry, I apologize, Mr. Richard, your foot. I forget. I think this is not a conversation for you."

"Mr. Richard, I have decided you will adopt me."

"Mr. Richard, did you see the Internet, they shot those hostages? I want to be a man of peace, Mr. Richard, and I pray for Al-lah to show me how. Don't you, Mr. Richard? We can be men of peace together, *in sha allah*."

"Mr. Richard, my older sister is feeling better, and now she's not so mean to us anymore. You could consult my sister's doctor, Mr. Richard, he could help you too. Then someone might like you."

Hakim is a talker, his mouth running out like a bathtub. I think I attract these people, because I don't like to talk. He tells me stories all of the time, usually about his childhood, and sometimes about the war, but most of his stories start one way and then go another, and that's when I stop listening. I have more important thoughts. Also, if I'm only half-listening because I'm working, or reading on my break, I don't notice the story's different, and then when I do notice, I realize that the story is about something else, and that it doesn't matter, because Hakim doesn't remember what he was saying when he started.

When Hakim talks, I try to picture Africa, and I can see the dry plains and huge shade trees falling over with their heavy canopies, like enormous umbrellas that broke, and the kinds of animals on TV or on a safari coming to drink at the watering hole near the big tree, eyeballing each other. One of them's going to eat the other. I know what Africa has to look like, and even though Hakim's stories are different, and I try to see what he describes, I still have my image.

Hakim's family lived in a city. His father worked in an office doing import/export work to help the country of Ethiopia, and his mother worked in a clothing factory, on a machine, until she had too many children, four young children, three close together in age. Then she stayed home, which saved her life.

When the war came, soldiers overran the city on armored Jeeps and in convoys of trucks, and they were brutal, house to house. It was awful everywhere. There were so many soldiers. It was like Vicksburg, only worse. That first night, Hakim's father hid, barricaded in his office. Hakim and his oldest sister had to stay together at school, they couldn't go home. Telephones were down, so no one knew where anyone was. The city was on fire a lot. That's like Vicksburg.

The first soldier to break into the office where Hakim's father was hiding was no older than a kid, with big, scared eyes and an old Russian rifle—I know about those kinds of rifles, they're advertised all over the back of the magazines—and boots too big that didn't belong to him. The story's not the story without the boots.

Hakim's father was behind his desk when the soldier squeezed between the plywood boards the office staff had hammered up, gun barrel first and then hands, and then arms, his body squeezing through sideways, and then the boy soldier's young, bug-eyed face appeared. In the dark office, the electricity cut, he was not a good sight to see, he was so scared and ready for killing. Scared people are the worst, Hakim says, and everyone was scared. Hakim's father was a big man, and he tried to hide behind a desk, but the desk was too small. So the young soldier could see Hakim's father, and in his little boy's voice, the soldier barked something at Hakim's father, who stood up very slowly, raised his hands, stepped one step sideways, two steps sideways, out from his desk, and said, "I surrender."

Hakim raises his hands to tell the story. The boy soldier was shaking, Hakim said. His father didn't know what else to do. Everyone else was still hiding; the women in the office had put a chair on a desk and climbed into the ceiling to hide, and the other office workers had replaced the ceiling tiles and taken the chair away. If the office burned, the women would be trapped, they would burn to death in the ceiling.

Hakim's father looked at the boy soldier. "Boy," he said. "Do you want to surrender?"

The boy soldier raised his rifle, probably an old AK-47, and then he shot the desk. He shot Hakim's father's desk again and again. The recoil sent the boy backward and he was knocked around with the gun's power, but still he shot and shot until the cartridge was empty, all of the rounds until the bullets were gone. The smell of the gunpowder made Hakim's father cough, and there was smoke from the barrel of the gun, and the darkness in the room felt worse. Hakim's father was worried that one of the women in the ceiling would cough too.

Then the boy soldier fell to his knees. In his own language, which Hakim's father didn't understand, the boy soldier said something that must have been like "I surrender." Hakim's father was safe.

Hakim's father was killed not long after the city was taken, probably soon after the boy soldier surrendered in the office. I don't know how Hakim's father died—Hakim doesn't tell that story. He thinks the story of the boy soldier killing the desk is a much better one. *Atta-tat-tat-tat-tat*, Hakim tells the story of the boy soldier killing the desk.

When Hakim first arrived at Bing's, he was a charity case. Somehow, his sponsor and his cousin and the Bing family were connected, and Hakim was hired. He was less talkative then, or he just wasn't talking to me all that much. He was like a newborn. One day, I saw him pull pieces of supermarket fried chicken from his pants pockets and eat: he had stashed supermarket chicken legs in his pockets, he didn't know any better, and the pants might have been from yesterday, who knows how old the chicken legs were. When I saw that, I was glad again that Monica and I never had kids.

I see the girl turn the corner of aisle sixteen—Storage Tools, Casters/Glides, Shelving, Closet Hardware—although really, I only see her black hat. Luckily, she's tall. I can keep track of her this way, without being too obvious or closing down my register. Frank wants someone on a register at all times. Makes sense, we're a hardware store.

What doesn't make sense: the girl. We have a very specific clientele, and she's not one of our regulars. What could she want? I would prefer Hakim return from his break, or wherever he is hiding, and I could tell him to follow her, or to scurry up to the office and check the security monitors—or, he could even just walk up to her and ask.

Hakim will know what she's doing. He's almost her age.

Seeing the girl's hat, and her skinniness, then seeing her disappear again, down aisle fifteen, makes me think again about Tony Malone. When people die, sometimes they get bigger in our thoughts. I don't know how to explain that. When a man dies badly, and a funeral can't do justice, that's what I think. Although I can hear Monica telling me to stop sulking, which is what she thought I did all of the time instead of talking, that I was making everything worse. If I worry more than other people, it's because I think more, because I don't talk as much, that's what I would tell Monica. Reading military history is enough to make a man a worrier, I would say. Visiting Mrs. Malone every other Sunday—that's plenty, too. It's no fun there, even if the Steelers win.

Everyone suspects I don't have any worries. Not talking means not complaining, so who would know anything about me? It's true I don't have much happiness in my life, that I like working at Bing's well enough, that I really miss having a dog and I would get a different kind, not a Mini Schnauzer, and that when I see a kid on a bike,

I think about Tony Malone, how different he was after the Vietnam, and I wonder how different he would have been after the bike accident, if he hadn't died.

How different would I have been after fighting in a war? Soldiers who like fighting don't like civilian life, and today, they're even more unhappy because of the VA and all. I hear they're killing themselves all over. Tony Malone didn't mind being home, at least not when we were hanging out drinking beers, especially during football season. That Steelers team of '76 was the best—we both agreed on that. What a year.

I didn't know what to say to Tony Malone after he came back.

The girl has reappeared at the end cap of aisle twelve, where the Galvanized Center is just past the nuts, bolts, screws, and nails. I can't tell if she's standing there and looking at something. What would a girl like that look at, I wonder.

"Mr. Richard, do you think the Fourth of July parade will include any Muslims?"

Hakim makes me jump, sneaking up behind me from the Register One side of Register Two. I fall a little, catch myself on the edge of my tall chair, and then steady up by grabbing the Plexi divider, that's better. Hakim knew he'd snuck up on me, the shit. Now's not the time, I should tell him.

"Mr. Richard?"

"That girl." I indicate with a chuck of my chin the girl who's standing still in the middle of the store, in the wide aisle back there, looking away from us. "Check on her."

I hear Sal and Walonda coming down the stairs together from the office, and Sal's saying something, Sal who loves to sing under her breath, especially around the holidays, who wears those chunky sweaters that she knits. Sal who's pretty knowledgeable for a know-it-all and for a cat person. I wouldn't have married her, I often think.

Raymond, her husband, always seems unhappy. He's a Redskins fan, although I think he used to like the Niners, and that could make a man unhappy, without someone like Big Ben to root for, a real quarterback on the Steelers in Steeler Country.

Walonda's okay, although she doesn't like me. She acts friendly, but when we're alone—which doesn't happen very often, as she only comes into the store every other Tuesday—we don't have anything to say. I don't think it's a racial thing. I think I'm just the old guy who works here.

Sal and Walonda are almost at the registers, Walonda carrying the big ledger, sliding the ledger into a flat nylon bag and then opening her briefcase as she gets ready to leave, the books done.

The four of us stand there—I don't know how to talk about what that feels like, all of us, with time kind of breathing for us.

Hakim says, "Mr. Richard thinks that girl is stealing."

I look at Hakim.

"What girl?" Sal, of course, is ready to take charge. She likes when Frank goes to lunch, or I do, and she can rearrange my drawer.

"The girl there—" Hakim points grandly.

"Don't," I say.

"Mr. Richard!" Hakim fakes being outraged. There are Cheez Doodle crumbs on his red vest. That's what he was doing.

"Hakim," says Sal. "Go see."

I am unsure about Maryland, where I have always lived, because of the Civil War. If I weren't a Steelers fan, or if I liked baseball and the O's, I would feel differently about Maryland. Maryland was a border state, with slaves, and President Lincoln had to issue all sorts of orders and decrees to get the Maryland people to fall in line. Then there was John Wilkes Booth, who shot Lincoln—he was from Maryland. The Battle of Antietam was fought in Maryland, with McClellan's blunders allowing Lee's inferior numbers to survive. I've read about that a lot. I've been to the battlefield and walked the lines and the creek. I was reading about it last night before bed.

It's like Antietam when Hakim goes to check on the girl, only different. Sal, Walonda, and I stay at the registers, curious, as Hakim reconnoiters.

Maybe after the girl left was when I thought about Antietam, now I don't know.

Hakim comes back, the look on his face different, his mouth open a little bit. He comes up to the registers and leans in very closely to speak, his breath on me, which I hate. "Mr. Richard," he breathes. "She has a big knife. On her belt. Like inside, slid in like that. A really big knife."

Danger is a drug, it can make feet go numb, or lips. It can make a man high, make his thoughts drivel, nothing matters that mattered. Danger makes a person not care about what happened before, we're here now, and that's where we are. Danger shines a light into your eyes, it's blinding. Everything feels like it's right now.

Hakim repeats himself in that loud whisper, like in the war movies when someone's coming, so that Sal and Walonda can hear too: "She has a really big knife. She's holding it. Crazy girl. We call the police."

Walonda swipes her cell phone on and then stops. Suddenly the girl is walking toward us, her head down again, and it's not safe. I can see a little bit more of her, over the pruning and potting display that Frank had Mark make for the summer months. I can see the girl's left earlobe, her neck, and she's so skinny, she's not there. I see her slowly: I imagine everything she must feel.

Where's Frank? I think that thought slowly too.

When the ambulance comes for me, for all of us, when Sal and Walonda are stabbed and die in each other's arms, and Hakim, who has survived Africa, dies at Register One—he's sure to die with a lot of noise, and with all sorts of drama—I will tell them that I was right all along. I will say to Monica, on my deathbed, as I try to hold all of my intestines in, where the girl has stabbed me, "I told you so, Monica."

The girl is almost here.

Hakim puts his hand on my arm, above my elbow, and squeezes me, too hard. I am thinking about Hakim, how Hakim needs to live, the boy has to bring his mother and sister up from Toronto, the boy needs to grow old and get fatter on his own Funyuns in his own hardware store, the boy has to be here. Some people deserve to live more than other people.

"Mr. Richard," Hakim says very quietly. "Mr. Richard," he repeats.

I can't answer.

"I must tell you something, Mr. Richard."

The girl is upon us now, coming toward all four of us, we're useless in this war. I'm sure her hand is on her knife.

"I am not from Ethiopia, Mr. Richard."

"What?" I say. I don't understand.

"I am from the Sudan. Sudanese. My father…my father…" Hakim looks like he's crying. "My father was a bad man. My father… he has killed. He killed people, Mr. Richard. They are dead people. They are mine."

In the military histories I read, the photos of the aftermath of battles are the worst. Sometimes, I admit it, I skip these parts, the pictures at the end of the pictures section, even though I like the books with pictures. Maybe I would not have been a good soldier. The battle-field pictures show so many people who didn't expect to be there, thousands of dead people who always look surprised. But there's never really a discussion of what happens in the moment danger arrives, or when it ends just like that. I guess it stops being really military history the moment it ends.

The girl shuffles by us, turning her head to look at all of us, right into me, she's so sick and sad, and she leaves the store without speaking. I don't know if it happens slowly or if I'm speeding up or what. Her hand was on the knife the whole time, I saw, but she never cared about us. I have never been so grateful not to matter.

Hakim squeezes my arm harder, he's crying without making any sounds, and then I look at Sal and I start—I think I'm the one who starts it all—to laugh. All four of us begin laughing, then we are laughing hard, for our lives, we stand there like the remnants of an army, laughing, people who will never be good enough, I will never be good enough, just laughing and laughing, and it's out of control, our laughter, the four of us standing there.

Four people laughing can make the laughter keep going. Just laughing makes one of us laugh, and catching another person's eye sets us off again. Hakim's face gets puffier, and the tears make his eyes go small, and I hand him a couple of tissues from my customer box, but that only makes him laugh harder, which makes me laugh harder. It's hilarious that we all need tissues. Walonda snorts and then laughs harder, snorting is hilarious, she takes a couple of tissues, I've never liked Walonda this much, and Sal clutches her side, she's got a stitch from laughing.

Then a customer comes in, a guy I recognize, and all four of us look at him, take a big breath together, sharing that breath, and then we lose it, we're laughing even harder, another round, and the customer smiles. Who knows what he wants, who can help him. He's shaking his head at us.

I'm right, she was going to hurt us, but she didn't, and that makes me laugh more. The laughter holds us together, the four of us who don't belong together, except here with our customer, who's laughing. The customer too. The laughter makes us safe, the laughing makes us okay, it's life and it's funny.

THE MISSION

Picture a little paper napkin in a diner, one of those napkins from a metal dispenser, the cheap ones. Pour water from a glass onto the napkin. Soak the paper napkin in a puddle on the countertop. The napkin turns gray when wet. Pick up the napkin and twist it tighter and tighter even though it gets mushier, until you can't anymore. That's me.

I'm on the bus. Christmas, the girl next to me, is asleep already, her feet stretched out on that pull-down footrest, the spring-loaded one that always snaps up and wakes me if I zone out. She was asleep before the driver finished making his dumbass announcements.

A bus is the best little universe. I love the bus, and here, finally, I get to feel alone in the cone of my own reading lamp, the light's all mine, with my own on/off switch. It's the only place. If my seat-mate's a pain in the ass, I wear my earbuds and pretend I'm listening to music, move my lips like I'm singing as I stare at myself in the window. I amuse myself because it's just me. But tonight I really have something to say—or maybe it has to be spit out. I have to tell what's inside me, even if I'm just going over the details in my head and the words are driving the highway all night like the bus, over and over the words on the wet road, owning nothing, move along, passing through. If the words are loud, well, it's probably about time, but if the words come quietly, so thick on my tongue that no one on the bus can hear me or understand, that will be okay too.

It's possible that I want Christmas to hear me because she's just a kid and she's dying and she won't tell anyone my secret. I'm careful that way. Maybe when she dies, she'll take my secret away; my story will be told, finished, she'll take it wherever the fuck dead people go, and I'll be free. Because it's because of her that I'm leaving Saxon Hills. Because her name is Christmas, and she made me use my safe money for two tickets, one for each of us.

Her name is Christmas. I knew when I met her that something was going to happen. She was a present for me.

We're heading up from Lily Pons to 340 toward Frederick, where there will be another bus to another bus, and eventually a bus to Pittsburgh instead of a bus that I won't take, the one that goes to Baltimore, to my parents' house, where I haven't been in three years, where there's a life I don't deserve lived by someone else with my name, Sarah Wasserman. She's nineteen, like me, she's living with her parents for the summer, Donna and Trey, she's studying to be a nurse at Towson State, and she's got a new boyfriend and a night job as a hostess while she volunteers part-time at the hospice off the Danton Pike. She's a good person. She wants to have children, but she's not sure if her new boyfriend does, and maybe he's not the type. She won't marry him. She feels too young for her life, anyway. She's what didn't happen to me.

The memory that comes back flashes in my head if I go to sleep drunk, which I do. A memory itself means nothing, and this one's pretty vanilla, no gore or blood to wake me up. I'm sixteen. I can see the firefighter in full gear—the boots, the mask he's got in his hand, his helmet bobbing, the mixed-up feelings in his eyes—chugging up the hill to the Seventh Street apartments to where I'm sitting on the front stoop and probably screaming. I don't remember screaming. It's a steep hill. He's out of breath. He puts a hand on my shoulder as he clunks by, saying something into a walkie-talkie, asking me if I'm all right, telling me to stand somewhere else, go stand in the middle of the street, *Step over there where it's safe, Miss.* There's squawking when the other firefighters arrive a minute or an hour later. I remember each of the sounds the way I remember a song I don't really remember, the notes playing at the same time together. But it's the one firefighter's face I remember most—his eyes, his panting as he arrives at the top of the hill.

For whatever reason, that's the memory that won't disappear, that feels the worst. Shitty things happened after, but I didn't see: I never saw the landlord, Mrs. Cassavettes, when the EMTs brought her out on the stretcher, so I never saw how burned she was, and I never visited. Her burns weren't fatal, just god awful, or so I was told. My parents wouldn't let me see her.

She was burned because I had gotten hammered, because the fire in my pothead boyfriend's apartment upstairs had started in an electrical outlet, caught the drapes and his gross old used-to-be-green couch, and became a death trap—and because when I called 911 and fell down the beaten-up stairs and ran myself through the burning hallway and rolled around outside, I gave the operator the wrong address. My address, not the Seventh Street apartments. I sent the fire department to my parents' house, five miles away. I was too drunk to remember where I was, and they couldn't tell by my caller ID, or from GPS, for a reason no one explained.

Her full name is Mrs. Margaret Isadora Cassavettes. Mrs. Cassavettes liked to leave her door open a little, and if she heard someone come in, she would call, "Who is it?" in a kind of singy song. She had an accent. We used to make fun of her, me and my boyfriend, Alexi. The lying douche who never spoke to me again, who went down the other way, down the fire escape, may he be in his own hell, while I pitched past Mrs. Cassavettes' apartment, her door probably open already at 8 a.m., down the front stairs and out the door, me too drunk or too chicken or both. All I had to do was yell "Fire!" and she could have saved herself. She heard everything in the foyer.

Remember that napkin from the diner, the one all wet and twisted? Throw it out. That's me.

Among the many bad things I have done since the fire, most are lost somewhere in the high, swirly forgetting of the last three years. Most, but not all. When I let the shitty memories get too close, the firefighter's face on his body and other people's bodies, there would be screaming, which got me tossed from shelters. Even in a shelter, people need to get their beauty rest—that's a fucking joke, right? Living on the street, I was copping drugs, stealing, and sleeping with a kind of crowbar in my hand, an iron rod I found in the trunk of a car, don't ask what I was doing there. A person doesn't belong in the trunk of a car. But I showed that rod around, waved it at people, in case one of the creepers got a bad idea and tried to crawl into the blankets where I curled up to sleep. Until I lost the rod running from the cops one day, and then I didn't have it.

Many of my actions over those three years will only be remembered by the people I hurt, most of whom I only stole from, which I've done a lot, and that's what they'll remember. I know. Because a bad memory can overwrite another bad memory, like a file on a computer, the original gone. Worse things always replace nice things, given enough time. Getting erased, I call it.

I thought I would forget, drown my guilt with drugs and whatever, and that I'd be poor enough to pay for my sins, like some sort of fucked-up martyr. It hasn't worked. Being shit poor is only being shit poor. There's nothing else to living like this, no alternative when you're in it, no cure, nothing good happens to your conscience or your soul or whatever makes you feel bad. Not you—me. I haven't learned anything except how to get to tomorrow. I don't fucking know what you've learned.

Money's part of the problem, that I've figured out, although it depends what kind of money we're talking about, because there are different kinds of money. Most people think that money is only cash, or credit, money now or money later. But drugs are a kind of money. Drugs are something to be paid in, or paid with. A Z-Pak buys a handful of Oxy on the street, but in a parking lot in the burbs, a Z-Pak can get you a shirt from a girl's duffel. Those are two different prices. You can shop in Memorial Park with a pair of shoes you're willing to give up, steal a necklace and trade it for a takeout thing of meatloaf—the diners in the strip malls are good for that kind of deal, the cooks who take smoke breaks out back always dumping food that isn't theirs out the back of the kitchen. So if the same thing buys different things, and is worth a different amount in different places, then there are different kinds of money. That's logic. It's not just bartering, it's money, baby. What's it worth to you? I got it.

People want money to be money, but it's not. Some money's better than other money, that's what I think. Some people are better than other people, right. Rich people's money is worth more than poor people's, even though that seems backwards. Gas on the corner costs less. Trust me, I know.

But I don't know what to do with this girl on the bus, or what this trip's going to be worth, or how some chick named Christmas fits in my story. Even with just meeting her, I'm all screwed up, and now I'm more screwed up, and it's her fault. A girl named Christmas who doesn't say much, who's skinny from the chemo and whatever but won't talk. She's so pissed, and who can blame her. I guess that's part of her effect on the world: she's totally pissed, and I'm totally pissed, but her being pissed is worth something because she's dying for real.

•

I met Christmas at the Farleys' three weeks ago. I've been living with them since last October, almost ten months together in the old house in the woods those crazy fuckers call The Mission. They painted "The Mission" on the foundation facing the woods; you can't see the words from the front walk, but they're there. That's how they like it, the Farleys, being there but not being seen yet, just planning for now.

When I came to live at The Mission last fall, it was just starting to be cold: there had been an early snow in Saxon Hills, super powdery, a mean kind of snow, and I was hanging out behind the mall most of the time with a guy named Ger and a couple of girls I didn't know, freezing already, when someone said we should check out The Mission, the Farleys had it going on. What the fuck was a Farley? I didn't care. I was so cold. One of the girls said the Farleys were taking in street people. One of the girls said, "Nerd-Ass, let's check out the Farleys."

Sometimes I go by "Nerd-Ass," sometimes just "Nerd," but I don't usually let people call me Sarah. My names come from the fact that I scrounge the racks for paperback books and I've always got a couple with me, usually ones with the covers torn off, even only parts of books with like a hundred pages missing, and they're all stupid books, just to read. I don't talk about it—the books aren't anything, and I'm no student. But you care about a thing, on the street, and that thing can become you, sort of. People think I'm a nerd because I've got half a paperback book in the pocket of my jacket, and I know that's dumb, but it works too. A nickname's a kind of money. Once I sold a paperback that had a cool cover to a girl on a cigarette break behind an Eckerd's for a box of tampons. She thought the book must be good, since I was selling it. I played pitiful, cramps and all, and that helped.

The Farleys are a fucking cult, maybe forty of them, and I think more in other Farley houses in other parts of the country, that's what people say. Most of the Farleys live in the upstairs rooms of The Mission, although a couple have rooms that they share downstairs. It's a kind of rank or military thing: when a Farley gets promoted to the upstairs, they become Super Farleys, or some such crazy bullshit. Five or six of them have jobs in Saxon Hills and pretend lives out there. I think a few might even live out there, and really pretend, but come to the nighttime meetings at The Mission, and those ones, they're Secret Super Farleys. Those ones, the Farleys call them "Normals," and everyone thinks it's funny.

The Farleys are nice to the street kids, though, and to strangers. They take in anyone, they'll feed us, take our share of the diddly we get from Social Services, as though the fucking government gave a shit about us, and the Farleys make it a group thing, living all together. Everyone matters to a Farley, but not as much as a Farley. We're not allowed upstairs: only the Farleys go upstairs. That's where the singing is at night, and the lights they try to hide with extra thick curtains and a couple of boarded-up sheets of ply. We can hear the Farleys go at it, singing and stomping and tapping, and there's something wild—right over the edge of crazy—that we can hear through the ceiling, all their made-up hymns about the messiah.

Apparently, Farley himself is going to show up soon. He's coming back to us. He's going to save us. What a fucking relief that would be, I say. It's in each of the songs they make everyone sing if they want dinner:

Far from here he roams
Man who knows
Man who knows
Farley is alone

Man who roams
Man who roams

When he meets the beggar be
Man who knows
Man who roams
Farley gives to thee
Man who knows
Farrr-llleeeyy

When he meets the child who cries
Farley knows
Farley roams
He shall dry that eye
Farrr-llleeeyy

When he sees our dire fate
Farley roams
Man who knows
Our souls shall he embrace
Farrr-llleeeyyy

Far from here he roams
Man who knows
Man who knows
Farley is alone
Man who roams
Man who roams

Our souls shall he embrace
Our souls shall he embrace
Farrr-llleeeyyy

Farley's not Jesus or Mohammed, and he's not the son of any god I've ever heard about. The Farleys don't believe in God, not really, or in any kind of salvation or afterlife. They don't seem like terrorists to me, but I don't work for the government: since the government hates me, I hate the government. And here the Farleys are, waiting and singing. They want to be saved by Farley, and they're fucking banking on it, he's coming any day, but he's probably just a Normal, that's what most of them think. He hasn't been here before, so he's the mystery guest. Who knows what will happen when he gets here? Farrr-llleyyy.

The stories about Farley are good ones, and the Farleys who tell those stories, they get that batshit look in their eyes, like it's the only truth and they're going to hit you with it like you're a melon and it's a big stick. They rub their secret lucky medallions with their thumbs, just like gamblers or like that pimp in O.C. I didn't want to know, when they told stories about Farley.

I don't sell myself, by the way.

Once, and it's probably once upon a time, Farley was walking along the highway, on the side of the road, like every homeless person ever. A storm was coming: he could see bad news clouds, and lightning, and he could hear the thunder, and the birds were all flying and screeching. There was no place for the birds to go. The birds were flying into each other in the sky, the weather was so bad. It was a religious moment. So what did Farley do? He took off his clothes and walked right into the storm.

When the storm was over, Farley came out, and he was covered in feathers. The birds had given their feathers to him, the Farleys say, and he was protected by his feather bodysuit.

The birds, man, the Farleys say, and roll their eyes and rub their medallions. They gave themselves to Farley. Don't you see? I don't see. In other stories, he has no feathers at all. So what's the deal about the feathers? Why didn't Farley keep his feathers, since they were so important?

Once, Farley was in DC, and the President was there, and the President was eating lunch at a counter where there had been a protest—it was like during the sixties or something—and Farley served the President a hamburger. When Farley handed the President a hamburger, Farley asked, "Sir, do you think we can stand up now? We have sat at this lunch counter a long time." The President apparently began to cry, who knows why, Presidents aren't like that, and he answered Farley, "Young man, you're standing up already. You're living a good life. You keep asking those questions, son." At least, that's how the Farleys tell that story—especially when they talk about sitting down and standing up, which they do a lot during their evening services. They sit down, they jump up and stomp their feet, and then they stand up and sing.

I'm guessing, because that's what the Farleys sound like from the first floor—for all the months I lived there, I never got in upstairs, although I tried to sneak up a few times. I even climbed one of the trees one night and tried to spy in, thinking they'd be distracted and maybe I could see. I just wanted to see. I wasn't going to do anything. The Farleys are good about their privacy, though. The Farleys know who's a Farley.

Services can go eight, nine, ten, eleven hours. The Farleys must be on fucking speed, maybe Dex or some boutique thing, because a lot of them go to work the next morning right after services—which I guess helps being even crazier, if you never sleep. I've been there, in my head. The street's no place to sleep. I wish they'd sell me what they're on.

At The Mission, my job was laundry. The Farleys like to keep clean, and they need their shirts and vests ready every night—they wear the same clothes each night for their services, and those clothes get pretty skanky, with all the sitting and standing and stomping. For two meals a day and a place to sleep, with three other girls in a little room that used to be a dining room when The Mission was a farmhouse, I did the laundry in a big tub. Four days a week, with a fifth day reserved for listening to different Farleys teach us Farley stories and fucked-up songs. It wasn't very hard work, just boring—I always get the boring jobs, but I know to quit them, that's my MO, and probably my whole future, it's already going to happen, that's how the future goes. But this wasn't bad: living at The Mission all winter kept me warm. Saxon Hills is too cold when the wind comes knifing down that valley like it's cutting into your face.

The weirdest part about the Farleys is that there's no Farley leader at The Mission, or at any of the other houses, far as I can tell. There's some kind of Council of Farleys, and they meet and decide who does what, and whether I would ever get to be a Farley, and who has to be a Normal, and who does the laundry and who does the cooking, and who has to leave. The house rules can be weird, but they're the rules, and it's the Farleys' house, so they get to say and you get to behave. They're nice people until suddenly they're not, and then they're fucking dangerous. I don't know what weapons they have stashed, but I do know that a couple of boys downstairs tried to steal from the Farleys and disappeared damn quickly. Farley justice seems a lot like street justice. People will cut you, they'll break your arm with a shovel or something. You're a girl, you're in more trouble. If it's over money, you're done. I admire that.

I was only going to stay the winter, but I lived with the Farleys longer than I expected. Doing tubs of laundry, hanging all of The Mission's clothes on the lines strung around that dining room—the old dining room was the laundry area too—was just work, and work's only work, boring, but so's life. When the weather got better, I could do the laundry indoors and hang it outdoors on lines strung between a couple of big trees. It was spring. I could stand outside and shut my eyes, and the laundry would be hanging there like all of the Farleys together, around me, or really all of them in the night upstairs, that's what I imagined. Shirts and vests drying and flapping in front of me and behind me, and hidden inside those open, spinning lives, I could just disappear. That was my favorite.

I don't really know how to explain what I have been feeling, or why it's different, but for the past month or two I've been able to go away, in my head, even though remembering at night still makes me scream in my dreams, and I'm still drinking. I can't tell what I'm feeling. I'm always so stupid about figuring it out myself. It takes a cancer case named Christmas to make me want to understand— Christmas and her stupid hat.

Picture a backpack, one of those gray Army/Navy ones that used to be cool to carry in high school, made of heavy canvas, the kind that opens and closes with buckles and straps everywhere, kind of Metal, and seems to have everything inside. I know those backpacks well, because the Farleys bought a bunch at a sale in town, and the Normals all had one, so you could always recognize a Normal somewhere else. Picture just one of those backpacks, and how everything a person has ever done or felt can go inside, can be buckled inside and carried along—it's what we do, carrying all of our memories and shit. Reach into that backpack to find something. Let's say you're looking for a photo album that you had printed at the mall, family photos from a barbecue the day before the big annual family reunion, and reach around in the backpack without being able to see in there, and you're grabbing around and you find everything else there is—it feels like you're touching all sorts of things you had forgotten, pieces of your old life that you don't recognize—but you can't find your photo album, no reunion shots in the little book. That's how I feel. That's me, the life's the backpack, and I can't find what I'm looking for, but I can touch everything else, pieces of me.

•

Christmas didn't need a place to stay. She has a room at her Aunt Nikki's, who sounds like a totalizing bitch wonder. Christmas' mom didn't want her anymore. From what Christmas says, she was fucking up in school, and stealing, and her mom thought she should change friends and schools, and her mom had a new job, and Nikki doesn't have any kids, so here we are, Christmas in Saxon Hills. I don't know how much of that I believe, but no one tells the truth. Her name's not Christmas, and my name's not Nerd-Ass. Although I did tell Christmas when we got on the bus that she could call me Sarah.

I won't ask about her treatment plan. I know that phrase. I was going to be a nurse.

So what was Christmas doing at The Mission? I think she was doing what most of us do: she was running. She didn't have her stuff, though, just a dumb little purse with bears and sequins on it, and her knitted hat, and her plaid. She always wears that ridiculous plaid, even when the plaids really, really don't go together. Really don't. A girl can be on the street for three years, I told Christmas, and still want to throw up when someone wears all those plaids together.

She had a honking big knife, too, but she ditched it once she learned about the Farleys' rules—how dangerous it was to bring a knife into The Mission. So she'd stash the knife in the crotch of a tree near the house before showing up, and grab her blade again at the end of the day.

The Farleys were sure Christmas was going to be a great Farley. I mean, holy shit, she wasn't even going to live and they wanted her to be a Farley. They didn't treat me like that. I think it's her cancer thing, that's why. I think a Farley who's only thirteen, who joins and then dies, would be good for the Farley cause, like some kind of ad. I think the Farleys wanted Christmas as a mascot.

Everyone wants to be nice to the dying kid, or at least make all of the right moves, bob their heads and make that *Awww* noise you hear from the same people who probably kick their dogs—but watching TV or something, even those people, they see a dying kid, and *Awww*, even when the kid's made up, those people are still like *Awww*. And a lot of people aren't made up, right? We're real. Still, they can't help themselves, they make that noise, which means it's what they feel.

Man, emotions and people, yo. The worst feelings we have are more intense than the best feelings. They're bigger feelings. We feel hate more than love. People are susceptible to bad feelings, more likely to be jealous instead of being happy for someone. Like I might want to kill myself instead of feeling like this has to be the worst and it can only get better. All of the bad feelings sink to the bottom of the lake and we don't know how to swim—okay, that lake thing's bullshit, I know. Feelings have nothing to do with lakes or swimming, I was just thinking about that because of Christmas, and the day we went to the quarry. But bad feelings are so easy, they're everywhere, they're in me more than any other feelings, and I know the whole human race is like this. I've seen.

Good feelings are hard to keep. Like you have sex with someone you love, and you have a good feeling—and everyone can have that feeling, it's there, just have it. Or kids and how cute they are, and how sad it gets when a young kid's going to die. That's a real feeling, even if it's an instinct, an *Awww* you can't put into words.

I met Christmas, and before I knew it, I was making the noise, *Awww*, because I felt the noise too.

●

Before the Farleys eat, they sing this song:

Oh, Farley, Farley,
Thanks be
For the Earth our bounty
For the Sun our friend

Oh, Farley, Farley,
Thanks be
For the river and wind
That bring me thee
Farley, Farley

The Farleys end their food hymn with a crazy little series of finger taps—*tap, tap, fist, tap, tap,* and another *thanks be.* Always, at The Mission, that crazy Farley touching and tapping, touching each other, touching and tapping in some kind of code meaningful only to them. They don't do it when they're in public, and the Normals don't either. It's just the Farleys with the Farleys in private, when they admit to each other that they're Farleys. I wish I knew what the Farleys know—but really, I just wish I knew something. I don't know shit, and I think that's permanent.

•

The fourth or fifth day after Christmas showed up at the The Mission was brutal, a heat wave, and the nights hadn't been any better, with killer humidity and no wind and the kind of hot that makes me just lie there with myself. It had been one of my dull workdays, and I was sweating and awful all day, moving garbage bags of wet laundry out into the yard to hang up. I had sprained my pinkie too, bent it backwards as I dropped one of the bags of wet laundry. I was bitchy. I smelled bad, which I usually don't care about, but I was on my period and I smelled me.

That evening, before it got too late, Christmas and I and three of the Farley girls and two other kids living at The Mission had arranged to go to the quarry for a swim, about a mile down the path through the woods. The quarry's cool. There are really tall, chunky cliffs on two sides of a series of deep pools and rocks to jump off and long, weird fish that you can see from above, swimming slowly down there as though they were on black-and-white TV in that super dark water. I love those glidey fish. The fish slide and turn for no reason, they're free.

Most of us didn't have bathing suits, just underwear. Christmas had a bathing suit—someone must have told her to bring it—but her suit looked like last year's, because the crotch was too short and the waist was bunchy. Her bathing suit had a big yellow flower on one shoulder, like a fake medal, the rest of the suit kind of orange or red. She must have bought the thing before she got sick, and taller. Not that a bathing suit would have fit her string body anyway, all skinniness and really pale skin. She's that age when nothing fits. She had just gotten her boobs too, and they must have hurt, they were real high up on her chest, and I thought they were going to be big, depending what the cancer did to her and when.

It had to be cancer. She'd had chemo for sure, because she had those gray lines in her lips, and while she wouldn't take off that knit hat, you could tell she had no hair, and her eyes had fallen back into her head, like they were looking at big shit we'll never know. Or won't see for years, if we're lucky. I don't know why dying people get to see what's out there, even though they're going there soon, you know?

She wouldn't talk about it. I tried, but no. She just said, "I'm fine. Shut up." Then she went behind a tree and changed into her bathing suit. She still wouldn't go in the water, she'd only sit on one of the big rocks and sulk. Finally, she put her pants back on, over her suit. I was looking at her now and then as I swam with one of the Farley girls. It felt good not to smell me. I was also trying to get away from one of the boys from the extra back bedroom at The Mission, a street kid I didn't know who had started looking at me close. He was creeping on me. So I'd swim away, and I would look over there and see Christmas and her big pout and her tall, skinny-ass body, and I felt bad, and I was also glad never to feel her feels. The feelings I had were all combo.

I was trying to make some sense of this girl. I knew what I was like at thirteen—because at sixteen, when I burned Mrs. Cassavettes, I was the same person I had been when I was thirteen. That was part of my problem. I was still thirteen in my head, immature and totes self-centered, only I had become sixteen and dangerous because of my body and sex and my wanting everything and being a bitch to get what I wanted. I was not a cool sixteen-year-old. All the time, I was tweeting like I knew. Plus Alexi had hot shoulders, and tats on his neck, and he was a bad boy and older, twenty-four, with his own apartment and good drugs. We did it a lot. He was the boyfriend my parents would never let me have.

Christmas didn't want anything. How can a person not want anything? I worked it, to get her to come in—I splashed at her from the water, I made a little rhyming nothing of her name, and got a Farley girl to chant with me: *Christmas, shiss-miss, kiss-kiss, kiss-kiss.* Christmas wouldn't get off that rock, and she wouldn't do anything but stare, and then scribble in her journal like she was keeping notes on all of us.

I had made sure she left her knife in the tree in front of The Mission. I knew about the knife already. I had seen the knife the second day, she was so bad at hiding it, and I had told her, yo, that's not cool here. When I was thirteen, I should not have owned a knife.

"The fuck, Christmas," I said, but she wouldn't answer, sitting on that rock. "Why'd you come?"

•

When Christmas and I got ready to go to Pittsburgh, she did me a solid. I wanted a Farley vest bad, a souvenir. The Farleys had been good to me, and I had gotten clean again living with them, no more drugs most of the time. Weed doesn't count. But the Farleys had kept me warm, even if they hadn't cared—I mean, they had taught me their songs, and fed me, and let me work and stay at The Mission, and sometimes a couple of them would party with me in the woods, which wasn't allowed, of course. I wanted to remember them, to have something from living there all winter. I like that.

Christmas got me a Farley vest in exchange for her knife. I don't know how she did it, because the Farleys cared a lot about their outfits and they didn't need her knife, so who knows how she talked them out of the vest, but the day we were leaving, as Christmas and I were waiting for the bus, she gave me a vest. I think they didn't want her to have that knife either.

She would have made a hell of a Farley, for however long she lived. She was important to them, important enough to get a vest. I was thinking it was good that the Farleys weren't into secret Farley tats, because Christmas was so skinny, and she might not heal right. A vest works.

Christmas and I were waiting at the bus station—it's not a building, just a roof way up high, like most bus stations, so you can get dumped on if it's raining sideways, and there are some benches I wouldn't sleep on, they've got that tilt to the seats and the heavy slats, which isn't comfortable, but there was a Coke machine. A group of local losers moped around, waiting for our bus too, and one of them was wearing a big Uncle Sam hat from the Fourth of July. Like that hat was the best hat ever and he was cool.

The gift was folded up and flat, and at first, I didn't even know what she was doing, why Christmas would be handing me this thing. No one gives me anything. I couldn't remember being given a gift. Someone always wanted something from me. Money would always be money.

I didn't want those losers to see what I was feeling. I spun around real quick and yanked at the zipper on my bag, which always sticks, and yanked some more, and then got my bag open and stashed the vest.

In my bag was another vest, one I had stolen from the Farleys a couple of weeks before, but I didn't tell Christmas.

●

Mrs. Margaret Cassavettes had been married to her husband Christos Cassavettes, who died ten years ago of a heart attack, before I burned her. Last week I went to the Saxon Hills Public Library, signed up for Internet, and Googled until I found his obituary from 2007. The article didn't say much about her, unfortunately, and it didn't tell why she had lived in the Seventh Street apartment building as the super or whatever, or much about their two kids.

The obit read: *Christos Cassavettes, aged 58, husband of Margaret Cassavettes, father of Sophie (Cassavettes) Tremblay and Hank Tremblay, of Baltimore, Maryland; Tasso (John) Cassavettes and his wife, Katina Fellinger, of New Castle, Pennsylvania, and two grandchildren.* The newspaper said that Christos had worked on the line at Alcoa before opening three restaurants in Western Maryland and he had been a deacon or something at his church. I didn't pay much attention to the rest. Flowers to some charity, thanks to some hospital.

Had Mrs. Cassavettes done anything at all during her life? Had she run one of the restaurants, or been the cook whose recipes they used, or cleaned houses, or worked in an office so that Christos Cassavettes could put in a hundred hours a week building his business? Had everyone ignored her too? When she had the two little kids in daycare, had she fucked around? That was a weird thought, the old-people-sex thing, although in the shelters, old people fucked and I had seen it, and once one of them wasn't a granny. Still, I didn't like the obituary: she wasn't in it. The life I ruined must have been a life. Something I've done has to matter, even if it's the wrong way. I printed out a copy of the obituary, just in case.

There was no Mrs. Margaret Cassavettes in my nightmares, and I felt bad about that, too. I wanted her to show up in Farley gear, or wearing the head of an animal, or dressed like my old rabbi, or to step out of a cable TV truck and be all *woo-ooo-ooo*, or to lie next to me when I closed my eyes. But even though she was my fault, I never dreamed about her. All I could get was the firefighter running up the hill, and I would wake up screaming, bye-bye joybird. There wasn't a way for me to feel bad enough. Mrs. Margaret Cassavettes wasn't the victim I saw, and I couldn't be the sinner who could be saved. No problem there, at least where I live: sin's not real.

Carrying around the obit fit my new idea about how when you're living on the streets, you're more like the people on daytime TV than the ones at night. People on daytime TV always have stuff they're hiding in their wallets or purses, and the producer finds out, and the host asks, and then out comes the obit. Everyone gasps.

Picture yourself with a house and a husband and a couple of little kids. Your name's Sophie Tremblay, married to Hank the Tank, and you're the daughter of Mrs. Margaret Cassavettes. Your mom and dad worked hard, gave up everything. Picture your mom all burned, lying in the hospital in the Burn Unit, taking skin grafts, and now you're going to have to move so that she can recover at your house. You're pissed. You know who did it, some high school girl who was drunk all the time, who thought blue eye shadow was retro enough to be slutty and cool, who said she wanted to be a nurse but didn't know anything. This sixteen-year-old girl, she would be the one sitting in the street in a puddle of dirty water from the fire hoses, and she could taste the ash from the burning apartment building. She wouldn't be smart enough to stand up and go get dry or sober. She didn't think to go someplace where no one would see her. She would have her boy-friend's jizz on her from last night. After that, she would keep trying to find the biggest puddle she could and go sit in it—not literally, of course, because that would be like drowning herself, and she's still alive, no matter that she tried to kill herself with drugs and all. She's such a loser, she can't even kill herself.

•

I suck at emotions. Not that I get angry like some of those psychos in the shelter, which would inevitably bring the cops, but emotions make me unable to do anything, to think or to answer questions, or really, just to be a person. Emotions are a prison. I told a social worker that a million lives ago. It might have been why I thought so much about Christmas and tried to talk to her at The Mission and gave her advice and shit.

She never asked for my advice, I know. Or, I know that now.

We had agreed to travel together. We paid in cash (my cash, I paid, she nodded yes) at separate times for our bus tickets, so that I wouldn't be abetting or doing something involving a minor. I knew about those laws. The cops and my parents had wanted me to rat out Alexi, say that he had raped me, because I was fifteen when we had started. But I wouldn't tell.

The plan was to get on the bus, get on the next bus, maybe there would have to be another bus, and go to Pittsburgh. The longer trip would be from Frederick through West Virginia, like twelve hours or something, but my geography sucks. Up to Hagerstown, I-70 through the mountains, Pittsburgh, we're there. Christmas and I had different reasons for going to Pittsburgh, but both of us were going. It was time for me, bye-bye joybird. I had stayed too long. Christmas, she was just beginning something else, I think, because she had decided not to be in treatment, to hell with the doctors and Aunt Nikki. That was the impression I had, but she didn't say much, Christmas, Miss-Miss.

She was sleeping like someone who would never wake up, with tiny breaths, her long legs stretched out, her hands across her chest, her knitted hat rolled down over her eyes, sleeping in her own bus darkness. I couldn't decide if Christmas looked more like a boy or a girl right then. She had that look, she could be anyone.

A person couldn't be anyone, I knew that, being anyone isn't a choice. I also knew that running away didn't feel the way it was supposed to, or how it was planned. There was no glory in it.

I had a bag of Doritos and a Coke from the machine. Maybe it was ten o'clock at night, I didn't have a watch or a phone, so I couldn't say, but I was hungry enough. I could see out the window, but there weren't any lights out there, we were in the mountains now, the world was gone. Some people on the bus were mumbling, someone back there was speaking Spanish. I don't know Spanish, or what would be out there in the darkness that I couldn't see. It was the same darkness in Spanish, in Mexico, or wherever I was going.

I used my teeth to open the Doritos. Then I did the little Farley thing before I opened my Doritos:

Oh, Farley, Farley,
Thanks be
For the Earth our bounty
For the Sun our friend

Oh, Farley, Farley,
Thanks be
For the river and wind
That bring me thee
Farley, Farley

Tap, tap, fist, tap, tap. *Thanks be.*

That Farley thing surprised the fuck out of me. Why was I singing like a Farley?

The Farleys had gotten to me. Was that so bad? I thought about doing laundry at The Mission, what it would be like if the Farleys let me go upstairs, how I could sing instead of pretending. I could trade in my pretending.

That was a big-ass thought, but not a Nerd-Ass thought. That was something Sarah thought. Next, Sarah decided.

I woke her up: "Christmas, come on. Wake up. Christmas." She grumbled, rubbed her eyes, stretched, and elbowed me on accident.

"Christmas, we've gotta get off the bus. We've got to go. I'm taking you back. You've got to go home. I'm taking you home...."

We had a ways to the next stop, and I said a lot more, but I don't remember everything. I talked and talked, the words didn't even feel mine, but I made Christmas listen. Maybe I told her about Mrs. Cassavettes, what if I did, the story had to tell itself to someone someday.

My Doritos spilled in a kind of explosion. Damn, there went my Doritos.

I was going to take her home to Aunt Nikki, who couldn't be that bad, and she was going to do right by Christmas, and Christmas was going to get treated and get better. She was just a kid.

Because I was going back, too, to get upstairs. I was going to be a Farley. They were the best people I had ever known, how they cared about each other. No Farley was ever alone.

I was going to be a Farley, and I hoped Farley would never come.

MY BEAUTY

When my mother said Saxon Hills would be a good place to live, she meant Saxon South, because that's where the black people lived. She was wrong. The idea that Saxon South was ever a leading black neighborhood was of course an invention, true to my mother's vision of race in America and the illusions of her generation. Instead, Saxon South was for years home to too many different people to call the area anything but poor, most of its residents mid-century immigrants with strikingly discordant origin stories, disenfranchised together.

In Saxon South, mixed-use zoning never worked, and the affectations of middle-class frippery served merely to distract from the cycle of poverty. As such, Saxon South can be seen as a yet another example of apartheid-by-real-estate in America, where the underemployed were jammed together with the underclass, mostly people of color but not only. There, boxed elbow to elbow, skipped by the census, victimized by the schemes of venal landlords and unforgiving public policies misnamed The Great Society, the people of Saxon South toiled. But toiling wasn't enough, and eventually the area "transitioned," as first crack and then meth picked off the most vulnerable.

Of course, my mother never lived in Saxon South. She would only go there to visit her sister, my Aunt Emily. Notwithstanding, Mother knew, or at least always had an opinion. To Mother, some

black people living near one another constituted a good neighborhood, necessary and sufficient. And now, ironically, she thinks she
lives in Saxon South—because that's where Alzheimer's has delivered
her, into the illusory embrace of a loving black community.

I cannot fault my mother for her beliefs. Born in 1941, she lived
her life strictly in the tight fist of a parochial life in Pittsburgh, growing up the middle of five sisters, her parents party and prey to equal
opportunity longings. My mother gave birth to me in 1960 when
she was barely eighteen, put herself through school as a single mom,
had a small career, and witnessed much of what she had hoped for
but could hardly believe: the glory of Dr. King, his shocking assas-
sination, and then, more than three decades later, the election of
a black president. These were her benchmarks, and proof of what
she dreamed, her City on the Hill in sight at last. What she did not
see, and will not now, is how the City on the Hill has been besieged
by the vengeful mob—for Mother is beyond knowing the horror of
today's news, a small comfort for which I am nonetheless grateful.
Mother has become too muddled to understand that the City on the
Hill is burning.

Now we have brought her here, in her dementia, to be a child
again in the gracious ranch home I have leased along the northern
edge of Saxon Hills. Everything imagined has taken the place of
everything real—and I'm with her once again, a child of sorts too,
but in my case clinging to a real life elsewhere. For the duration of
mother's decline, for this our shared portion, I've arranged to work
remotely, keeping atop various cases and only returning to Capitol
Hill as crises require. Still I'm nowhere here, acting nurse and son,
newly single. Thus far my confinement with Mother has also felt
oddly restorative, coming as it does on the heels of my break up with
James three months ago, finally exhausted by our mutually persistent
failure to be in love.

So I think I'm still working, and that I'm the same man, albeit in some kind of recovery. My illusions abide as well. If Mother wants to believe she lives in a black neighborhood called Saxon South, and that makes her happy, why not? Almost everyone she sees in her confinement is black. If I want to believe I'm convalescing rather than mourning, who's to say otherwise?

There are good reasons for these decisions—that's what I tell myself. Here, we're close to her sister, my cheery Aunt Emily, a person sad around the edges, who already moved out of Saxon South years ago when she lost a child to the horrors of addiction. Mother likes her home, entertained by regular visits from a home healthcare worker and the breezy presence of my cousin Shauna, whom I have hired to help out. And Shauna has been a delightful surprise—a fine young woman, a firecracker, socially competent, and far too nice to me. Shauna's been a good-humored addition to what might have become a charnel house. With her encouragement, I've learned to be an enthusiastic if bumbling caretaker.

Mother has been taking care of someone too, an oddity of the highest order. She now keeps a little doll tucked to her breast, a child's toy named Baby whose existence we all pretend not to know about, as per the advice of a good doctor. In the relentless miasma of her Alzheimer's, with false consciousness all Mother can muster, Baby has become her truest friend.

The conversations Mother has with Baby are the most difficult for me to accept, but I eavesdrop like any good horror fan. The fact that Mother doesn't recognize me matters, and hurts, and yet the wounds aren't mortal, her befuddlement indifferent, not about me. But when Mother questions Baby, and holds Baby up to hear an answer, I feel Death drawing near, a wave of darkness closing over Mother's being and shivering mine.

"Baby, do you remember that Irish girl? Momma cleaned for her...they were on Beechwood, near the ice cream man. They were so fine at their church—we went there once, sat in the back. Baby, you weren't more than four, 'cause I was six. Someone had a new car—it wasn't Daddy. Who had the new car, Baby?"

I'm sitting on the sofa in the living room, Mother choosing to sit in her wheelchair nearby, even though she can still walk. Mother thinks I'm reading the paper. I'm on my iPad, which she hasn't figured out: it's got to be the *Post-Gazette*, because she can ask me for weather updates, and the weather's become one of the few subjects about which we chat well enough. She doesn't know I've got the camera on, the tablet poised on my leg, aimed at the little scene, and I'm making a movie to show the social worker (a camera that lets me feel like a sniper, or Instagram paparazzo, ever ready to upload the next disaster).

Baby gets a ride in Mother's grip, up to Mother's ear, the doll's dress nonchalantly smoothed by Mother's trembling hand. "What's that? Yes, ma'am! Baby, you are so right! It was that Mr. Telwin, the one lived just over on Pocusset. His little girl and you wouldn't speak, after that day. That was an *incident*. Your daddy was sure mad, Baby. You don't like making Daddy mad."

Baby goes back into Mother's bra. Mother looks up at me. "Honey, do you think I could have my dinner?"

"You just ate," I say.

"I did? But I surely didn't!"

There are so many complexities to this simplest of conversations, I stop filming. I press the button on the iPad and end time with a little *ping*. "Honey" was the name of Mother's late little sister, who lived in Spokane, an aunt I never knew. But Mother has called many people Honey throughout her life, including me, her only child, and it was always the endearment she used to address white children she met and liked. Who's Honey now?

Mother was just served her dinner by Shauna not a half hour ago—a nicely prepped plate of pot roast and peas, mashed potatoes with gravy—but she only nibbled at the food, turning the peas into the mash, more hiding. Mother's asking for her dinner has become part of the war Alzheimer's wages: Can I have my dinner? I'm not hungry. Can I have my dinner? I'm not hungry. I didn't want that. Can I have my dinner? That's not my dinner. I would like my dinner early today. I'm not hungry. Can I have my dinner? Please, may I have my dinner now? It's dinnertime, don't you think? I would like my dinner and then my dessert. Please may I have my dinner? Can I have my dinner now? I don't like that.

Much of the Alzheimer's literature speaks to the prospect of such repetitions spiraling down to some new state and bottoming out in anger, but so far, we've been lucky. Mother's confusion has been true in its precipitous plunge into childhood, falling freely past the snarls of emotional conflict. Alzheimer's can make a person furious—all of us, really—with phosphorescent rages at the ready. I am frightened by this future, although I wonder what would happen if I merely pretended to be angry, and yelled back? A question for the social worker.

•

In another world, I am still my mother's son, and she remembers with what pride she saw me grow up and succeed—and I was so proud to make her proud. I remain grateful for what she sacrificed, a gratitude I tried to share with her not long ago, and then watched as my feelings slid off the dumb exterior of her Alzheimer's, her affect impervious. Perhaps I shouldn't have tried to thank her, for how it felt after; perhaps better never than late.

In that other world, Marcus Johnson, impetuously named after a man from a library book she had never read, would not be gay. Not Millie Johnson's only child and singular hope, no sir, not the one who got out, went to American and then to Howard Law. Once I came out, and over the years of our strained silences (guarded phone conversations, boxes of Jordan almonds on her birthday), Mother would forever reduce me to the sum of my accomplishments, not a man but a résumé: "This is my son, Marcus. Did I tell you about my son, Marcus? He's a Howard man. He's a lawyer for the government in DC," pronounced the Southern way, *Dee*-Cee.

I can still see myself as a kid in Pittsburgh. On a hot evening just a week ago, after waiting impatiently as Mother cooed to Baby through another endless meal, I made a little cairn of crumbs on the counter as I cleaned. That pile of crumbs set off a long-lost memory—a cataract of feeling from deep in childhood, a stunning vision of Hulk, the gaunt mutt I found in a vacant lot and rescued, and loved. Hulk, who slept on the smoked green glass coffee tabletop when we weren't looking. One Sunday, Hulk had apparently gotten into our dinner, chicken bones scattered on the kitchen linoleum when we came home from church, a neat pile of bones deposited right in the middle. Hulk claimed to be innocent, from the satisfied and wide-eyed grin the forever hungry and too-skinny dog gave us. Who put all that garbage here? Hulk barked with dogged mock outrage at the offending remains, and my mother and I laughed and laughed.

I haven't remembered Hulk so vividly in forty years. That's what Alzheimer's does: it drags everyone back, not just its victim. The past is portentous, legible as the future in the figures cast by chicken bones. Or maybe the past is an old dog in need of putting down.

"I'm glad we've come to this place in your feelings," says my therapist. "It's good that you're not hating her anymore."

"But I want to." I try not to pout.

"Yes, of course. And maybe you can again when she's gone. But now you can't." She pauses. "So what will you put there instead of hate? Hate digs a hole."

Neither of us speaks. On the bookshelf, my therapist's ticking clock performs its maddening, steady march through each of my rationalizations.

The astonishment of my mother's Alzheimer's is that she has returned in her mind to the promising life she had before me, albeit in a Saxon South she never inhabited. Will she grow up, get pregnant, and raise me once more? Will she live long enough this time to cast me out again? What direction is she going, and at what speed? Can I slam the door harder? If we're doing this again, what's my exit strategy? Hate digs a hole—so what does love do?

My therapist says that for too long I've been the guy who chooses the path of most resistance, emotionally, to win the game I call my feelings—an unhealthy choice, and never a path to happiness. Such insights keep me traveling to DC each Friday to talk through my troubles for $300, and then treat myself to a night on the town. In DC, having not yet sublet my apartment, I can cab my way back from anywhere I cruise, do what I want. Therapy and then sex, words and then none; I know the ways my desires mirror one another.

For all of my self-interest, and believe me, there's plenty, I'm an affable guy, agreeability my profession. For years, my work for the Fed has involved negotiating restitution for what one or another person (or persons) has perpetrated against an injured party, as I pursue a middle way, reconciliation my bag. Usually, my cases include a client or firm taking umbrage, the wronged party's peevishness most of the problem. In a negotiated process, reconciliation affords each party dignity: reconciliation assures us that we were right to feel wronged, because someone is always wronged, the process alone redemptive *a priori*. Ridiculous, really—I work to reconcile the claims of others, and now live a life of unclaimed injury, Mother's rejection my constant companion.

She has Baby, but she's the baby here, and that's no fun. I miss hating her; it was so much better.

Less fun: the suspicion that I was never wronged, no matter the horror stories in my memory.

•

Cousin Shauna claimed the smallest bedroom, an eight-by-ten-foot box painted lime green by the owners of the house, a boisterous family of six relocated by Alcoa to Akron. Mother's bedroom is across the hall, a larger, bright blue box formerly occupied by twin preteens, complete with stick-on glow-in-the-dark stars glued to the ceiling. We discovered the stars shortly after moving Mother here: she likes to lie in the dark and tell Baby about them.

Mother's bedroom faces out back, with two windows that look upon a long and deep yard cutely adorned with half of a split-rail fence—a decorative accessory, although the logic of its location in the backyard confuses. Who cares, if no one sees? Nevertheless, there's the rail fence, six lengths of architectural comment.

At the far back of the lawn, beyond the fence, the woods begin, signified by the onset of scraggly underbrush, long grasses and shaggy weeds, and a bed of maidenhair ferns the deer won't eat. We are in deer country. The white-tailed deer appear regularly, parading through my cocktail hour. Sometimes they materialize much later, deeper in the night, to invade my insomniac haze as I stand at 3 a.m. in the living room. Sometimes they don't come at all. But when the deer do come, the picture windows make of their showiness a marvelous display, and I am their glassed-in, appreciative audience. I love those deer—I would say so happily to any therapist. To a deer, I could commit.

The white-tailed deer is primarily active during twilight. It's my favorite time of day, too—when I get to leave work (schedule permitting), hit the Metro, and aim myself toward a dirty martini with extra olives. It's a time to do what I please. Dinner with friends in Adams Morgan, dancing at the Mill in S.E., I wear a suit to work and a different outfit later, changing with my clothes. I feel the gift of twilight as a biological boon, like an alarm that goes off in my blood.

Naturally, the deer in Saxon Hills wouldn't know me from Caesar, or love me back; nor do they stand for any real need of mine, despite the fortuitous hour of their arrival, everyone just in time, pretty enough for a cocktail. The deer don't care—which also means that the deer don't judge me. It is July in Maryland, in an endearing ranch house I have arranged for Mother to live in as long as her illness agrees. Perhaps the world will let the two of us misunderstand each other in peace.

The deer come most sundowns, and I wait for them by bracing my body, breathing through my mouth, jittery and anxious. The deer stand in the backyard, or they leap through, and that's all. Nothing is different when the deer go. Sometimes I wonder whether there ever were any deer.

I have a crush on one particular doe, more reddish along her backside than the other females, with an asymmetrical splash of color that runs from her neck at a jaunty angle across her chest. She looks like she's wearing a sash: she's my beauty. She's a recent mother, with two fawns that gambol about like awkward wind-up toys, their white spots playfully dramatic, furry polka dots or even stars. All of the deer have milky white stomachs and long tails with white undersides, and all seem to have a ring around each eye. Even though the Greeks and Romans named no constellation after the deer—only after her nemesis, Orion the Hunter, whose belt I can see from the backyard, sometimes, around dawn—the white-tailed deer who visit seem to me of a decidedly cosmological order, inevitably transitory and yet earthbound, servants of the ancient gods and their ready passage through the western Maryland sky.

It's like watching soft-core deer porn. When the doe and her two fawns show up as a trio, I am at my happiest. I pour my first Beefeater's and sink into a plush, ugly chair facing the broad backyard, Mother napping before her simple dinner and muttered evening of relentless television. All of the woodsy world's a sight for my pleasure: the windows square the scene, the deer framed into focus. I gaze upon the animated backyard diorama as the fading light bends to obeisance and the gin slides down my throat. With the deer there, in their benevolence, Nature makes a case for a god I have never known. Atheist though I am, their wary intelligence seems an argument for belief.

The two fawns could be related, but as Cousin Shauna says, "That's just silly, all the deer are." One of the fawns—ever so slightly smaller—has a habit of prancing to a halt a pace or two behind her sister, then scurrying up and tucking her head into her sister's long neck, as though seeking some kind of protection, with a little nick and a tilt. It is a religious gesture, although I can't place the image exactly from my youthful, sexually distracted touring of Italy and its ubiquitous churches. Perhaps somewhere in Assisi? The larger fawn seems the proudest of the deer: she never bends her head unless to eat. Even when she eats, she seems so sure. The larger fawn is also the least watchful, the calmest of her generation. How has she come to be a calm deer? How would a calm deer survive?

The movements of the white-tailed deer have been documented broadly. In wooded northern climes—the kinds of woods and meadows we in the nation's capital have seen developed into boomburbs—thriving agricultural habitats support ten deer per square mile. In sparser surroundings such as Saxon Hills, white-tailed deer have become "varmints," as the guy at the local hardware store disparagingly called them. (All I asked was what do the deer eat.) In suburban areas, the deer have become a plague upon the passionate gardener, whose heirloom tomatoes are forever at risk.

That the white-tailed deer is a herd animal makes sense to me. In my own relationships, and in the kinds of passing erotic encounters I once favored socially, monogamy fell prey to more generalized desires. I too was more of an animal, less reflective, my pursuit of beauty carnal and fraught, although sometimes I still like being that man.

My mother is somewhere in between states of being, at the moment, one animal becoming another.

In therapy last week, I mentioned the idea that my mother had abandoned her humanity as she failed more often to recognize the present. "That's bullshit," replied the expert. "People choose all the time not to recognize the present. It's a coping mechanism. It's how I make my living, Counselor. It's how I pay the bills."

I answered: "But I'm all about the present."

My therapist smiled, which is much like my therapist laughing, or as close as she gets. "Yet here you are, and there's work to be done. You're here because you think the past might be worth rehabilitating." And then she added with a bigger smile: "You're not getting off the hook, sneaky human. No one's cured."

When the doe and the two fawns arrive as part of a herd, something else altogether happens to my backyard world. There's a kind of military appearance to the power and majesty of the flashing bodies of so many deer, the red and brown and white fanfare of their fur, and to their shifting and dashing. They run and run and then stop, bound into our yard, and then run and stop, and stand, and run again, a madcap choreography. It reminds me of a platoon cut off from command, a faraway general barking orders into a dead radio, small groups of soldiers massing uncertainly with neither instruction nor inclination to proceed. A herd of deer that stops running and poses, poised—they seem to me all readiness and no plan. Now what? they seem to ask one another.

I have counted eleven deer in our yard at one time, although rarely a buck of any great size. They seem commonly to be women and children—which I said once to Shauna, who continued to humor my city mouse terminology, as she responded with her usual tenderness, "Oh, you loopy doopy. They're not anything. They're deer. Let's just watch a little TV."

My identifying with the deer resides in a simple desire: I want to be someone else. To step into the yard in their midst, to be acknowledged as someone a deer could know—a slight flick of an ear, hello, as the deer continue to munch upon the heads of the landlord's columbines. We would toast each other, me with my Beefeater's and the deer with their flowery hors d'oeuvres, share a moment of pure being. It's of course an absurd wish, as my wishes tend to be. I have only once tried to greet them, stepping outside to welcome my beauty. The result was an immediate rout. How they fled from me.

Yes, I know, everyone wants to be someone else—and Mother's failing, yes, I know, I know, which makes me wish most of all for her safe passage, wherever she goes. But one of the curiosities of Alzheimer's is how it incites such grief in its caretakers preemptively. Mourning comes early in these parts.

I'm keeping it all together, though, aren't I? That lie feels good.

I would imagine my mother has a similar desire. Her infantilized toy friend seems to indicate a need to relive a past that never happened, in a changed shape and form. Mother's memories appear so sweet—how could life have been that sweet? She and Baby beat a path back to postwar Pittsburgh, where my granddad swept steel shavings in the mill and my grandmother cleaned toilets when not too pregnant, and everyone wore little hats wherever they went. I'm not making up the hats: I have seen the photos, the suitors in their snap-brimmed trilbys, the sisters in tri-corner bonnets with a bit less flair. Which gives me an idea: I'll get my mother a hat. Perhaps I'll get a little hat for Baby too, and pin it to the doll's head when Mother's asleep. I'll try not to stab the doll in the eye. The thought makes me laugh aloud, which earns a little look from Shauna.

•

Until her Alzheimer's changes again, there's a surprising lot to do. In the night, Cousin Shauna and I surreptitiously slip to Mother's bedside and snatch Baby, whose little brown head juts from Mother's nightgown. I hold the flashlight aimed away as I light the scene indirectly and Shauna eases the doll from its slumber.

Baby, who smells like her old lady, needs a bath. The original packaging for Baby said to wash the cute and cuddly doll weekly, and do so during your three-year-old's nap. The doll—an African-American sleep aid, whose eyes curl to a close when we lay her body down—is safe for little girls. In the lab, the prototypes were subjected to pull strength and choke tests, the filling polyester and flame resistant (not the same as flame retardant, my lawyer self knows to note). But Baby does not fit into a toilet paper roll: the standard opening of a human child's mouth is said to be roughly the size of a toilet paper cardboard tube, and as such, dolls like Baby are made larger to prevent choking. When I read this, I understood that Baby could easily fill Mother's adult-sized mouth, and choking could ensue, and no one would be at fault. No litigation would be warranted by such an accident.

What cracks my bell is the historical anomaly: Baby is black. I know well *Brown v. Board of Education*, and with the sixtieth anniversary of the ruling having recently passed, the case has become prominent again—especially now that the news is the news. Professor Kenneth Clark did the heavy work with the children and the different-colored dolls, and the great Thurgood Marshall did the rest, broadly inferring from the solid data and arguing that the separate but equal statute of *Plessy v. Ferguson* violated the Fourteenth Amendment in the case of minority schools. My mother was the right age to have had one of those blond, white dolls, shaming the household and confusing any little girl who loved the fake girl's rubbery, alabaster skin. The real girl could never be as lovely as her doll. My mother is the wrong age now; she's of no age, I think, just dying along. But at least Mother is dying with a sociological and legal correction cradled in her arms.

Baby hears what Mother will never tell anyone again. All of the sweetness in Mother is saved for Baby. The memories have become Baby's, whispered to Baby, memories that have risen again through the Pittsburgh slush, such as the one time the sisters went to the pictures together on a Saturday and then for ice cream floats. (Mother was never a fan of the movies when I was growing up, so the details of this story come as a surprise.) But now she's in my movie: I play back the video on my iPad later, cue the tale told to Baby, and turn up the volume. The memory of the trip to the picture show is now mine. All of that impractical detritus of a life lived practically, white-collar poverty its denominator, Mother shares with a tiny doll who cannot keep a secret. I film Baby when I can, the too-late repository of Mother's better intentions. I tell myself I'm filming for the doctor, but that's not true; it's not a documentary, I'm just rubbernecking.

We got Baby for Mother at the suggestion of a previous home healthcare worker, a portly, acne-pocked, sympathetic young man name Darren who only worked with us a few weeks, who I wished were cute, but who made a number of great suggestions nonetheless, including shopping for Mother at NiceDolls.com. Not a porn site. (Darren was the one who suggested binge-watching *The Good Wife*, and in the third season, I'm still grateful.) Darren also suggested that Mother take the back bedroom, that if there were wildlife in the yard,

Mother might like to watch. As Darren explained it, giving Mother a back bedroom, with something to see that changed slowly, could keep her safe. If Mother were distracted, she might not mosey into the street, curious about her long-gone childhood pals. Too often, Darren said, when the Alzheimer's patient begins to roam, she has to be moved to a safer and more supervised facility—a move that tends to accelerate the patient's decline.

What Darren didn't know was that the deer were here for me. Mother has her Baby, and I have competitive balance. Someday, and boy do I hope it's soon, she and I will each run away with our secrets.

"You're kidding," my therapist says, when I tell her this. She sits up: an unusual gesture for her. She seems a little keener, suddenly. "Where do you think you'd go?"

"Into the woods," I say. I'm trying not to be a cliché. "With Stephen Sondheim. Away."

"Oh, just get drunk when she goes to sleep," my therapist says. "Your mother needs you."

My therapist is occasionally brutal. She's a good therapist. So I get drunk while Baby's in the washing machine (drinker, drinkest, drunk), as the doll tumbles in the dryer, and then take Baby out back with my next martini to look together at the night sky. Though the sun's down, it's still hot out. The sky's too overcast for stars, and the deer wisely steer clear of me. I'm very hungry, or drunk enough to think I am. Working out makes me hungry, even just exercising alone in my room, no matter what my trainer says. But drinking's just like working out, isn't it?

All of these people, Baby included, my therapist included, have more to say about my life than I do. I know they're trying to help me; they see what it means to live with Mother, and to watch her go so slowly. But I wish they would all back off, too, or that James would call. (He chats amiably enough when I call him, but we both know this only goes one way.) All of these good people are certain of what's right for Mark. Because of course I'm Mark. Marcus was just my stage name in Mother's little play, way back in Pittsburgh when Baby was a doll.

"Baby," I slur exaggeratedly, holding her up like Yorick. "You've got it made."

In the morning, I find an empty jar of olives and a crumpled bag of corn chips on the patio out back, along with the shiny, sharp shards of my martini glass sparkling on the brick. Did the deer enjoy the chips? Unlikely, based on how I feel this morning. Cousin Shauna clucks at me, but she's got nothing; it's just another hangover.

At least I remembered to put clean Baby back in Mother's clutches before she woke. I might have been fall-down drunk, but I wasn't stupid. Or maybe Shauna did it, picking up after me.

The white-tailed deer is an athlete. Weighing between one and three hundred pounds (I weigh under two hundred, when I'm lying), the white-tailed deer can run at speeds up to thirty miles per hour and jump ten feet in the air. While there's little cause to treat the deer allegorically—they're not my guilt, they're not my redeemers, they're not here to transport Mother's soul, they're not emissaries preparing us—I find their athleticism striking in comparison to my own, a symbol of something nonetheless. I can't run or jump. In fact, just from wear and tear, I'll probably need a knee replacement soon, happily relying upon my Civil Servant healthcare, unless some elected buffoon takes it away. Of course, I wouldn't eat a twig if you offered me a decent paté. (I often find the chewed-off stubs of branches at the edge of the woods.) By comparison, more flamboyantly, I would absolutely wear my gorgeous antlers for show. Like that of the ram or the elk or the peacock, my horny plumage would bear the standard of my virility. Word on the street (read: the Internet) is that the antlers of the white-tailed deer are for rubbing. I get that. If I'm going to rub or be rubbed, I'm going to look good.

Of course, I have explored my sexual habits with my therapist—it's one of the best parts of therapy. We analyzed together what looking good means, and what I find attractive in a man, both body types and outfits. What James was into, when he wasn't into being vain. What I like to do in bed. What kind of guy I think is hot. Not surprisingly, I like the bad ones, at least for short-term encounters. That Friday session with my therapist was a Top Ten therapy moment—talk as foreplay, before my cruising began, to discuss desire and then go hunting for its object. Later, I was aroused for hours.

The bad men validate my badness, naturally, and pose no long-term threat to my social order. Everyone agrees it's a hookup. Bad's not the same as stupid: I am a man ever ready with condoms, despite what a bad man may want, and James and I were always safe.

The deer know I'm watching. They know I wait for them, that I keep to my side of the glass, that Mother joins me on occasion, that Cousin Shauna is learning to enjoy the time of day and sure does like those delicious cocktails I pour, and that there's something deer-like in humanity's collective behavior at dusk, our own crepuscular habits. I know as much about them, I think, tallying data, as they know about me. From the wild side of the window, we're sedentary, circumspect beings not easily frightened, our watering hole bountiful, our foraging easy, the refrigerator bright with produce. The deer might even see I'm learning to be kind.

Cousin Shauna's so good with Mother, I am in awe. Shauna asks direct questions that elicit on-point answers, runs the meeting well, leads her patient carefully. Mother trusts that Shauna makes sense, even if Mother often calls Shauna "Hattie," which was Mother's own mother's name. Shauna seems okay with the fact that Mother is now a child: it is a truth universally acknowledged that Cousin Shauna will make a good mother.

Me, I don't get a consistent name—Honey sometimes, Moo-Moo, a childhood nickname, and even names I don't recognize. I think Mother's Alzheimer's gets this one right, actually, my life never quite fixed. Although at times I miss the name Marcus. Because it was in fact Marcus Aurelius who said, "It is not death that a man should fear, but never beginning to live." How the hell did my mother know that I would be that man?

Mark suffices, low-key and agreeable.

In the cells in Mother's brain, in the victim of "the Alzheimer's" (which is what Shauna calls it, with the deterministic morbidity of the definite article), acetylcholine has begun to break down. As the doctor in Pittsburgh described the disease to me and Aunt Emily, memory's like the surface of sand at the beach, at the water's edge. The wave comes, and everything floats in the wave, carried here. We pick something from the wave, and we remember. Now the wave recedes and deposits driftwood and bits of plastic and seashells upon the bubbling sand. That's what it's like when the nerve cells in the brain are isolated, they devolve to detritus. Until, eventually, there are no more waves.

I appreciated this doctor at the hospital in Pittsburgh, whom we saw early on. I admired the pressed jib of her, the manner in which she communicated the relative uselessness of the drugs—Aricept, Namenda, high doses of Vitamin E. The doctor was informative, a fount of confidence and pessimism. We were given timetables and charts, Emily and I; we were shown the grim future, the potential for years of limbo. I have always liked theologians, less so theology.

•

There's a deer on the chaise longue in the backyard, long legs and black hooves restful and akimbo. It's the most absurd sight I have ever seen—a deer on a chair—but I can't be that tanked, can I? It's either too early or too late. With my martini glass in one hand and the big shaker in the other, the jar of olives in my pants pocket, I stand aghast at the door to the patio. I can see the flashing of white, and fur, and flesh. There is a deer lying on my deck chair.

But now there are arms, and now there are hands. It's not a deer. It's a girl in a hat. What's she doing here?

With my butt, I bump open the door. Cousin Shauna's gone for groceries, Mother is in the living room in her wheelchair, and I'm here in the sweaty twilight with a deery girl in my borrowed backyard.

"Can I help you?"

She twists around to look at me but doesn't get up. "No. I'm just lying down."

"You're…" I don't know what to say. I step fully onto the red brick patio, pour a good martini, put down the shaker to add my two olives—and when it's all poured, I extend my hand politely, guests first. "Would you like a martini?"

"I'm thirteen," she giggles.

That means no.

"Would you like a Pringles?" she offers in return.

"No," I smile. "Thank you." I place the olive jar on the glass table and ease into the other chaise longue. She's in my chair. It's a good martini.

Drink slowly, I tell myself too often.

"I thought you were a deer," I say.

The girl looks at me, just turns her head. Something's in her gaze, and she's so thin, like Mother. I think the girl might be sick too.

"Who lives here?"

"No one," I say, the quick answer a surprise to me, too. "I mean, we're temporary. We're tenants. My mother…" The sentence ends badly. "I'm leasing the house for my mother. My cousin stays with us. I go home to DC on weekends."

None of this information could possibly matter to the girl. What is she doing here, eating chips and acting in my backyard movie? We sit in our chairs. There are crows somewhere.

After a while, the girl asks, "What does a martini taste like?"

It's something to do. "I'll get you a glass," I say, jumping up again.

Inside, Mother asks a question I don't hear, and I call out, "Yes." I aim myself at the breakfront and the stemware. Cousin Shauna has her own special glass, so I take another, a different style, one with swirls. Cousin Shauna's glass could be a Murano, another example of Shauna's recent education, the ruination of young Shauna, her Bildungsroman.

Out back again, I pour. "Here."

"Thanks." She sips. "Whoa," she says, and coughs.

"Do you like it?"

"Definitely not," she says. She takes another sip.

There's a lot of quiet and a little noise in Nature, bugs or something. We drink. She coughs.

"So." I perch at the edge of my lounger. "I'm a lawyer, and I want to ask you a few questions. Would that be okay?"

"Sure," she says. "But I don't like to talk."

"That's fine," I say. "The gin will help."

"I'm not a dumb kid," she says.

"That's good," I say. My third martini is always my favorite, until the next one. "But you're a teenager, right?" She giggles. I know so little. "Do you hate your mother?"

She looks at me. "That's...no..." She lets out the word. "I just can't be there. There's too much...I hate Aunt Nikki. Bitch."

"Oh."

"Do you hate your mother?" the girl asks, returning the favor.

I like this girl. I look over my shoulder, and the girl looks too. We can see Mother in her chair, talking to Baby.

"That's her?"

"Yes."

"Do you hate her?"

"I probably do. Or I did. I used to. Hell, I don't know."

"That's confusing," she says. "What's she holding?"

"It's a doll. She's got the Alzheimer's," I say. "It's hard to hate a sick person."

"She's dying?"

"We're all dying," I say.

"Wow, don't say that. That's not cool," the girl says. "You don't know."

She's got on big black boots unlaced at the top, some kind of leggings, and plaid shorts over the leggings. There are buckles and snaps on her little black vest, like tribal markers sold at the mall. She's wearing an ugly knitted hat—well, it's all ugly—and she looks to have no hair. She's sick. I imagine she smells bad.

My martini has gone too far. "You're very mature for your age," I say, to help.

The girl shakes her head. I don't know if she's agreeing. She wedges a little stack of Pringles into her mouth.

"Would you like to stay for dinner?" I ask. "I was just about to cook. We can do better than chips—and I can't only drink. I'll have a nasty hangover."

"I don't eat fish," the girl says, still chewing.

"No fish." I smile. "I'll whip up a little something. I'll call when it's ready."

Will she stay? Will the deer recognize her?

It's just past Mother's dinnertime. I can make linguine with jarred pesto and a mixed greens salad from the prewashed box. Mother will have pasta with a dollop of tomato sauce, which is bound to be an adventure and will lead to a washcloth bath—but Shauna will be back to take care of all that. Shauna the clean-up crew, the miraculous, sure cousin ready for the wiping up.

I'm drinking! There's a houseguest! I turn on my iPod, sync the Bluetooth speakers, and groove to the new D'Angelo while I putter in the kitchen. I waited fourteen years for D'Angelo. How long can I wait for Mother?

The appliances are ancient. The electric stove works well enough, although it's not very sophisticated. The burners are hard to regulate; they heat up slowly and then suddenly they're too hot. Nonetheless, thirty or so minutes later, we have dinner. I wheel Mother to the table, though she's muttering a little aggressively, and I call the girl in from the patio. The three of us settle at our places. I open a bottle—nothing special, a little white Burgundy—and with a silent nudge and a smile, I offer the girl a glass.

"Yes, please. I'm bombed. You left me out there." She slurs a little. "Olives taste like fish."

Dinner's good enough, better than Pringles, or the girl's just hammered, her smile cockeyed. Either way, she chows with gusto. Mother eats two bites, then stops, maybe even dozes, then stirs again and plays with her food. I have given her a fork and spoon for her pasta and applesauce, along with a tiny glass of wine—she's not supposed to drink, but we have a guest—and Mother seems pretty happy.

In slow motion, it begins: years of slow motion bring us to this. With a shaking hand and a spoonful of pasta and sauce, Mother's eyes widen in confusion. Something has scared her, something she cannot make sense of—her hand shakes more, tilts, and then she dribbles food onto her front and down her housedress, Baby in there somewhere. I forgot to give Mother a bib.

Mother begins to whimper.

"Oh no," the girl says. "Lady, it's all right. Lady…"

"It's okay." I wave the air, comfort everyone. I stand to go get something.

"Baby," Mother says.

"It's okay." I step toward the kitchen. "It's just a spill. We'll clean it up."

"Baby!" Mother is more insistent.

"Be right there," I call from the paper towels.

"Let me help," I hear the girl say.

When I turn back from the kitchen doorway, I see the girl standing and reaching toward Mother, napkin ready to wipe the mess, Mother clutching Baby, the doll splattered with spaghetti sauce.

Then Mother's slapping at the girl hysterically. "Get off me, you fucking bitch! Cunt! Cunt bitch! White cunt bitch! Fucking cunt! Whore cunt! Cunt licking, white fucking, white fucking bitch! You're hurting Baby, you fucking white bitch!"

The girl freezes, looks at me. I'm sure my mouth is open too.

The girl throws down her napkin and runs, banging open the patio door, into the woods. Her arms flail, her white legs flashing.

I watch the girl run. She's away.

She should have stayed, and I should have run.

Mother's screaming.

Run, Marcus.

MEG'S TEAM

I go to all the games. Sunday afternoons, the boys play pickup double-headers at Rockerson Park, Tuesday night league games are at Findlay Park, Wednesday night league games are at Findlay again, and then Friday night league games are at A.B. (That's what everyone calls it, although the park's named A.B. Wo-je-ho-ee-woah-ee or something.) I bring different seat cushions for the different seats in each ballpark, hand warmers and space blankets in case the temperatures drop, and pack the cooler with healthy snacks for between innings or between games at the doubleheaders. I bring the first-aid kit. Of course I travel to all of the regional tournaments, but that's another story, and different guys and girls are involved on those teams. I always keep the book, which means I'm the scorekeeper. Everyone knows that's what I do: Meg keeps the book.

I write the travel team's newsletter, and I post updates on injuries—Senior Softball is a game of subtraction, my husband Bryson likes to say. Bryson's a pitcher, so the newsletter's called *KnuckleBalls*, which Bryson thinks is funny and wants to believe he made up. During the offseason I compose and copy memory books, knit bat hats, monogram nameplates for the other ladies' cushions, embroider the sleeves of Bryson's teams' jerseys with each player's initials (or with his jersey number if, God forbid, one of the boys passes, so that everyone will be remembered), and I organize—although I don't always host, because that would be greedy—the annual post-season get-togethers, as well as the holiday potluck.

I have been ejected from the ballpark three times this year. I'm not proud of that fact, but when the ump's wrong, don't ask Meg to keep quiet. All three times, I was right. I was at Findlay the night we lost Jackie Jean to a heart attack—June 6, and yes, that's D-Day, which seemed to me ironic, when I thought about it later. I wish I could have done something, but I don't know CPR. I remember her husband Vince's mouth opening and closing, kind of like a fish wanting air, one of those koi you see in a manmade pool in Vegas or at a really fancy indoor mall where the buses drop you off to shop at Black Lion. Vince held Jackie Jean's hand. The dirt of the infield looked like it was blue and swirling—not the reflection from the ambulance light, but the dirt itself swirling, if that makes sense. I'm very specific in what I remember. Bryson says it's one of the reasons he married me, but he married me because I got pregnant a million years ago.

Being this involved in Bryson's life gives me joy. I have more joy than anyone I know. I make cute things, I add touches of life. I get to think all of the time—the girls are always saying I look like I swallowed a peanut butter sandwich, that's their little joke about me. The girls say I tighten my lips when I'm thinking, and they can tell Meg's got her thinking face on. Even when I'm cheering, the girls say I look like I'm thinking about something, Meg's always thinking.

But this is a story about a little girl named Christmas—what a ridiculous name—and how she's dying, and what I did for her, not a story about me. Which is how I feel about Senior Softball: that it's always a story about how the boys did, who won, who got All-Star in the tournament, or if Bryson didn't hit, how grumpy he'll be when he gets home. To the extent that I add the flair that makes life more enjoyable, sure, this is about me, but not in the ways a person might know right at first. Just as I did for Christmas, that poor girl. She needed me. I know, I've had four kids, and I have wonderful grand-babies. Knock on wood, step on a crack, no one's had cancer, even though Mikey does have colitis, which is no fun at all.

I'm an artist. I studied drawing, painting, and graphic design for my Associate's. Crafts are how I show I love everyone, and I love everyone a lot, all of the time. I'm so filled with love, I'm about to die of bursting. It's like the Michael's slogans, how the sayings at the ends of the aisles alternate between "Great Price" and "Things We Love." My art qualifies as "Things We Love," and of course, I don't charge anything, not even for supplies, so "Great Price" makes sense too. It's free to be loved by Meg. I just appreciate when I'm appreciated. Being inspired at my crafts table—that's my favorite thing, when I've got a bag of foam balls and a bundle of pipe cleaners and craft paints and my hot glue gun. I could do that for hours.

Back in high school, a lifetime ago, where Bryson and I met, an art teacher said to me in Art Club once, "Meg, you sure care about everything. It's so sweet you make things to show it." That stuck with me, even though that was the same art teacher who got arrested for selling marijuana out of his Corvette. Here I am, just making things—it's not caring, though, it's bigger than that. It's love more than love, if that makes any sense. But it's not boring Christian love, I didn't learn that, my parents weren't churchie. When I tried going to church with a couple of the girls from the bleachers, we just sat there with nothing to do. Singing to the baby Jesus who isn't even there? Love means making stuff. It's called "making love" for a reason! See, Meg's always thinking.

I worked in insurance, so I know what's what. Before I had my Christy, Missy, Mark, and Mikey, I was the receptionist and then the co-manager of reception at the State Farm Office in the Henderson

Building, Henderson Insurance, run by Old Man Henderson and his bad seed, Gordo. But I had to get out of there. They couldn't take Meg's opinions, that's what I learned, and I couldn't take Gordo slobbering on me, which didn't stop even after I got pregnant. I can only put up with so much from a man like that. Big deal that I was already eighteen and legal. I knew not to tell Bryson or one of my brothers. Nothing good could come from Gordo being beaten in the parking lot. I handled it myself.

The first time I met that girl, Christmas, she was lying about the creek at A.B. Park when I went to rinse out the boys' cooler after the Friday night game. They've got a hose that runs from the back of the snack shack and restrooms to the creek, and it makes sense to rinse the cooler at the creek, because that's where the water runs. It was hot, even for July, and that child smelled like liquor. I knew I smelled something forsaken as soon as I stepped behind the snack shack, and that's saying a lot, because the public restrooms are right there. She was drunk, her butt in the creek, and she wore godawful clothes and a hat that didn't say anything. What's a girl like that doing that for? That's what I asked her. I said, "If I'm not Meg O'Daly! What's a girl like you doing that for? What's your name?"

"Christmas," she said. "I'm Christmas." She mumbled something else, which I think isn't right for a girl. We girls need to make sure the boys understand when we talk. She's got a lot to learn. Then she retched.

"You go on, get out of there," I told her, and I meant the creek, and I meant for her to get over here. But I had to turn around and let the boys know, head out without me, I'll see you at home, I've got my Kia. I'm thinking I've got my space blanket too, once I get this skinny thing washed up. If need be, I'll close down the fields—I know how to hit the lights if the Parks and Rec young man with the big beard doesn't come by on his golf cart. I can do a man's job.

Because I'm an artist, I see the world differently. It's not like I'm Bob Ross, I'm just someone who makes things for others. My art has purpose. When I put self-adhesive rhinestone stickers on Christy's book covers for nursing school, I did it because her sad patients needed bling in their lives and everyone else had given those sick people gifts that don't last, flowers and balloons. If a girl's in chemo, she doesn't want her *Get Well Soon!* balloon to deflate overnight, or to watch the pretty flowers on her puke stand wilt and die, even I know that. She wants to think about what tomorrow's sunrise is going to be like, how pretty the world is going to be, and will it rain the day after. She just wants to know there will be a day after.

Rhinestones are perfect for thinking about the future. Self-adhesive rhinestone stickers, the square ones you can mosaic on a clean surface in any pattern, even tip to tip like diamonds—they're beautiful like that, all lined up. They're art, they're like nature, they're glued there and so they're going to stay there. They're practical, just like me. I'm not going anywhere, Christmas.

It's like when I worked in insurance—art's like insurance. Take a ceramic mug. A ceramic mug's going to break, someone with neuropathy will drop it, or the mug will chip in the dishwasher, or there won't even be a reason, the mug will just be broken. We all wear down. If I just let the mug be broken, I haven't done anything useful today. Every day is a useful day, that's one of my mottos, I always say, "Meg O'Daly says every day is a useful day." So art's like that, and so is insurance. Insurance makes sure that we're protected, it's like gravity. Art makes sure that we have beautiful innocence in our lives, against all of that ugliness we have to see. Insurance helps us not be destitute when bad things happen. Art is like that—but it's for the soul. Insurance for the soul, that's what I tell everyone art is, because they're always asking me those questions when they see my art, those "What is it, Meg?" kinds of questions.

My favorite art project lately has been making little replicas of everyone on Bryson's Beaver Hunters—that's his traveling team, they're called BBH to be polite—out of FloraCraft Foam Mousse • Espuma. I take one of those three-inch foam balls and I make it look like a softball. I hand-dip a base layer of bright lemon-lime; I hand-glue the ribbon to look like the stitching of the ball. Then I use other sizes of FloraCraft Foam Mousse • Espuma, different-sized foam parts that I attach with hot glue, and I decorate with bits of cloth that I've sewn on my Singer Sew Mate, and I make tiny replicas of everyone on the team. Rafael's stringy hair (he plays first) and Keith's white head (he plays second). Their faces are painted to be faces. Their uniform numbers are on their backs. Only when everyone's done do I carry the whole team like that, in a cardboard box, to the field, and I sit them down on the bleachers next to me—they lie on a green swath of cloth, like grass only nicer—and they cheer on the real players. I can't say how happy it makes me to see those little FloraCraft Foam Mousse • Espuma players getting rowdy in the stands. Better than any vodka tonic! All the girls *ooh* and *ahh*. What I don't tell the girls is how many times I had to make Scottie, the big DH, because he has such a funny face, kind of a sideways face. I must have thrown out five Scotties.

I understand what it means to be better than I am, to want the FloraCraft Foam Mousse • Espuma replica of Scottie, the DH, to look like him. It's not just pride, which I do believe is a sin, even though I don't go in for those sins. An artist needs for herself the thing to be beautiful—then it can be beautiful for someone else. The girls are always asking, "Why'd you do that, Meg?" and I want to say, "For me," but that's too much the truth, and they wouldn't understand. Only another artist could.

There is just one course of action when a pukey girl's stinking with liquor and she's half in a creek, and the person who knows better is standing there with a hose. "Christmas, dear," I say, "we're going to clean you up."

She looked at me like I was the Devil and his friend Daniel. She was hollering at me to stop, but I didn't pay no mind, I've had kids, and I know the back end of a pig from its cute little ears. I used to make pigs, I was on a pig kick. For a year there, all I made were pigs, out of pipe cleaners and poly stuffing tucked into pink terry. They were cute too, but a woman can only make so many pigs before she goes crazy—pig crazy, Bryson called it. Pigs aren't useful the way art needs to be. Pigs aren't people, although that girl, Christmas, probably smelled like a pig before I hosed her off. I did like the googly eyes of all of those pigs—gluing on those plastic googly eyes was my favorite when I was pig crazy. No matter what Bryson said, I had my reasons, and so I stopped making pigs once I realized that they were all beginning to look like Grandpa Colin, who was a right sonofabitch to Grandma Jean, even for those days, way back when, when it was okay for a man to be a right sonofabitch.

Here's what I think about the girls and the boys: it's like we're playing a game, but one team only gets to have eight players to the other's ten. That means we're two down in the field—probably a second basemen, and only playing three outfielders instead of four—and we've got two automatic outs at the bottom of the order. That's the girls' team. I raised my kids to think differently, to make sure everyone gets a chance to play, the girls and the boys, and I come out to Bryson's game because this is my time too. Just because I'm not an athlete doesn't mean I'm less. I'm making my art, and I'm showing how much love I have, and it's tough tweeties if someone can't understand what a girl has to offer. Because sometimes one of the girls in the stands will say, "Meg O'Daly, I know, let's get a girls' team and play on Thursdays!" and I'll say, "Now, you listen. We do a man's job, and we let the boys play games."

I have another saying, and it's a real important one: "If you don't want Meg O'Daly's opinion, don't ask her." It's gone a long way to making sure Bryson and I are still married, forty-four years and counting. He's had to learn a lot about me, information a man might not want to have. For our fiftieth, he knows already he's taking me on a cruise, and I'm going to bring home a little umbrella for every drink I get—although I did see that Michael's is carrying those little umbrellas now, and all they need is a splash of paint, and presto, you've got a theme. Most likely, one of the girls will think that's a good idea, to have a Hawaiian party at holiday time, when you need to be thinking red, green, and tinsel. That's okay, she's entitled to her opinion—so long as she doesn't ask me, we should be fine. I'm not in charge of all the holiday themes. Bryson will say, because he always does, "Why are you coming to me, Meg O'Daly, when you need to be telling all this right to her!" He means well, but he doesn't know how to be part of a community, how to get along with everyone. "Just pitch the ball," I say sweetly to Bryson. "I'll take care of the rest."

That girl, Christmas, showed up at the end of our spring season. We weren't having our best season—a couple of the boys had injuries, and one, Rocky the left fielder, looked like he might be finished—but we were in the thick of the standings. We had already made the playoffs. That's a little joke in Senior Softball: if you lose every game, no matter if you're playing rec ball or competitive, you still make the playoffs, because everyone makes the playoffs. There's always a round robin tournament at the end, either single or double elimination, and doesn't it just squeeze my heart, how often the worst team wins it all. I'm not supposed to like when that happens—Bryson hates it, putting in all that hard work, and being the captain, and being on the best team, and then seeing the worst team with the trophy—but I have to say, it gives me a little shine. Of course, I yell and stomp with the other girls. I know my job.

The boys had just won a squeaker, and it was the game after the Fourth of July charity tournament our All-Star travel team played down in Rockville, and some of those players, having played six games over the weekend, were looking their age. Just because jocks play Senior Softball doesn't mean they're younger than anyone; six games is a lot. Looking older isn't as bad as feeling older, I always say—even though some of the girls wouldn't agree. Like that Mandy, who paid for her boobs, which everyone knows, so it's not even gossip.

I made Christmas stand there, and I hosed that girl down. It's a professional style hose, the water's cold and the pressure's strong, which made her do a little dance—she covered her chest with one arm and tried to cross her legs, but also used her hand to protect herself down there, and she hopped around and turned her back, or tried.

I love how water changes things. I've got this little waterfall in my breakfast room, a plug-in kind I bought myself for my birthday, and it makes all of those little pebbles shiny and wonderful. With a person, looking clean changes other ways we look. Christmas kept looking younger and younger in the hose, tall and skinny and sick and barely a baby. I had the funny impression that if I kept that hose on her, she'd wash away.

I had towels I could fetch, and a space blanket. She took off her hat—that was a shock to see—wrung it out and put it back on. She's not very smart, I thought, to put on a wet hat. She just stood there shivering.

I remember thinking she should not be drinking liquor. When I'm sick, drinking liquor makes me feel worse. And what if I had cancer. Meg O'Daly, that would not be fun.

I went to turn off the hose and get the space blanket in its foil pouch. The towels were folded on the backseat of the Kia, and the space blanket was in the Rubber Maid first-aid tub I keep in the trunk, so I had to go to the parking lot. "Stay here," I said to her. "You stay here." But I should have kept my eye on her. Any teenage girl named Christmas is bound to be a hellcat.

Life's funny, how people surprise you. You can give someone a gift—you can make them a housewarming combo bouquet out of the nicest silk flowers, add in a touch of spray, and use the vase that was in your collection, maybe from that condolence call you got when Dad died and the girls wouldn't leave the kitchen, they just stayed and stayed—and people can still look at you like you're Typhoid Meg. Like you were giving them a bomb or something, handing them a piece of crap (pardon my language, it's a little problem I have at times). "What people?" Bryson likes to ask, even though he's just teasing. He's a good man, my Bryson.

I was doing right by Christmas, but she was a wild child, and I should have known better. When I came back behind the snack shack, with the towels and the space blanket, shaking and snapping out the wrinkles as I turned the corner, she was gone. I wouldn't say ungracious if I didn't mean it—and I wouldn't mean it, except for that word she yelled at me, from the woods behind the creek. That wasn't very nice.

●

The second time I saw Christmas, I thought to myself, Meg O'Daly, this can't be true. There I was at Michael's, buying DMC Embroidery Floss, because it was on sale, off-season, and I had just turned the corner and made the most fabulous discovery near the restrooms, and darned if there wasn't Christmas again. It wasn't more than a few days later, but she looked pretty much the same, almost as wrung out. She looked like she was still standing there all sopping wet and shivering, covering her girl parts, except she was dry. Of course, the little girl could have gotten her period, she looked that pale. It can hit hard when it first hits and you're that skinny.

Michael's specializes in the best notions. Every holiday season, I send a note to the Michael's corporate office, telling them how much I appreciate them and what they do for their customers, how they think of the best items to sell, but this year, my note would have to be extra long. In the back of the store, on a shelf right where I could see them, were cardboard boxes already labeled: Secrets, Ideas, Things. What a great world we live in, I might have said aloud. "Meg O'Daly, it's a great world!"

"What?" Christmas was rubbing her hands together. She was taller when standing right before me.

I stayed in her way. I wasn't letting her get by me, not this time. I'm a person with some width to me.

"Look at that. Isn't that amazing."

"What?" Christmas said again. She did a little shift to the left. "Those boxes?"

I did a little shift to the right, blocking her way. I've raised four children, and I knew how to handle this one. "Okay, smarty," I said. "Let's see what you know." I took her by the wrist, skinny as a piece of string. "Get two boxes of each and follow me."

I moved her hand to the shelf, and I stood there and nudged her until she began to take down the boxes. Two each: Secrets, Ideas, Things. When she was done, I turned around and marched away, toward the front of the store and checkout.

I knew that girl would follow, because she had my boxes. Plus she was just the kind to make a lot of noise, dress in those awful clothes, grumble on and on, and then want to behave, to be good. She was only a child. She would follow me all the way home, especially if I offered her cookies or cake. Which I did, and she did. I told her to bring the bags from Michael's to my Kia, and then to get in, come with me, I had treats at home, and she looked surprised at every step, but she did what she was told.

Score one for Meg O'Daly.

•

We sat at my crafts table in what used to be Bryson's den, before he converted it into my art room. He never went in there, when it was his den; all he needs is a desk for his computer. It's much better now that it's my art room.

I gave Christmas some Oreos, and she seemed pretty happy about that. Everyone likes a good Oreo. I served on my Fourth of July plasticware, even though the setting was from a couple of years ago. The cookies weren't in the right colors, compared to the good old red-white-and-blue motif, but some things in life aren't right, like this girl having cancer, and losing all of her hair, and dying. She was a good girl, and I got sad to think about her dying. So I talked to her instead.

"Look at all this, won't you? We'll each have a box for each: Secrets, Ideas, and Things. You can come here and use your boxes any time you like. You just knock on the door, and if no one's home, I'll show you where the key rock is—it's in the garden, it's an As-Seen-on-TV Hide-a-Key rock. The ones that hide the key?"

I realized that I was talking too much. Meg O'Daly, I told myself, don't scare her.

"Would you like some pop with your cookies? I've got Sprite and Dr. Pepper."

Christmas had a mouth full of Oreos. She nodded. Her eyes were kind of watery. I wondered if that was the cancer, making her eyes soupy like that.

"Dr. Pepper?"

She nodded.

"One Dr. Pepper, coming right up."

I went alone into my kitchen. Bryson had just redone the wall-paper borders, and the yellow of the daisy pattern was new. Maybe I should have him do it again, make the wallpaper borders more green to go with the kitchen chairs. I had done the chairs in light green vinyl—a lettuce color. My kitchen was my second favorite room in the world, and the colors here had to make me happy.

That girl had me confused, if you can believe that. I had been standing in the middle of my kitchen, holding an empty glass in one hand and the big bottle of Dr. Pepper in the other and staring at nothing, just waiting for the world. I don't know how long I had been standing there; something in me had stopped moving. I wasn't the Meg O'Daly everyone knew.

The Dr. Pepper was open already. Bryson had been at the Dr. Pepper again, so this was likely a different bottle. It was one of his secrets that I wasn't supposed to know. He would buy Dr. Peppers to replace the Dr. Peppers, and I was supposed to act like I didn't know he was guzzling pop late at night, when he did his lineups and team emails, even though the doctor was worried about Bryson's sugars. Good thing he didn't think I was stupid—we could both just pretend that the Dr. Pepper was the Dr. Pepper.

Then I decided, because being wishy-washy isn't me. I am the luckiest woman on the planet to be standing in such a beautiful kitchen, and I had to do something. Something right.

I sat her at my crafts table. I could hear the central air, the water in my little fountain in the breakfast room trickling over the pebbles, the stand-up electric room freshener whirring, the cute Swiss clock in the hallway ticking, and my own breathing, *huh, huh*. I was hearing things very small.

Let's get going here, I decided.

We sat at the table, facing one another.

I looked at her, poor thing. I bet she didn't want to be treated like she was a poor thing. I said, "If you were dying real soon, would you choose a box which says 'Secrets,' 'Ideas,' or 'Things'?"

Christmas didn't answer. She sipped some of Bryson's Dr. Pepper. The Oreos were gone.

"Me, I wouldn't care."

That got a look back.

"But if I had to choose, maybe I'd want 'Secrets.' Because there wasn't going to be anyone to tell my secrets to."

I made my right hand flat, and I pushed one of the Secrets boxes a tiny bit toward Christmas, maybe just an inch. She still hadn't said anything.

Okay, I thought. Not that one.

"Or, maybe I would want 'Ideas,' because no one was going to know my ideas, because I was going to be dead."

I made my left hand flat, and I pushed one of the Ideas boxes toward her, then stopped pushing. I clasped my hands together and laid them on my stomach. Here's a church without a steeple, I told myself.

I made myself sit there.

Christmas' eyes moved, left to right, Secrets to Ideas. Right to left. Left to right, and that's where they stayed. She had chosen: Ideas it was.

"Okay," I said. "This one's yours."

I took the lid off of the Ideas box. Inside, there were dividers; the box had a plastic insert and little compartments. The dividers were each wrapped in plastic, how cute was that.

"My word!" I said to Christmas. "It's just like a person inside. All divided up. It's just like you and me!"

On the shelves along the wall—I had Bryson build them this past winter, when he was sitting around doing nothing again, another winter with Bryson waiting for spring—I keep stacks of construction paper and card stock in different colors. Not that I have a stationery store or anything, but I do like my craft papers in so many ways. Christmas wasn't big on chatting when crafting, some girls are like that, so I got up from the table and went over to the shelves.

"If I were to give you squares of paper, would you be happy? You could draw on them or write Ideas for your Ideas box."

Children who don't answer make me nuts. But I had to be patient. I could almost see the girl think that she was thinking she had to get out of here, that this crazy crafts lady was going to murder her with a pair of pinking shears. I knew exactly in which drawer I kept the shears, and she was right, if she didn't answer me, I might kill her. I had to make myself wait, and that was hard.

We both waited.

"Purple," Christmas finally said.

"Purple!" My voice was a little too squeaky. "Purple," I said. "I just happen to have purple, and we can use the big paper cutter and make squares out of it, and then it can be yours. You can have as many purple squares as your little heart desires."

"Rmm-ou," Christmas mumbled.

"Speak up, dear," I said.

"Thank you." She raised her head.

"You're welcome."

I decided I wouldn't murder her with the pinking shears after all. That was a funny joke I told myself just then.

But then I wondered, if I were dying, wouldn't I want to die right away, instead of waiting for it? Kill me, I thought.

"What are all these for?" Christmas had gone to use the restroom, and was calling from the trophy hall.

"They're trophies," I said.

"What for?"

"Senior ball. My husband plays."

There wasn't an answer. Christmas appeared in the doorway of the crafts room. She had a piece of something stuck to her cheek.

"I hate sports," she said, and moved to sit back at the table. She had work to do with her purple squares.

"You've got something—" I pointed toward her cheek. "There… almost…there!"

Christmas didn't laugh. A healthy girl would laugh, I realized later, after she had gone. Anyone healthy laughs at a thing stuck to her face. Dying makes people not funny, that's what I think.

●

I showed Christmas where the As-Seen-on-TV Hide-a-Key rock was, and how to let herself in through the breakfast room side door. I showed her where I would put the Secrets, Ideas, and Things boxes, on a little shelf just for her. I told her I'd leave a snack for her if I went out, that she should help herself, and that I often went out, because of Senior Softball and Bryson's league schedules, which were coming up on the playoffs, and she was welcome to come by anytime. I felt like I was talking to a stray cat, saying, "There will be a saucer of milk for you, Fluffy." What do strays die of? I'm not a cat person.

Once Christmas left, I thought about calling my phone chain and getting the girls involved. I thought a long time, sitting at my crafts table, cutting purple paper into squares to put into the Secrets, Ideas, and Things boxes, for her to find if she came back. I hoped she would.

Squares are perfect. I held one up. I turned it around, but that didn't matter. Then I decided to handle this situation myself, even though the girls on the phone chain like helping and they rely on me to tell them how.

This girl needed the Meg O'Daly touch.

•

Because I'm an artist, I understand what being different is like. Take jewelry, for example. I don't make a lot of jewelry, but when I do, it's because I'm inspired. I find that inspiration makes me different from other people. It doesn't occur to Bryson to sit at his crafts table and make jewelry as a gift for someone. That's my own thinking.

I use Stringing Enfilage/Enhebrar—the kind that comes on the card, I like the rainbow-colored—if I'm making necklaces. For earrings, I work with jewelry wire, and use 4mm jump rings and spacer bars and findings. I have nylon-covered round-nose pliers for opening the jump rings without scratching the metal, and once the rings are open, anything can be hung there and made pretty. My granddaughter Shayla loves making earrings. But as I tell Shayla, a girl's got to have pierced ears to wear earrings, and I don't make clip-ons, those are for beginners.

Here's what I think about wearing earrings: a girl wants to fit in, and she wants to look unique, but if she looks too unique, she won't fit in. It's just how society is. The boys are telling the girls, "I want you to look pretty," but they don't know what that means. A girl has to say what she wants and to decide how she looks. I grew up, and Daddy never let me want what I wanted. But Bryson's good, and he waits for me to say I'm ready before we go out.

My girls and boys, they grew up knowing better, although I'm not so sure about the oldest, Mark. He's in sales and he's just like my dad, one of those men who thinks he knows. Mark wouldn't act differently if you paid him—although he likes his money, that's obvious. He's a good salesman, my Mark, and he and Margie have my favorite grand-twins (okay, they're the only ones I have), even though they live so far from here, but I think that being in sales makes Mark feel like he knows better all of the time, telling a customer, "You want to have this generator because it's the best one on the market at the best price," whether or not that's true.

I think Mark's a bit opposite of me. I say, "Meg O'Daly, you've made something for someone, and even if you love it so much, you've got to give it to them. That's your job, because you're an artist."

When I make a present for someone, I try to picture that person a lot. I close my eyes and I open my eyes and I unfocus on the person, which helps me see the person. I want the person to be visible, to be smiling at me. Christmas kept coming up invisible, to me, and it wasn't because of her skinniness. I couldn't make myself see her. I didn't know who she was—I think it's because she's a young girl, and not a grown-up yet, and she's not one of my grandkids, and she's so wild, such a feral little thing. Which is why the earrings I made for her didn't work.

Nice earrings, too. Once I selected the findings and chose the spacer bars, I turned some silver wire around a little cylinder or tube or whatever it is, and then I added red wire next to the silver, for a striped effect, and I used my pliers to make a loop out of the red wire, and then I hung a little silver ball in the loop. Not real silver, of course. I think I made these earrings—picturing Christmas in my head—with the ball at the bottom because I was thinking about what a little kitty would wear. Like a bell on a collar.

I made two mistakes with these earrings. First, she wasn't a little kitty. Christmas was a different kind of person than that. I got that wrong. Second, I don't like cats, so why would I make something out of love for something I don't love.

Another way that crafting improves a person, an article said, is to help with "mental challenge and problem-solving." I agree completely. I appreciate a good mental challenge, which I think must be because I'm an artist. I like trying to solve things with art.

In the meantime, whenever I went out, I put a plate of Oreos on a dish and left it on my crafts table, with a matching napkin and a little note that said, "Welcome!" That's all the note said. Each time, the Oreos were still there. Then, on a Tuesday afternoon, when I went to stock up on Gatorade powder for the boys' game that night, I came home and the Oreos were gone. Christmas had been there—the thought made me smile, and made me think of Santa, too, even though that girl and Santa couldn't be further from one another.

I had done right and not left the earrings for her, but I had to make something. That girl was sick, and I had to love her somehow. She had asked to be loved, by coming back for the Oreos.

A necklace was wrong, mittens were wrong, a little coin purse was wrong, a tooled belt was wrong, a glasses case with lots of bling was wrong (although one of my favorite gifts to give), a blouse with embroidered collar points was wrong (too cowgirl), a lampshade was wrong. The mental challenge continued.

Christmas came back on Wednesday. She waited for me to go out—she must have been hiding nearby—and she ate the Oreos again. This time, I found the dish in the kitchen sink instead of on the crafts table. The Secrets, Ideas, and Things boxes were all in the same place.

Christmas came back on Friday. Oreos gone, and the dish in the sink. We were having something together, like we were leaving messages. Maybe she was coming into unfocus a bit more.

I called my daughter Christy, the nurse, in Columbus, Ohio, and told her about Christmas.

"Her name's like yours," I said. "I should have named you Christmas."

"Mom," Christy said. "Joe's due home soon and I'm working tonight."

"I know, I know, this won't be but a sec. Be sympathetic for a change, would you? What should I give her?"

I had to leave too, since the drive to A.B. takes fifteen minutes and the game was starting at 7:00. Bryson wants his Gatorade when he wants it.

Christmas was changing my life in so many ways.

"I don't know, Mom. Make her something. Like you do." I could tell Christy was exasperated. "Make her something she'll wear. Look, I've got to go—"

"Of course, honey. You tell your Joe his mother-in-law says hi. That should surprise him plenty. Happy trails to Joe from me."

I went out again on Friday, and Christmas came and ate the Oreos and cleaned up after herself, fourth day in a row. I was beginning to wonder if she might like a different kind of cookie. Maybe I would put two kinds of cookies on the plate. Maybe if a person's dying, she only wants her very favorite cookie all the time.

Bryson's Friday night softball team has a few different players than his Tuesday night team. Some guys who play Senior ball aren't retired, and they can't play during the week for work reasons, but they like the weekend warrior routine. Some of them are real good, too, and the Friday team, "Oldies But Goodies," OBG, they're fun to watch. One guy, R.J., used to play college ball, he's a beast in center, and he hits it out two or three or even four times a game. He grunts when he hits the ball, which makes us girls smile.

Bryson's OBG team has OBG hats that I ordered through a website, and OBG logos on their jerseys custom made by Willard Smith at The Craft Maxi Mart. CraftMaxiMart.com does the best custom labels and logos, and Tom Smith's my guy on the phone. Since OBG is sponsored by MotoRivals, the European sports car place on North Central, there's money enough to pay for Tom Smith's fancy work. Sponsors are important.

I was packing Bryson's extra gear and a hat for a substitute player, late Friday—the game was at 8:30—and I looked at the OBG hat, and the logo, and there was the answer. Just like that, I knew what to make. Christmas was in luck. Christmas would come early this year, I told myself, but the joke didn't make sense, even though it had Meg O'Daly love in spades.

•

I can't do anything but keep the book when I'm keeping the book. The official scorer for each team has to watch every play and use the System 17 method that the Official Quick Tally™ Scorebook requires, and to show the ump the score if asked, which happens at the end of each half inning but sometimes more often than that. I know this is boring for most people, but not for me. That night, though, for the first time I could remember, I didn't want to keep the book. Which shook me up a little: Meg O'Daly was going through something.

I wanted, instead, to be knitting. I knew the hat I was going to knit for Christmas. Although I probably had to stop at Michael's for more purple yarn.

Everyone else at A.B. Park was so alive. The center fielder, R.J., would hit the ball and grunt, and for once, it seemed to me the saddest thing I'd ever seen.

•

I'm a knitter, so knitting a hat doesn't take me very long, and even if I want a more sophisticated hat than a basic beanie, the work's easy. There are lots of patterns on the Internet—including "Inside Out Chemo Cap," which I would never make for anyone. I woke up extra early that Saturday morning and went right to my crafts table, drinking my coffee and wearing my art clothes, sweatpants and an old shirt of Bryson's. I like getting dressed for work, for my job; it's like going to an office, where today I would be knitting Christmas a purple hat.

It's a funny moment, isn't it, giving a gift? "Here, I made this for you"—that's a wonderful thing to say, one of the best in the world, as sayings go, everyone should feel what that feels like. I know what I'm talking about. But there's something to those feelings that isn't logical. I make a hat, it's Meg's hat while I'm making it, and then it's not Meg's hat anymore, it's someone else's. When I see that person put on the hat, I think, "That's my hat, I made that." So I own it again. Gifts come back to me that way.

Tom Smith at TheStudio.com made beautiful patches for me last year, for the shirts everyone wore at the charity tournament we played at the beach, even the wives and girlfriends. (The ones from GreenStreetArts.com weren't as nice, and a little more expensive. We made that mistake the year before.) The girls and I all agreed that Tom Smith makes the most beautiful logos and arm patches.

Once Christmas' hat was done, which meant I decided not to block the fabric because it would stretch the ribbing too much, I sewed one of the red patches from Tom Smith onto the folded cuff. The girl could roll down the edge and not show the patch, if she chose. Only she and I needed to know what it said. That was important.

The patch said, "Meg's Team."

After a nice lunch of tuna salad and one of Bryson's Dr. Peppers, which maybe I shouldn't have taken, but it was in honor of Christmas, I thought a lot about how to give the hat to Christmas. I thought a lot about her face, and the moment she had that piece of something stuck to her cheek. I especially thought about that moment, and how she didn't laugh. It occurred to me that while I was sitting in my breakfast room, holding her hat, she could be outside waiting for me to leave, that she might want her Oreos right now. She could be out there—the day was sunny and hot, weather I like, now that the Change has stopped for me, thank god, no more hot flashes—but she could be sweating all kinds of tomorrows because she was dying. Maybe that was why she was drunk in the creek, because she was sweating, drunk, and dying.

I decided to put the hat in her Things box. I would put the hat in the Things box and then go for a drive in my Kia. I didn't know where I wanted to drive, just to drive. Maybe I would see something.

It wasn't a Secrets hat, or an Ideas hat, just a purple beanie I had made for her. She would find it when she found it.

I took down her three boxes. That made my curious.

She had been busy, that child. There were purple notes in her Secrets box, on the purple paper I had cut up for her. I read them all.

I hate you, the first one said.

Hose Lady owes me a phone, the second one said.

You broke my phone!

I didn't know I had broken her phone. Was that when she was in the creek? She probably dropped it, I didn't break it. Just like a teenager to blame everyone. I could leave her a note and tell her she broke her own phone, and she could be responsible for once, and buy herself a new phone.

That's not Meg O'Daly, I told myself. Maybe she was responsible.

I read another note: *There's water in my phone bitch.* I wondered if that was the first note. I couldn't tell the order. But the thoughts mattered. So I just stacked them up and reread them.

I hate Hose Lady.

This is a stupid house.

Why do you care?

I don't care about you.

ppl don't care.

I'm going to steal a towel.

Mrs. O'Daly are you reading this?

This is fun.

No one cares b/c there's no trophy Hose Lady.

I hate Aunt Nikki.

Aunt Nikki's a bitch mom.

Mrs. O'Daly may I have more Oreos? See I'm nicer than you?

I hate my life.

Mrs. O'Daly your grandkids must love you b/c they don't know you.

Hose Lady I'm not your pet.

Mrs. O'Daly you're reading my Secrets.

Purple's fun.

Damn straight it hurts.

Hose Lady where's your husband?

I hate my life.

I hate this house.

I hate my life.

Dr. Peppers make my nose tingle vm when I drink fast.

I hate I can't stop.

Hose Lady thank you.

FIREWORKS

No one ever remembers what I look like. I'm tall, I'm short, I have blue eyes or green or brown, my hair stands up, my hair is moussed, my hair is cut short, my nose is flat, pointed, wide, sloped, I'm white, I'm Italian, I'm Latino, I'm Jewish. I have a weak chin, I need a shave, I have sideburns, I have a birthmark below my left ear (true), I have long fingers, I always wear fingerless gloves. I'm quiet or I'm talkative. I'm a loner but I like people. I've got some of these characteristics, different ones, depending who's asked—it's amazing what people can't remember about me. If you ask my girlfriend, Liana, I'm good-looking, I have sexy wrists, which she says matters. She's got a great body, and she's too good for me, I admit it. She's going to be a badass math teacher once her student teaching's done and she gets her certification.

I'm a combination of invisible and really invisible. If you want to know if I'm good-looking and you ask my dad, he'll say who cares. Ask that girl, Christmas, who I am—I'm the guy, Sam, who caught her shoplifting, who plays *Minecraft*, and who talked her into doing something totally off the chain.

I like my anonymity. It's like a flavor you can't identify on your sandwich, what is that flavor? When you nuked the two $3.99 fake-ham-and-fake-cheese sandwiches in their wrappers at the

MiniMart gas station—where I'm the night manager, like Apu on *The Simpsons*—without reading what all was on the sandwiches, you had no clue what you were having. Then once the sandwiches got hot enough to eat, you ate them, standing right there. Steaming in their plastic, they wouldn't taste like ham or cheese, or anything I'd call food. They're food stuff: a person should know what they're eating. Sure, you were too hungry to wait, and you were abso-tooting-rooting-lutely drunk as stink. Even though I was stoned, I caught you, and because you didn't have any money, that's stealing. I don't care that you're dying or whatever, or that you're just a girl, or you're gonzo. I don't care that you call yourself Christmas. I've got you now, I can talk you into doing shit, and no one will know I'm behind it all, that's the truth. I've been waiting for you, Christmas. That's what I told her, and it worked.

I knew she was bombed because you know. I get stoned most nights before I go to work, but not when I come home, I'm straight by then, and I don't smoke up again. I know that's backwards. Remember, I'm the guy you can't remember, the one you expect to get stoned *after* work, chilling, but no way, this guy likes sleeping it off and then getting up in the afternoon and thinking in his brain before he goes back to his slave job. *Minecraft's* better. Hanging out with Liana's better. Googling is better. Planning is better.

On "Silly Evil Genius," my favorite web cartoon, the bad guy's always planning, but he comes up with the dumbest shit. That's why the cartoon's funny. Lester, the Silly Evil Genius, can't think of anything really evil to do. I know why he's like that. Lester's got no ex-girlfriends. If he had ex-girlfriends, he'd have lots of evil ideas. Ex-girlfriends are the source of wars—just look at Starbuck in the *BSG* reboot.

I've got three ex-girlfriends, the most recent being Deedee, who dumped me four years ago. We were going to get married, that's what she said. But *Smash Brothers*, boom, I'm dumped. Normally, like other normal guys, I would be a little pissed at Deedee, but being who I am, being pissed takes a long time. It's slow. I'm a planner, I'm an evil genius, and I love revenge, and I love anonymous revenge even more, and so I wait and wait. I wait four years, grooving on the slow thing.

I was always this guy, the one who tied your shoes together when you weren't looking, who had his costume six months before Halloween, who knew what mailbox he would booby-trap next summer, who wrote someone else's name in the wet concrete of the sidewalk. Being an evil genius means two things: one, do funny and low stuff to people who hurt me; and two, don't get caught. Now that I'm older, I have changed, I have grown up. Now I have introduced the notion of patience into my evil genius schemes. Patience makes revenge more satisfying. Waiting and waiting and knowing I'm going to screw up Deedee someday—see how I don't say "fuck up," I'm more mature than you know—that's the best. Of course, I don't intend to screw her up so she gets hurt or anything really bad happens, because I'm not a psychopath and I'm careful about what's a felony, but doing something funny and mean, that's my long-term goal. Even if I have to make many small evil genius moves along the way to other people, to keep myself entertained. *Thatthh entertainment*, as Lester likes to lisp.

Here's what I think about fitting into society. Other people, especially other people who play *Mortal Kombat* or *WOW* or *Counterstrike* or any of the other FPS or RPG games and especially *Grand Theft Auto*, the kinds of people who lose their minds to their Xbox or PlayStations, they might be dysfunctional, but we know who those gamers are. The cliché is that they're fat and live in their moms' basements, but that's an oversimplification. Those gamers, they're recognizable because we can see their secrets, there's nothing to make them invisible. They don't know how to hide. A weirdo is a type.

They're at the mall, they're online, they're vulnerable. We see them lose their brains when there's a Gamergate—but we know them, they're knowable, and that makes them vulnerable.

No one knows who I am. I'm not a gamer, a slacker, a pothead, a nerd, a twink, a jock, or a Dilbert. I'm not Apu. I shower, I dress in polo shirts and skinny jeans, respectable as a business student or the manager of your local Sunglass Hut. I have no visible tattoos when I have my clothes on. If there's a party, I'll be there, sure, and you'll talk to me, but you won't remember our conversation. It's what I do. If I have something smart to say, I keep it to myself.

Liana changed who I am, of course. We don't live together yet, and that's cool with me for now, but just hanging out with her, I've got less time to be an evil genius. I know I'm a guy, and guys are stupid when they're horny, but it's not only the sex that makes her special. I have learned to go into my body, and into hers, and disappear, be gone. In fact, that's a good way to have sex. Although I'm not sure if this is right, it kind of feels like swimming.

Hanging with Liana means I have to make another set of plans that aren't evil as I prepare for events that I can't predict. I know, that sounds backwards too, but when you're with another person romantically, and now the future's got definite possibilities, you really can't know what will happen. It's like some weird unpredictability factor in a game. Like in *Minecraft*, you're playing multiplayer, and you're concentrating hard because there are too many spiders, when suddenly some Internet bozo you don't know humps along and wrecks everything you've carefully built, and then you're homeless and the zombies kill you. That kind of brutal, no-prisoners vandalizing in *Minecraft* is called a "griefing." In life, my family priest, Father Massima, would call it "fate."

Both Liana and I believe in fate. Liana grew up Catholic, like me, only hers was a big family in Colombia. Her father's American and her mother's Colombian. Dad was a Marine doing a thing down there, and that's how they met. I've only met the moms once, when she visited from Atlanta, but the dad's not talked about any more. I don't think he's dead. Liana shut up when I asked, and she did that evil eye move, reaching for one of the saint's medals she wears on a little gold chain, and giving me the death stare. So I didn't ask again, even though I'm curious. I think she'll tell me eventually, but we're not at the point where I can put it there and expect an answer.

My idea of fate is different. *Minecraft* teaches us to die and die and die and eventually live. That's fate. Every day is like that, that's what I think, and one day, it will be better, but a man has to practice to get there. You have to practice for fate. Which is a little like what real Catholics believe, but not the ones who are evil geniuses.

I grew up here, Sam Vinieri, the baby of the family, little Sammy V, who became just Sam except to his mother, she still calls me Sammy, even though I'm twenty-six. My mom and dad are both good people; he's in tool and die and she's a secretary, although Dad's had trouble keeping work since '09, bouncing around various jobs. My older brother and two older sisters went to College Park, and the smartest one in the family, like ever, my sister Julie, is going to be a pediatrician. Another older brother died in the Gulf—Bruce. I miss him.

I'm more normal than you on the outside. Being an evil genius requires that I maintain all appearances, that my actions appear natural. So I apply to programs—that's the magic word when I talk to my mom, "programs." See, Mom, I've applied to a program in leadership and business through the Knights of Columbus. Hey, Mom, I've applied to a program to be an EMT. Look, Mom, I've applied to a great program in social work. I'm convincing. I actually have a BS in Psych from Frostburg State—my favorite course was Environmental Psych, taught by Berkey, he cracked me up—and I look so plain no

one knows I'm a college boy. Sometimes I even apply to these programs. Liana likes me to have ambitions, and it's fun to fill out forms
together. When she's not looking, I finish and close the app without
paying the fee: I have stuff to do before the world makes me actually
normal. Smart, right?

Liana knows nothing about my being an evil genius, or my secret
revenge plans, or that I ever think about Deedee. Of course, Liana
had to meet Christmas, but that became part of the whole thing.
Christmas, now that's a screwy kid. She was cool with the plan from
the beginning. If she doesn't die soon, she could be an awesome evil
genius herself.

There's more to being an evil genius than planning and punk-
ing people. It's a way of looking at fate and reality and the rest, of
showing people who they are. That's how I think about it: I'm here to
show you who you are. I'm here to help.

For instance, I might be at work, and let's say I'm not stoned,
because I know the cops who patrol the neighborhood have been
coming around more often, checking front and back, due to smash-
and-grabs being on the rise. I can talk to them when I'm stoned, but
I don't always like to, since they're cops. They're kind of innocents,
too—I don't know how to explain that about cops, but they are. They
believe in the badge and all.

Get this: I'm in the MiniMart alone, I'm in my booth, behind
my bulletproof glass, the blunts and the Powerball tickets safe too,
and an old couple comes into the store. Let's say it's one, one thirty
in the morning, and they're decked in evening wear—they're really
old, like Tillie and Tino in that game, *Hall of Reapers*, the two Sages.
I like those Sages; they've got cool whisper cloaks. So this old guy
in my store, he's in a tux and she's got some fluffy fake fur on, even
in this weather, and I can see the dark green of a poofy dress underneath. They're kind of awesome. They could be fifty-five, but I bet

she's younger. Her earrings are long and yellow and sparkly, even in the pissy yellow MiniMart.

I'm guessing they want bottles of water, now that they've put gas in the Lexus. I play the mirrors—if I were stoned, that would be even more fun, watching the customers in the round, weird mirrors, following them in one mirror and then tracking them in another. Sure enough, they're reaching for bottles of water in the back, heading up to the front to check out.

Here's the evil genius in me. When I saw them at the pumps, topping up the Lexus, I took a twenty from the register and came out from behind my counter and and laid that twenty-dollar bill on the floor in Aisle 3. Now they're coming up Aisle 4, perfect. Watch and learn.

"Um, ma'am, sir. If you look down there, we've got a two-for-one on Perrier." I'm pointing from inside my bulletproof booth. I tap on the heavy plastic a couple of times to indicate where. The straightest path to the Perrier is down Aisle 3.

They turn to look. "Yeah, down there," I say. Tap, tap.

What I want most is for him to go first, to be a little bothered he missed the two-for-one Perriers—he's a dude who notices stuff like that, that's how he got to be where he is in life—and for her to follow, and then for her to see the twenty. In my experience, he'd just pocket it: he's an old guy in a tux. But she would have to hold up the bottom of her dress to squat or scooch down, use her left hand to keep the dress off the dirty floor of the MiniMart, and scoop up the $20 bill in her right, and that would take a decision and a little effort, she might feel she earned the free money.

I want her to have to choose what to do, once she picks up the money. I'm not taking twenty bucks from the till and screwing up my count for just anyone.

She's the kind of woman who never sees how safe she is. She lives with cameras everywhere, she goes all sorts of places where she's being watched, where there are security people scarfing Bugles in bulletproofed booths and back rooms and looking out for her, but she doesn't know about any of that. She never thinks about it. The world is totally her world, it's gated for her, and the twenty is hers, if that's what she decides. She doesn't have to look around once she picks up the bill to see if anyone's watching or if she's doing wrong, she's that sure. What she wants is hers, that's how she rolls—and really, she doesn't even have to think it. Money says she's right.

I want to make her look around, and then I want to see what she does with the twenty. Will she walk to the coolers along the back wall, turn, and then come down Aisle 3 again, and drop the bill where she found it? Will she pocket the cash? I don't think she has any pockets, looking at her dress. Will she return the money to me, turn in the twenty, here you go, young man, this was on the floor? I worry that her life has taught her to skate moments like this, not to see a decision as important, and I want to change that, I want her to have to make the call, to think in a new way.

Maybe I can see a little perspiration forming on her forehead, although I can't see her face very well, and it's possible she's sweating in the small of her back, in her armpits. Her makeup was already pretty smudged when she came in, probably from dancing at the charity ball they went to, the silent auction where they bought that dumb watercolor they'll never hang in their pool house. It's been a hot July and tonight's hotter. I'm making her be a different person in her life right now, even though she doesn't give a cat's crap about a measly twenty bucks, from the look of her, and she hasn't had to think about paying in cash in forever. Her lipstick probably cost forty.

My plan's working. The guy in the tux cruises Aisle 3 without seeing the twenty, headed for the bargain Perrier, walking faster now that he's got a goal, he's a goal-oriented guy. He's all about the game of life, Mr. Lexus. Got some cheese? He's a good mouse.

The woman's slower, really slow behind him, maybe because of her dress and wrap, maybe she's tired, she switched from Champagne to gin, and that couldn't have been a good idea, she might even be a little wobbly. Yes.

I see her see the twenty.

Flash, I'm ready, I have my keys, I come out of my booth, pull the door shut behind me: in just a couple of strides, I catch up to her as she's bending down to pick up the money, her back to me.

When she puts out her left hand, for balance, clutching her purse, and straightens up again, I'm right there, close enough.

"Ma'am?" I say. That's all.

"I…"

I wait. Evil geniuses wait.

For sure, she crushes and balls the twenty as she does a slow one-eighty to see who I am. She's even older up close, not bad-looking, pretty mouth, her hair piled up like that, done up, a little dazzle in her eye, and clearly at least a little drunk. The way she looks at me, she looks smart—that's even better, I think.

"Ma'am. The two-for-one deal is good on chips too." I point to the end-cap, make myself more invisible.

She's not going to show me the twenty.

That's it, how I run the world, change her life, reveal to her herself, her moral failings. Her guilt. I show her her fate.

When he pays, she adds two bags of Lays (baked, of course) to go with the two Perriers. She's twenty dollars richer, and she thinks that matters, it's better for the buzz, which is life sometimes, its own buzz.

•

Liana is coming over later, my roommate Anders is at work, and I'm playing *Minecraft* and Christmas is watching. Christmas is thirteen years old; that gets me. I can pretty much remember being thirteen years old, watching my older brother Bruce play *Call of Duty* before he went off to Iraq and got killed. We were in the playroom, and maybe one of my sisters was there too? Makes sense, but I don't remember—there was usually a sister around, but maybe not. In my memory, it's just Bruce.

It's not a memory I can control.

Christmas says, "Do you have anything to eat?"

"Hold on," I say. Even though I'm in Survivor mode, and it's early, I have to pay attention: the Creepers will blow themselves up, and then I'm dead.

She sits on the couch with her legs crossed. She's been here an hour; she came over just after I woke up. The air conditioning in the apartment's been struggling, making a puddle on the floor, which I've got a towel on, and Christmas and I are both too hot. We're drinking pop, that helps, but I can't drink too much pop on an empty stomach, I get the acid.

"I'm hungry," she says.

"Hold on, hold on." I use my sword to kill a Creeper. "Bam." I pause. "I'll get us a pizza," I say.

"Pepperoni," she says.

"Pepperoni's gross."

She slaps my shoulder. What a teenager.

Hanging out with Christmas means I have to act like a thirteen-year-old boy, but I also have to treat her like an adult. It's a challenge.

"No hitting," I say. "Remember?"

"You're a dick," she says. "Pepperoni."

"You're a douche," I say. "Now…who's the evil genius here?"

Christmas giggles. "You."

"Right. Don't you forget it." I hit her shoulder.

"NO HITTING!"

Christmas likes to sit on my couch with her legs tucked under her, making her tall body short. She never takes off her boots, which bugs me, it's hot in here. She can sit there for a couple of hours and write in her journal while I play *Minecraft*, and we don't have to talk—impressive for a kid, I think. She's super extra-skinny, scary skinny, and the chemo or whatever has made her hair fall out, I presume, so she wears a purple beanie that says "Meg's Team." It's a dumb beanie, probably from the Salvation Army. That kind of makes the beanie cool, I guess, one of those hats that's cool because it's dumb. I never could figure out how to be cool by being dumb, but she's got some of that happening, even being just a dorky teenager.

I've only known Christmas for three weeks, but we've spent time together, usually like this, when I get up in the early afternoon and the kid just comes over and hangs out. She writes in her journal and then stuffs it in her dumb purse. It's happened like four, five times.

Mostly, Liana's sympathetic, but she's tough too.

"Be careful," Liana said last week.

"I've never had a little sister," I said.

"You're crushing on her, that's all," Liana said. She was getting ready to leave. She tells me important stuff right before she leaves. "I know you," Liana said. "You'll get over it. But she's crushing on you too. And they're unreliable at this age. I was..." Her thought went away, like she was remembering. "You'll see. Just be careful."

I had my elbows on the counter in the kitchen, my face leaning on one hand. I stayed there.

"Lula-Lu," I said, 110% charm, Liana the only one. "It's more than that. She's here for a reason—it's July, there's no school, she doesn't know anyone, her aunt's a bitch...she's a mess. She needs someone. She just sits there and I play *Minecraft* and we talk. That's it. What if she dies, like, tomorrow?"

Liana looked right into me. She can change what I feel with that look. "She's not a puppy," she said. "You can't have a familiar." The look done, she slipped her phone into her purse and put on her sunglasses, applying her lip gloss without using a mirror, the conversation over. She waited at the door.

"That's funny," I said, coming around the counter to give Liana a peck on the cheek, my hand on her hip. "Bye, babe."

"Bye."

But I didn't think it was very funny, actually.

Letting Christmas know that I'm an evil genius became part of the plan before it was planned. I had waited a long time for someone else to help, but I didn't really know that—until there she was, scarfing down those sandwiches in the MiniMart, stealing, and I had to do something to change her thinking, too. True, I didn't know about Christmas when I made the plan, but now I've adjusted. I've got Christmas covered.

The pizza arrives, half pepperoni, half pineapple and ham, and free jalapeño poppers. I give the guy a good tip. I'm a good tipper.

Christmas doesn't smile when she takes a slice, but I can tell she's happy. "Mmm," she says. Then she looks a little embarrassed to have made a yum-yum eating sound. She reaches for a popper.

"Mmm," I say too, to help.

She's so skinny. On top of being sick, she could have one of those eating disorders too, like she's going to puke after. Christmas just bites and gulps her food, she's awful, like she's grunting or something. That kind of thing, my mom would rap my knuckles with her spatula—manners, Sammy.

We eat some more, and I try not to watch. Then Christmas asks, "When are we going to do it?"

"Soon," I say.

"She doesn't know anything!" Christmas takes another too-big bite of pizza. Her mouth's full, and the words garble. "Rhut's her name arren?"

"Deedee. Why can't you remember that? Dee-deeeee. And she hasn't thought about me in forever," I say, thirteen years old too. "She's totally into someone else."

"Evil genius," Christmas says to her slice of pizza. "What are we going to do to her?" When I don't answer, she does for herself, "I know, I know, you'll tell me." And then, looking toward the kitchen, she asks, "Is there more Pepsi?"

"Lazy dweeb," I say. I un-pause *Minecraft*. "Get it yourself. Get me one too, please. With ice, in a glass."

Minecraft's cool. In *Minecraft*, if you choose Survivor mode instead of Hardcore mode, when you die, you can respawn. That means you get another life, you haven't lost, you can go to the house you built and it will still be there, and when you find your corpse, you can rummage around and collect all of the resources you accumulated before dying, your minerals, meat, and sticks. Or you can go back to your farm and grow more pumpkins and cacti. So you get to start again from where you were, basically.

I don't believe in reincarnation, no way that's true. I believe in fate, I believe in free will, I believe in evil, but not Satan. I believe in God but not the God my mom talks to at Mass, and not the Holy Virgin, and not the blood and the body, and not Jesus Christ, Our Lord and Savior.

I don't worship *Minecraft*, like some people do in the chat rooms, or the way the weirdos talk on their player blogs. It's just a game. But I get what those weirdos are thinking. You don't have to worship something to see it's religious.

I wonder, as she's watching me play *Minecraft*, while we're sweating in my crappy apartment eating pizza, what the hell Christmas thinks of all this. If she weren't thirteen, I might ask. Her life's like she's bad at *Minecraft* without even playing.

•

There's more to being an evil genius and having a plan than anyone can know. Naturally, I have to make contingency plans—if she does this, I do that—but it's more than just preparedness, this isn't the Boy Scouts of America, good night, Felicia. There are levels of difficulty, ways to understand achievements in relation to aspiration and effort, it's more experimental psychology than hard science. When I make an evil plan, I design three or four mini contingencies inside the possible outcome, I make goals for myself and my subjects, backup plans for my backup plans. I learned that in school, in Experimental Psych. What's important, too, is to set a few goals that will never be reached by anyone, because the world's not perfect, no world is. I'm not changing fate, I can't do that. I'm showing Deedee what her fate has always been.

The plan for Deedee includes two big bags of fireworks I bought three years ago at Phantom Fireworks, when they had a pop-up sale in the Big Lots lot. I've got a couple of packs of Blue Streak Rockets and Fiery Frogs, one rocking box of Shagadelic Mojo 16 Shots, and the pièce de résistance, a Bada Bing Bada Boom 19 Shot box. I don't know very much about fireworks, aside from Googling the Grucci family, who turned out to be kind of cool. They're good old Southern Italians, a thing my mom and dad always appreciate. The Grucci family did the fireworks at the Olympics in Beijing in 2008, and that was my favorite. They're a sixth-generation family business, which I consider American by now, and I care a lot about America and what's American and who, since my brother Bruce died for America. Then last year, holy hand grenade, Batman, politics went crazy, and then the government even changed who gets to be American. I can't decide what I think about all that, especially since it's changing again every day.

I keep the fireworks in the basement of my building, in a corner storage area the landlord let me lock up, all of that gunpowder just sitting there. I like to think of the fireworks waiting, how they're waiting there like me, getting ready. Like I'm gunpowder inside.

Sometimes I wonder what would happen if the basement got too hot, like in weather like this, and the fireworks went off—I would be in trouble, but it would be an accident. I've also wondered what would happen if I went down there and lit the fireworks on purpose. I'd probably get caught, the investigators would be able to tell who did it from my DNA and they would CSI everything, and I'd probably go to jail, or at least pay restitution. I've done my research. Arson in Maryland is a misdemeanor, unless there's over $1,000 in property damage or anyone gets hurt. There are other options: I could light it all, then turn on a hose to put out the secondary fires. I could save everyone.

I'm not going to light the Bada Bing Bada Boom collection in a bag of dog shit on Deedee's doorstep and run away. I'm not a child, which she conveniently forgot when she dumped me, when she called me an "immature little twerp." We were at River Walk, and she shook me off, she wouldn't hold my hand, she was really pissed, we were in the mall and everyone was watching us. I think we were standing in front of Old Navy. I hate Old Navy, I hated Old Navy even before that day, and she called me a little twerp and she screamed that she never wanted to see me again.

When she ran away from me, I yelled after her like a moron, "I'm not a little twerp. I'm a…I'm a…" and then I yelled the dumbest thing ever: "I'M BIGGER THAN A LITTLE TWERP! I'M MATURE!" I was so confused. "FUCK!" I yelled.

One of the aspects of fate that really gets me, one agreed on by the Catholic Church and the gamers who play *Minecraft*, is that fate's both predetermined and in an individual's hands. That's stupid. You can't change what happened, only what you think about what happened, not to mention the whole contradictory combo burrito Father Massima calls Confession and Absolution, forget that. You can't wipe life out. I don't know any decent video game that lets a player go back in time and change the past in order to make the present and the future different, like the *Terminator* movies or *Continuum*. In pretty much every game, if you're reborn, you respawn, and then you start from where you were popped. Starting over is a new game.

I would change the past, probably, even though I've got Liana now, and I want the future to include her. I'd change Christmas' past, for sure. It would be enough, in life, to let that kid reboot.

Which makes me think about Bruce again: he died in Iraq, he gave his life for me. I'm not so narcissistic to think he did it only for me, but he did do it for me. He told me that, kind of, I think.

I don't know Christmas well at all, Liana's right, but the girl's almost the age I was when Bruce joined, she's only thirteen. What would I give for her? What would I do for her? What should an evil genius do for someone he barely knows?

•

I haven't been stoned in five days, and work has totally sucked as a result, what a snooze-a-thon, but it's all part of the plan, being clear-headed. I've been working out, doing free weights in my living room, curls and all. My eye's on the day, next Saturday—Deedee Day, I call it, although I'm not telling anyone that stupid joke. Part of being invisible is knowing not to share every dumbass thought, every joke or nasty comment I could make, or any emotions that can get a guy in trouble. I have emotions, but I only let them out a little, spin them out, and only one at a time. People can hurt you.

Christmas is hanging out in my apartment again, sitting there on the couch like everything's fine. I'm beginning to get that Liana's right, the kid is crushing on me, but so what. There's nothing dirty or creepy in how I treat her—in fact, I think it's kind of the opposite,

I treat her like an adult, even if Christmas wants me to behave like a little kid most of the time. Maybe we treat people really better when they're almost dead. R-E-S-P-E-C-T, that oldies song always seems to be playing at the MiniMart. I like that song.

In *Minecraft*, there's a mode called Creative, which I don't like nearly as much as Survivor. Creative is like ultra Survivor, in a way, since you get unlimited resources and you don't need a crafting table and there's no crafting grid. You can destroy everything in Creative, which bothers me, since no one's that powerful. Sure, I know people aren't the same as games, and we're not God, but rules teach us. In Creative, you can fly, and the coolest things can happen when you fly, which is why I sometimes play in Creative.

There's one sun in *Minecraft*, because it's not such an alien world that the planets multiply or anything, although it's not Earth either, since there are zombies and pigmen and dragons and Endermen. It's a fantasy that's like reality. There's one moon, although you don't ever go to the moon, or at least I've never been there. The coolest thing that happens, though, is that if you fly really high in Creative, you can fly above the clouds, and then there's a moment when the sun and the moon look weird—it looks like there are two suns. I think it's a glitch, even if the *Minecraft* Wiki says the illusion's due to the render distance being too small. But on the Wiki, players also say that changing the render distance doesn't have an effect on whether you see two suns.

Two suns. I love that. Every day is two days. Maybe one of the days would be a secret.

"Stop," Christmas says.

I didn't think she was paying attention.

"Right there. What's that?"

"It's two suns. I'm in Creative. But it's not really two suns, it's just a bug."

"Whoa," Christmas says. Then she writes something really quickly in her journal.

"I know, like, dude."

"Don't be such an old guy, Sam." Christmas isn't looking at me.

"Whattaya mean?"

"'Dude,'" she quotes. "Like, dude? Like that's really neat."

She's making fun of me. It's good, I think, and kind of irritating.

"Look," I say. "I can jump down and fly over here."

Christmas puts down her pen. She's watching the game closely, like she cares. What the hell, I think, and so I ask: "Do you want to play?"

"What?"

"Do you want to play?" The game's on pause and I'm offering her the laptop. "You can sit here."

She scowls at me. I said something wrong. "What?" I say.

She's starting to cry, oh no. Now she's really crying. The faucets open.

"What? What is it? What did I say?"

"Just…don't look at me. I don't want to learn anything," says the girl with cancer. "You're an asshole."

This is a serious moment, I think. I don't know what to do, so I sit there. She cries. There might be words in her tears, but I can't make them out. After a little longer, she seems to calm down.

"I'm sorry," I say. "I'm an asshole," I say.

"You're an asshole."

"I'm an enormous asshole. The biggest."

"The biggest asshole." She's starting to smile a little, maybe.

"Sorry," I say again. "Dude, like, I'm sorry."

"Fuck you," Christmas smiles at me. "Dude." She pulls down on her hat, yanking on the left and then the right, then rolling up the front a little, adjusting as though it matters, serious, but doing better.

I save. I can come back to the game later.

She needs something, I think.

"Do you want to know the whole plan?" I say.

Christmas nods, her eyes open wide, the crying done.

"Saturday," I say. There are a boatload of crumbs on my lap, and I brush them off. Anders is a slob, so crumbs on the floor won't matter. "This weekend. It's happening. Let's go down to the basement. I want to show you something."

●

Liana and I met at Sullivan's two years ago. She was there at happy hour on a Friday night to meet a guy, not a blind date, but he turned out to be a donk anyway, and I was sitting at the bar on her other side, and I could hear him donk out, and so I started making wiseass comments and she started paying attention. When I leaned in a little, I discovered that her hair smelled amazing, but then I thought too close, too close. But she wrote her number on a cocktail napkin when the guy went to the bathroom—she even asked the bartender for a pen. I left pretty soon after, even with nowhere special to go. When I called her two days later, she asked me what took me so long to call, and she asked me where I'd gone, why I left Sullivan's so quickly, and I told her the truth. I didn't have anywhere to go, I said, but I thought I'd be chill and just go. You know, no pressure. Chill, that was fine with her, she liked that. I think her previous boyfriend had been a succubus (that's a gamer term; sorry to get so technical).

She's a little younger than me, but everyone thinks she's older. Liana's one of those old brains or old souls or previous life people—we've talked about that some. She's got amazing eyes that look blue one moment and green another, depending upon what she's wearing and her makeup and even the weather, if it's raining, and her eyes also change depending on what she's saying. I can never figure out the color of her eyes. Like if it's raining and she's saying something emotional—forget it, the colors will be blue, gray, and green all at once. It's true she has a rocking body, which makes me glad she's Catholic, because she could totally Instagram model, and then she wouldn't be mine.

When we first got together, Liana would keep a lot of herself private, she wouldn't tell me what she knows, all the wisdom and how organized she is inside. Of course, I didn't tell her that I'm an evil genius either. There's no wisdom in revenge, and I'm sure it's not very attractive, it's probably even a deal-breaker. I'm doing everything I can not to blow it with Liana. Cool, cool, I'm so cool.

But she's amazing—and the most amazing with little kids. When she meets a kid, in no time she's on the floor, she's laughing with them, and they're piling on her. All of the kids she's student-taught hug her every day, including students from before. My little cousins love her, and Francesca even made a big announcement last Thanksgiving, that Liana had to sit at the kid's table. Francesca's four—she can't even say her own name right, but she had to have Liana.

I want to have ten kids with Liana, or twenty. She's waiting for me to figure out my stuff first, that's what she says. It's true that I don't talk enough; she can't know what I've figured out so far. I could try to fix that, too.

But holy Lando Calrissian, her family, they're terrifying, even though I am Catholic too, thank God, because she has to marry Catholic.

When the moms visited, she cornered me in the stairwell in my building, on a landing, and there was no one else there, and she hissed at me like she was some kind of animal on the Discovery channel, "You're not good enough. She knows already."

I'm like, "Dang, Mrs. Costa. Hold on."

She was jabbing her finger in my face. "My Liana, she can really hurt you."

I didn't know what the hell that meant—she could stab me or something? "Mrs. Costa, I love her."

She backed off a little, into her own corner, and pinched her eyes at me. "I know all about you, Sammy the Nobody. You don't love."

"Mrs. Costa. I…I think we should go catch up. They're waiting for us."

"You don't love," she wagged her finger, jabbing it at me. She had to reach up to do that, she's really short. She kept saying it: "You don't love, you don't love…"

I backed up, backing up the stairs slowly until it was safe to turn away and keep going. Jesus, she was frightening. Called me "Sammy," just like that. Like every goddamn mother in the world is my mother. How do mothers do that? Any mother in the world can make you feel like that.

•

I'm off on Saturday. The plan calls for the thing to happen in the middle of the night, when everyone's asleep and no one will see, it will be a random act of vandalism, only funnier. I tell Christmas I'll text her when I'm ready, she knows how to sneak out of her aunt's house, and we can go in my car, then we'll park a couple of blocks away and slip in with the fireworks.

For a long time before I text, I stand outside Christmas' house, leaning on the door of my Nissan, looking at the sky. That's already weird. I don't look at the real sky enough. There are a few wispy clouds, and not much of a moon, but a little light, and almost no wind, the air fracking hot and sticky, a nasty July heat wave.

I am about to change the sky. That's an interesting thought.

Maybe I should have gotten stoned first.

Over there, beyond those houses, that direction's East, and over there, that direction's North, toward the high school and A.B. Park, and the golf course next to the park, with the big hill we called Old Glory, where I used to go sledding with Bruce. I can only remember going that one time. Bruce was a lot older than me, and he didn't have much interest. Bruce wasn't my friend so much, just my brother.

I used to spy on Bruce and his buddies. Later, when I came to understand what being an evil genius meant, I understood that I had always been like this, that spying on Bruce, following him around in the woods where he used to hang out, that's how I learned my craft.

He never knew I was there. Or if he knew, he was good at hiding that he knew. Like me.

Damn, it's so weird to be thinking about him when I'm not.

She doesn't wait for the text. Christmas sort of runs from the house, her shoulders all hunched up, her head down. She kind of crab-walks standing up. She has on her combat boots, black pants, and a plaid shirt, really dark, and her purple hat. As instructed, all dark clothes, just like mine.

"Hi!" she says in a stagey whisper. I've never seen her eyes this wide.

"Dude," I say.

She hits my shoulder. "This is sooo cool! Dude!"

We get in, and I start the car, put it in gear. I'll keep the lights off. Then I reconsider and turn on the headlights.

She's really, really jittery. She's making a little fist with one hand, and then opening it, and I want to say stop, or touch her hand to help, but I don't. She stretches over the seat to scope the fireworks in the back.

"Seatbelt," I say.

Deedee Smith lives on Winston Court, about a half block south of where the Heights begin. I know she's home: I cruised Winston on my way over, nice and calm, an ordinary evil genius driving down the street, and saw her truck, a red Ford F-150, parked in the driveway. Target acquired.

Christmas is acting really weird, not just jittery but something else. Now, as we drive, she keeps pulling her left leg up, under her, and then changing her mind and straightening her leg again.

"Chill," I finally say.

"*Shhh*," she hushes me.

"Jesus," I say.

I don't know if the air conditioning is broken in Deedee's truck, but I do know she likes to leave the little sliding window open, the one between the cab and the truck bed, and that's all we'll need. It's a simple plan: light a boatload of fireworks, toss them in the little window of the truck, and stand back. Maybe the truck will blow up—that would be too big, but wild. Stand back and then run, of course; I'm not stupid.

I didn't tell Christmas that Deedee is black because who cares. I don't know if the cops would care, or if it would matter that I'm white and Christmas is extra white, but I'm not going to let them find out, this isn't about that. It never mattered to me, only moms notice that stuff.

We park on Timmins—three blocks away—grab the fireworks, one bag each, and I lock my car. Lots of people have parked their cars here, it's perfectly normal.

I didn't plan on the hot weather being so hot. I'm pretty sweaty as a guy.

Christmas and I walk ever so easily down Timmins to the corner, left on Eighth, past Dill Court, Harlan Court, and then left again on Winston Court. The street ends in a cul-de-sac, but not yet, Deedee's house down just a little ways, before the circle. There are more trees than I remember.

"Sam," Christmas says really quietly.

"What?"

She's not answering right away. "I don't…" She doesn't finish her sentence. "I'm sorry," she says, although I can't imagine why.

Here's my evil genius plan. The fireworks, the truck, Deedee, revenge—none of it matters. I'm here to let Christmas feel some danger, the rush of the adrenaline, to get all toasty with life before she dies. I know how those feelings feel, so I have taken full responsibility. A girl can't just die, she has to feel it all.

One house from Deedee's. "There," I say, and point with my chin. That's dumb, I realize, not only is it dark but she's not looking at me.

I stop, Christmas stops. We're there. We stop.

Someone's standing next to Deedee's truck.

"Sam," the person says, stepping up. It's Liana.

"What the fuck? No!" I say. "What are you doing here?" I hiss.

"Sam, you can't do this."

"What? Liana!"

The three of us are standing there. I bet Deedee's inside the house, sleeping like nothing's happening. I look at Christmas, who looks away.

Liana's also dressed in really dark clothes, and she's wearing a Pirates hat. She never wears a Pirates hat. Where'd she get that hat? Is she wearing my Pirates hat?

"She told me," Liana says.

"Who?"

"Christmas. She doesn't want you to do this. You're hurting yourself, Sam."

"You told her?"

Christmas kicks her foot, at a rock or something. She's not looking at me.

"C'mon, let's go." Liana puts her hand on my arm. "I know the perfect place."

"You're ruining it," I say, meaning both of them.

"C'mon, Sam." Liana tugs gently on my arm. "Let's go. I need you to go, Sam. Let's go. Sam, this is me. It's me."

What should I do? I want to think, or decide.

I'm really thirsty—I notice that.

When all you want is time, there's never any time. When all you want is the future, and the future's different, that's fate too, you can die a little each moment, in each thing that happens, but that's okay. If there are people with you, I think that's better, unless it's not.

The three of us are on the football field behind the high school. It's the middle of the night, I don't know how late, my phone's off because they made me, and the sky looks like it's been turned off too. The screen's off. We drove here, Liana led, and here we are.

I'm an evil genius, I try to repeat to myself. I am, but I'm not.

"How do you do it?" Liana's got out the Fiery Frogs and one of the two Bic lighters from the MiniMart, and she's looking at me funny. "Sam?"

She's going to light my Fiery Frogs. I don't know what to say.

"I want to do it," Christmas says, pulling the Shagadelic Mojos out of the bag.

"Sam? Shouldn't we light them all at the same time? The cops could come if we take our time. Sam, where's yours?"

"It's in my bag," I say.

I look at Liana, who nods. That nod tells me things. Okay. I look at Christmas, who takes her time, she was looking at something else out there, but then she finally looks at me. We look at each other, a long look, her eyes shiny. Something feels right.

Maybe I am an evil genius—I got Liana here, didn't I?

"I guess," I say. "Yeah," I say. "Together. All at once."

DEAR DOROTHY

When my mother and father came to the United States from South Korea in 1970 and moved in with my uncle in Los Angeles, and then I was born, and then my little brother, and then we moved to our own apartment, there was only a golden future to imagine, and not a No. 720 bus. That was the bus that slid, its right front wheel climbing up the back of a Datsun to avoid a bicycle, and then, catching air, the enormous red monster groaning up onto its left side, skidded along on two wheels, rubber shearing to the rims and metal tearing as it screeched down the sidewalk. Then the No. 720 bus took out a line of little trees and a couple of big palms, and finally killed two nice little Korean immigrants, my mother and father.

No one dies in the future we imagine. In the future they never went beyond, my parents stepped out of their new store on Wilshire on a sunny day in 1975, lowered the security gate and locked the Uline lock, and got ready to pick up their toddlers from Uncle's duplex. They were going to go home together and watch their kids grow up. Then my parents died.

I think about my parents' story a lot, take it apart, look again, wonder at the second act no one wrote. I try to picture it, and I can't, and I do anyway. Seeing the bus like this, I apparently resemble my mother, or so I have been told by Uncle—she liked to dabble in back-room fortunetelling. But it's more like telling the past. Get out of the way, it's a bus, I tried to tell them over the years. That didn't work. No fiddling with the spirits, no hollering across the divide, nothing would warn my parents on Wilshire. It's a bus.

Then I tried it as a movie, in film school. There I learned to call the story of my parents' death the "Do Not Touch" script—because that's the script that stays the same, the green-lighted pages sent from the writers' room to the producer and then into principal shooting. My parents' story was the one-camera documentary I always wanted to make, the one I saw in my head, until I tried doing so when I finally got the chance. But that didn't work either (for which actually, I'm grateful). My student film flopped in development, as soon as I failed to match the vision with the form, and so I quit making movies, choosing to teach them instead.

My mother named me Dorothy, after the one true Dorothy, the most American girl, Dorothy Gale of Kansas. I see it as a natural choice for my mother, an immigrant born in 1939 and obsessed with the United States. I have a Korean name, of course, Kim Mi-sook, but I have always gone by Dorothy, been Dorothy, and wanted to be Dorothy. Once my parents were killed and my brother Jimmy and I moved in with Uncle, Dorothy was the only name to which I would answer.

How awful it would have been if my mother had loved *Gone with the Wind*, another classic from the year of her birth. I could have been a shy Korean orphan in the Los Angeles public schools in the '70s named Scarlett, my kimchi thermos hidden inside a Tara lunchbox. Or, worse, I could have been named Aunt Pittypat—that could have happened—a new American christened after the insane, saccharine aunt who warns us with a shout, "Yankees in Georgia!" There are too many examples of those gaffes in cross-cultural communication, and not just in Hollywood, poorly translated howlers between new immigrants and their adopted ways, and maybe it's just me, but so often it seems like the work of off-the-boat Korean knuckleheads who think they've got America right. I consider myself lucky to be named Dorothy.

Still, I keep being reminded that life is probably a "Do Not Change" script. Now that I'm forty-two, single again, teaching film courses at the community college in the Valley, going to Wednesday night Pilates and the occasional Sunday morning Quaker meeting, and trying to find time for myself, so much of who I am seems written. The settlement money from the accident ran out years ago. Now the future's just the present, only longer.

So I thought I might start something, use what I've learned and maybe make some cash on the side. I want to have an egg to put in a nest, and ultimately buy a tidy house up near Sacramento, or better yet, maybe a two-bedroom in Sonoma. I love Healdsburg, my favorite town in California. I dream of a little house near the river, in Healdsburg, some place not LA.

Which is why I started DearDorothy.com. Few people know as much about *The Wizard of Oz* as I do, and I was tired of being that woman at those parties, waiting to show off her trick—ask me anything about *The Wizard of Oz*. Even then, or maybe even more so, people didn't want to talk to me. A website made more sense, especially with Phil Papadopoulos helping, the guy who's sort of the super in my building, who lives in the garden apartment in the back and who's a coder, the day job he does at night. We had my friend Ellen, a lawyer, draw up the deal, proceeds split sixty-forty, and since I'm the talent I get sixty. To start, for sure, we would have been happy with what the little-known Judy Garland made in 1938—the girl star was paid $500 per week for twenty-three weeks of filming, while the vaudeville veteran Bert Lahr was paid six times as much to be the Cowardly Lion. Girl stars were worth one-sixth of old white men, and probably still are. Granted, he was amazing.

The website was easy to build because I didn't build it. Phil splashed a picture of the movie poster on the home page—a shot we got off the Web, the poster you see everywhere—and I added some text, mostly fluffy PR stuff, and then we selected the tabs, which Phil said were the most important: Trivia, Toto Too, Dear Dorothy, Store, and Links. We knew the first two categories would get the heaviest traffic, and that Toto Too would have the shortest page views (because it's a catchy phrase, and cute, but it's mostly about animals in showbiz), and that Dear Dorothy would be the interactive page, a kind of message board/chat room. I'd provide Phil with weekly content for Trivia and Toto Too, and Phil would handle the Store and Links. The Links were the easiest to collect, especially with the seventy-fifth anniversary having just passed. Dear Dorothy—well, that's me, so I would reply to posts, be right about the movie, and try to bump our standing in the analytics. For the Store, Phil would contact vendors who trade in *The Wizard of Oz* collectibles and request a shiny dime for every item sold.

We agreed to go live only when every page had good content, once the links were working and there was something juicy to say— like a previously unknown, salty Billie Burke wisecrack about the raunchy midgets that we could run as a banner along the bottom of the home page, a teaser, with a link to the Trivia page.

The posts to Dear Dorothy we had to fake at first, to spoof interest and generate traffic. So we began, on a nice day at the end of June, the palm trees applauding in the hot wind off Santa Monica. I grabbed an okay bottle of Sauvignon Blanc to get us going, and agreed to meet Phil on the patio in the garden, to combine our limited imaginations. That's what I joked to him, that the two of us together make one good brain. It's a little true. I learned in film school that I have nothing to say.

Having lived in LA since the invention of skin cancer, I know all about SPF and lip gloss and water bottles and wide-brimmed hats.

I'm all West Coast, as Queen Bey says, *I woke up like this*. I was not quite bedazzling, headed out the kitchen door of my apartment on the third floor, down the stairs, when I changed my mind. Not these shoes: let's go with something strappy and Thirties. I found my pink mules with the feathers on the top and the peekaboo toe—I mean, they're not Jimmy Choos, and they totally clashed with the rest of my outfit, but I like that kind of drama in my clothing. It's also how I like my men, but maybe that's not a story for Dear Dorothy.

When I clumped down the stairs and into the garden, Phil had his laptop open on a low wooden table, and he looked kind of cute, deeply slumped in the big pillows of one of the curved lime-green sectionals, eyes closed. It was late in the day and hot and blowy. Phil was usually just waking up around this time. The propane fire columns in the garden were beginning to sputter—the landlords had put in six of the faux torches, after Joe and Kris in 2C got drunk on April Fool's and Kris bashed his head in the dark, earning seventeen stitches and a suicide cocktail party. That the never-ending California drought dictates strict rules for open fires didn't seem to bother the landlords; they paid for Kris' suicide margaritas, what a great party.

Me, I love sitting in the garden at the end of a day, reading or prepping for a class, cuing up clips from *The Manchurian Candidate* or just talking to Phil, sipping a cool white in a tall glass. There's even something about sitting alone in the dusk, the day growing darker, watching the building's tenants hurry around, absorbed in their lives and kind of sucked into the evening as it comes. I don't know. It's not magic, but it's special: I've decided the landlords are right, and the propane torches are worth the risk. Didn't they say on KCRW that the cure for the drought was a fire? I'm pretty sure that's what I heard—but maybe it was a PSA for quitting smoking.

A bottle of wine, a pretty yellow bow in my hair. In other circumstances, my girly heels might have threatened to turn the outfit into a cliché, to transform Dear Dorothy into a Margo Channing wannabe in her own *All About Eve* remake, but I'm too Korean ever to have been an ingénue, so I felt pretty safe. When I picture myself as a sitcom star, I'm mostly batting my eyes.

Phil wouldn't notice anyway. Phil's a trip, in tank tops and flip-flops and Smiths—he has a stupid love for both the pants and the band. He's maybe five years younger than me, and as far as I can tell, he's either straight or bi, but I've only lived in the building for eighteen months, which means I don't know all the secrets yet. Phil has secrets. He looks away when he's thinking really hard, spoiling the two-shot. He doesn't really care about his good side. And maybe he's a little pudgy for my taste, but so am I at the moment. He has nice green eyes. I would imagine he's going to get pudgier, and probably soon, and he'll no doubt be surprised by how that happens once it sneaks up on him. He gels his hair straight up at the front. He's very proud of his hair.

"You look…" Phil didn't finish. He was lying on the sofa, maybe half awake, one arm across his head. "Awesome shoes."

He did notice, that's nice. "I try…wine for breakfast?" I offered the bottle by the neck.

"My darling…" Phil's voice rose into an awful falsetto.

"Oh, God, what accent is that?"

"It's *Masterpiece Theatre*," Phil protested.

"More like *Disaster Piece*. Here, drink this magical concoction." I poured for us both, handed him a glass. I could see the screensaver on his laptop: Pacman, of course, old school, and maybe the GOAT, if you're a coder. "Honey, let's make some money," I said, plopping down next to him on the sofa, my wine sloshing, uh-oh. I wiggled my ass into the pillows to get comfortable, which made me giggle for some reason. "There!" I kicked off my heels with a flamboyant *ta-da*.

"You're genius at this stuff," Phil said, and gave me a little elbow dig. "I love it."

"This stuff?"

"Life," Phil said. "This stuff," he looked away.

"If only," I said, and meant it.

The first posts we wrote together were crazy easy. We wanted to make Dear Dorothy sympathetic and sincere and especially responsive to children, whose parents were naturally our target audience on the monetized website—Mommy's got the credit card. Phil had confidence in the commerce: he said he knew how to turn page views and click-throughs into any dream house I wanted, Healdsburg here I come. He promised, too, that my ex would never find out, that my alimony (LA for "rent") was safe. He promised. So we began.

Dear Dorothy,

I'm seven years old and I love you. I have seen "The Wizard of Oz" a thousand million times! I think I'm a good witch but my mom says there aren't any witches only fairies. And there's Harry Potter. She said I could write to you and ask. Please tell my mom the good witches aren't all dead.

Your friend,

Melanie McCall

•

Dear Melanie,

You can be any kind of witch you want, so long as you help people, like I do. Remember in the movie, when Glinda says at the end, "You've always had the power to go back to Kansas"? You have the power to be a good witch, Melanie.

The good witches can't all be dead! Tell your mom that if we believe, we can make anything happen. That's what I think.

Your friend too,
Dorothy

●

Dear Dorothy,
I just love the munchkins! They're so adorable. I know you became BFFs with all of them, especially with the three ballerinas in The Lullaby League. I want to join The Lullaby League! Can you tell me how?
Love,
Hannah

●

Dear Hannah,
Yes, of course you can join The Lullaby League! You'll make a beautiful ballerina. When you watch the movie again, make sure you're wearing your pink tutu, and put little flowers on your shoes. Then you can learn the dance the ballerinas do, and sing the whole song. Practice a lot. Don't forget to twirl! That's all it will take. You'll be in The Lullaby League.
The munchkins are little people, you know—and they're grown-ups. They might be adorable, but they want to be treated like grown-ups too. Can you remember that?
Please write to me again, and tell me what happens when you do the Lullaby League dance! I had to leave Munchkin City to follow the Yellow Brick Road, and I haven't been back in a long time, and I love to get letters.
Love,
Dorothy

•

The website went live on a Thursday night, with an eye on the TV schedule, as the movie was scheduled to air on TNT three times a day that weekend. By Sunday night, the website analytics were buzzing, according to Phil, and he texted and suggested we meet for a cocktail in the garden. There was a new Dear Dorothy letter—one we hadn't written, the first—which he had discovered once all the spam was cleared away. Ads and junk, Internet trash, like what had happened to the LA we all used to love.

Dear Dorothy,

I saw you once at the Winter Garden many, many years ago. You had such a lovely voice. I'm sure you didn't see me—you didn't seem to be "with it," as my Robert would say. It's nice to know you're better.

Best wishes to you and your family, especially to your wonderful Liza.

Yours truly,

Betty Undegraf

Sioux Falls

Phil made me a drink. He had read the post already, and he turned around his laptop so I could see, his poker face pretty good—until he saw the expression on my face, and we both lost it, laughing. We didn't know what to do, and so we laughed and laughed.

Sometimes, when I laugh, I get lightheaded. Finally, I was able to breathe. "She…" But not yet, I still couldn't finish my sentence. "She…" I sputtered.

"You've got to answer her!" Phil said.

"But… she…"

"You have to!"

"Okay, okay!"

I had the laptop open, the password entered, the world flat as the computer screen where Betty Undegraf slept in South Dakota, where I hoped someone was monitoring her vitals, because her meds had to be off.

I took a good pull of my drink, thought about Betty and Judy and Liza, and playing the Winter Garden, and typed my reply.

> *Dear Betty,*
>
> *Thank you. I always loved to sing "Over the Rainbow." Did you know that song almost didn't make it into the movie? After the second sneak preview, the producer tried to have the song cut, but his assistant and the composer and the lyricist were having none of that guff. "Over the Rainbow" stayed.*
>
> *Yours truly,*
> *Dorothy*

I posted my answer and spun the laptop around to show Phil. He didn't say anything at first, but the look on his face changed. He sipped his bad Tom Collins. Finally, "Cool," Phil said. "We're off to see the Wizard," he added. "Guff," he said. "Props for 'guff.'"

The letters began to be posted more regularly, mostly in the afterschool hours no matter the time zone, which, according to Phil, was a good sign. The questions posed to Dear Dorothy were totally darling. *Dear Dorothy, can you help me with my art homework? Dear Dorothy, I still drink Maxwell House because of Margaret Hamilton. Was she nice? Dear Dorothy, I live in York. That's in England. What happened to the jumper you wore in the Emerald City? I would love to see that jumper on one of the Obama girls—did you ever meet them? Dear Dorothy, do you like the Tin Man or the Cowardly Lion better?*

Admittedly, without telling Phil, I began to check the message board often, and then maybe even a little obsessively: on my iPad in the bathroom at Seafood City, in traffic on the 10, at home as the juicer squished my breakfast into a glass, and at the end of the day, one more time, before I went to bed each night. I had to see what people thought of me. I even left a screening in my summer school class of *Cabaret* (Bob Fosse, Dir., 1972, released the year before I was born, and starring Liza Minnelli, of course) to duck into the supply room in the Media Center and check the Dear Dorothy site, although there hadn't been any new posts that hour.

Then, a week after the site went live, with thirty-one letters posted already, including a reply from the mother of "Melanie," our first writer—a thank-you letter that I wrote myself, for kicks, because I like to write thank-you letters, it's *trop* vintage—the world changed.

I was in the Mean Bean, getting a caramel macchiato on my way to campus, a regular treat I give myself so I can slog through my Intro course, and it was 9:45 in the morning. I'm sure. I remember. "Purple Haze" was pounding through the speakers, and my bag was too heavy on my left arm, and my Mean Bean pal, Louie the screenwriter/dog walker/barista, was pulling my triple shot—all of this I can see clearly, a "Do Not Touch" moment. I even remember there was a little donation box for Cerebral Palsy on the Mean Bean counter. I might have been hungover.

With my free hand, I logged in and read Dear Dorothy.

Dear Dorothy,
I am thirteen year old. I have cancer. I want to meet you.
Yours,
Christmas Danzig

"Is this for real?" I didn't say hello when I called Phil. I'm sure I woke him up, but he shouldn't have left his phone on.

"What?...Hello?"

"Christmas! That's her name?"

"You saw." He coughed. "Excuse me."

"Three-shot caramel macchiato for Dorothy!"

"Here. Thanks, Louie…. Hold on, hold on, I'm getting coffee…" I had to juggle my phone and my drink and my bag, which felt like juggling what I was feeling. "No, no, hold on…shit…I'll call you back."

I went out to my car to sit and think. I had to get to school: today was *Birth of a Nation*.

I called him back: "Phil?"

"I Googled her," he said. "There's no one with that name, but I pinged her ISP, and it's in Maryland somewhere."

"Maryland?"

"I think it's real," Phil said. "You didn't write it?"

"Phil!"

"You wrote the one from Melanie's mother."

"How do you know that?"

He didn't answer.

"Phil. I've gotta go teach. I'll see you later."

"You have to answer her. She has cancer. Can-cer."

That night, Phil Papadopoulos and I had pretty good drunken sex. I was surprised too. And I'm telling the story out of order, the fourth act can't go before the third, but we had sex, and that's the part of the evening I remember the most, or sort of remember. That's the part of the night I want to remember. I brought home takeout burritos from the drive-through at Lucky Boy's, we drank a pitcher of Sangria, we talked about what to do with Dear Dorothy, and how she should reply to Christmas Danzig, and then Phil and I had sex. Well, twice.

I didn't know I was attracted to him. He was a good lover, really happy about it, and also noisy in a funny way. At first, I thought his noises were a joke—as though he were making all of these sounds to make me laugh, to relax me—but then I realized that he was into it, that the grunts and moans and half words were just Phil. He had a wide back from working out, which I like.

I liked the noises. I might have made a few noises myself.

It had been a couple of months since I had slept with a guy, not since Earnest Manny—that's what I called him in my head, Earnest Manny—the junior agent I met at a Quaker meeting, with dyed blond hair, kind of punk, kind of Euro, totally LA and oh-so-boring. Earnest Manny, who was always taking the red-eye somewhere. We had seen each other for a few months, three or four, over this past winter, but there wasn't any sizzle to the twizzle. I guess that's what you get from Quaker meeting.

"Now what?" Phil asked.

He was lying in his bed, and I was moving about the room in the low light of a single bedside lamp, a cloth thrown over the shade, all atmosphere and after-sex smells. I was getting dressed to go upstairs to my apartment. I couldn't tell what time it was, for sure after midnight, because I was worn out and sober.

"The usual…now we get married," I said. I patted his leg.

Phil smiled. "I knew I was good," he said, grinning.

"Don't kid yourself, Phillie," I said. My shirt on the chair. Shoes. Was I forgetting something else? "Korean chicks are the sexiest."

"True that," Phil said. He didn't know what to say next. "I'm going to get some work done," he said next, not to me, sitting up and reaching for his laptop.

"I'm going to write to Christmas," I said. "Like we agreed."

"You're fun," Phil said. "This is weird."

•

Dear Christmas,

That's awful you have cancer. Are you getting treatment? Do your parents think you'll be okay?

You know, this is a website, and we probably live far away from each other, but I'll see about getting together. Until then, I hope you wish upon a star and wake up where the clouds are far behind you. That would be somewhere over the rainbow—I'm sure you recognize those lyrics from the song!

Love,

Dorothy

•

Four more letters arrived that day, but none from Christmas Danzig. One of the letters was a rant—*You are totally appropriating the reputation of Judy Garland. She was treated so unfairly by everyone, and she was just a little girl. This site's a travesty, you're just trying to capitalize on the popularity of the movie, and you have no respect. Judy Garland was in pain…*yadda, yadda, yadda. I hate when people are so opinionated. At least the letter was unsigned. I would ask Phil to take it down.

That night, Friday night, Phil said he had a deadline. I wanted to believe him, so I did. He texted to say he wished we could "hang out together a lot." He also said he had fun with me. His nerdiness had some appeal. I wondered how long I'd last with him, what shoes I'd be wearing when we broke up.

We had sex again on Saturday night, right after takeout sushi, and then watched *Wings of Desire*, which I had to screen again for class the next week. Turns out it was his favorite movie—I expected *Blade Runner*, and I got Wim Wenders. We used my vibrator during sex, which turned us both on, and I came hard.

There were no new letters from Christmas over the next five days, I checked a lot. Okay, a real lot. Had I said the wrong thing? A couple of cutesy kiddie queries did arrive, which I answered politely, and with my Dorothy Gale trademark sweetness. *Yes, Callie, you can be Dorothy in the next movie, if you practice and practice.*

And then, early on Friday morning, a new letter from Christmas. I wrote back right away, and that day, we wrote a lot to one another. I don't teach on Fridays, so I never got out of my PJs, it was too exciting and scary. I had a responsibility to her, I kept thinking, but it was the Internet, so who knows.

> *Dear Dorothy,*
> *I remember the song. It's very pretty.*
> *My favorite part in the movie is when the witch melts. That part and the tornado. When the witch melts, the head of her army says Hail to Dorothy, and then the soldiers kneel down. They weren't happy she was in charge either.*
> *I think too many people are in charge of me.*
> *I want to melt, but not that way.*
> *What do you think?*
> *Love,*
> *Christmas Danzig*

●

> *Dear Christmas,*
> *I know how you feel. Everyone's always in charge of us—our families, our teachers, our bosses, everyone. I hate it too. I wish I could be somewhere that I'm the boss of me.*
> *You seem like a very sensitive girl. Do you cry a lot? I cry so much. I can't help myself. Whenever I see the movie again, I think I'm crying all the time. That's like melting.*
> *Love,*
> *Dorothy*

•

Dear Dorothy,

Yes, I cry a lot, but not anymore, I have cancer. It's dumb to have cancer and to cry about it, so I don't.

Love,

Christmas Danzig

•

Dear Christmas,

I hope you feel okay. I hope you don't cry too much.

How did you get your name?

Love,

Dorothy

•

Dear Dorothy,

In the movie, the actor who plays the Scarecrow also plays one of the famers, right? That dude's Hickory, and he calls himself Hick too. Everyone has a couple of names and is in disguise. That's what I think about life. No one's real anymore.

That's how I got my name.

Love,

Christmas Danzig

•

Dear Christmas,

Did you know that the Land of Oz was named "Oz" because the writer of the book, L. Frank Baum, couldn't think of a name—and then he saw his filing cabinet, where the files were labeled "O" to "Z"? Oz! He had a eureka moment.

I loved being in Oz, but I also really wanted to be back at home, with my Auntie Em. Isn't that weird? Kansas looks so black and white, and I still want to go there. I guess home isn't always pretty.

If you had a land all your own, maybe over your own rainbow, what would it be like?

Love,

Dorothy

At the end of the day, I texted Phil, but he had another Friday night deadline. I needed a break. I went to Cloud 9 and caught a late showing of the new Wes Anderson, even though I had already seen it in previews. It was still pretty damn good, and awfully twee. When I got home, nothing, Phil's light was on, but Christmas Danzig hadn't replied. What time does a thirteen-year-old go to bed in Maryland?

Something was wrong, I knew it: she probably wasn't okay. There was no reason she would write to me, a stranger, and kind of pretend I was real. I know, I know, the Internet, blah, blah, blah, blah, nothing exists and all those Blink! and Wink! and Think! books that say we can't tell who's what anymore, but this kid, a little girl named Christmas, she could tell. I was sure she knew what she was doing. But I worried she was dead.

Sex with Phil looked good for Saturday night. I booked a Pilates class in the afternoon—I had missed my regular this week—and rang him after. But I had one condition: sex, but then we had to go out together the next day, Sunday, like on a date, for brunch. It's the LA way. He's from St. Louis, so he maybe didn't know, but I'm not going to screw a guy more than twice and not have brunch.

Really, what I wanted most was to talk. I needed to be sober, not to be in Phil's apartment in the dark, waiting for my vibrator and his dick together, but somewhere in public, where there were other people, to see what the conversation would become, to talk through what was happening. Not that I could explain what I was feeling, except to say I wanted to be near other people, people walking around, eating and laughing and flirting, and maybe going back to their apartments to have afternoon sex. Something good might be happening with Phil, I had to admit that, but I also had to see it for myself in the daylight. Plus, it was important, a Sunday brunch: the world comes together at Sunday brunch. It would make all of us real. Even the Internet teenager with cancer, even me, Dear Dorothy. All of us needed to be real.

I didn't know too many teenagers, as my two nieces were younger—eight and nine—and my cousins' kids were worth ignoring, mall junkies, all about the brands and the boys. Some of my students were only eighteen or nineteen, so they were teenagers, technically, but the boys were the ones who acted stupid most of the time. The girls at community college tended to act older—they had jobs, which helped them pretend to be grown up, and to be old enough to do idiotic grown-up things. The girls in my classes lied more, too. In my classes, students tend to be schemers or innocents, and sometimes they were both, so young that even their schemes were innocent. Which is all to say that I didn't know what to expect from a teenager living in Maryland named Christmas Danzig.

I thought Christmas must be alone, with no one there, since she was writing to me. Then it occurred to me that I was just as alone, checking for her posts all the time. That was not a feel-good moment.

Sunday brunch in Santa Monica, at Eggs 'n Booze, my favorite place near the pier, Phil and I waited an hour for a table, sitting on a bench out front, away from the sun but hot. Even though I was prepared, twirly in my poppies sundress and white Grace-Kelly-before-she-gets-in-the-car scarf. I had made Phil put on a polo shirt I found in his closet, a lilac-colored golf jobbie that looked like it had never been worn.

"My mother gave me that shirt," Phil had said, staring at the closet. "Don't be my mother."

"C'mon, you chicken. Your mother doesn't have sex with you. Remember? Sex?" I goosed him.

"Yiy!" He hopped a couple of steps to the side. "Oh God," Phil said. Then he laughed really hard. "Oh God! You're so bad!"

He liked it, I could tell. He had a nice laugh.

Brunch meant hollandaise and a Bloody Mary or three: a mimosa's wasted on me, as is the Champagne headache. We sat outside, under a big awning in the back, the tables at Eggs 'n Booze too close together, the servers the best, even when I show up wasted at four in the morning. Eggs 'n Booze is rightly famous for its waiters, the gayest, a whirl of restaurant tuxedos that suddenly becomes a chorus line and sings show tunes in the middle of everything, trays hoisted for effect. I'm not a fag hag, but I love a good gay man.

"I used to come here a lot," Phil said. "When I was at USC."

"I didn't know you were at USC."

"I was going to be a lawyer."

"Really!" My ex was a lawyer: I hate lawyers.

"Wasn't for me." He lowered his eyes. "So…I wanted to tell you something."

Someone rang a triangle: that was the signal. "Wait. Hold on. They're going to sing."

The waiters were sashaying and hitch kicking together, flapping their server aprons around, shimmying shoulders, places everyone. The triangle was rung once again. From the back of the room, near the bathrooms, came a strong baritone, "*There's a bright golden haze on the meadow…there's a bright golden haze on the meadow.*"

And an answering voice, from near the bar: "*The corn is as high as an elephant's eye…and it looks like it's climbing clear up to the sky.*"

"*OH WHAT A BEAUTIFUL MORNING, OH WHAT A BEAU-TIFUL DAY!*"

All of the waiters were singing, and quite a few customers.

"What?" I had to shout to Phil, leaning across our table.

"I…" Phil was shaking his head. He took my hand, the sweetie. "That's Corey—that guy with the tats. He was my roomie."

"That guy!"

Corey was short, ripped, and too cute, right in the middle of the chorus line. He and Phil had the same haircut, gelled up in the front. Phil waved and Corey waved back, can-canning, and I felt pride, a different kind of pride, sitting with Phil and holding hands.

The baritone returned, easing his way toward the middle of the restaurant: "*All the cattle are standing like statues. All the cattle are standing like statues.*" The chorus line preened, vogued, and froze in their funniest faces.

"I…" Phil began again.

"WHAT?"

"Oh, forget it!" he shouted back. "*OH WHAT A BEAUTIFUL DAY!*" he joined in.

•

Later, reading the *Times* in the garden, lazing around while Phil did some work next to me, I realized that we had never really talked about Dear Dorothy and Christmas. Maybe I hadn't wanted to talk about them.

Our hips were touching. I could feel him, and could tell through his little workout shorts that he was getting hard.

Dear Dorothy, I told myself, *what are you doing with this guy? He's a keeper, and you're not.*

I reached for my iPad, and with Phil not paying attention, I logged in and checked the site. There were no new posts, so what's a girl to do?

I wrote a new letter to myself, Dear Dorothy.

•

Dear Dorothy,
How does the Scarecrow look so real?
Love,
Christmas

•

Dear Christmas,
We filmed The Wizard of Oz *in 1938, long before you were born. I was only sixteen, but they wanted me to play a twelve-year-old girl— even though you know that Dorothy is just six in the books—and so they tried a lot of different wigs and rosy cheeks and dresses. Then one of the directors, a man who only worked on the movie a couple of weeks, told them to get rid of all the stuff, to let me play the part. I had to wear a corset inside my dress, because I was already more mature, but that was nothing compared to what the other actors had to do.*

The Cowardly Lion's costume weighed ninety pounds! Everyone wore long underwear underneath their costumes in those days, too, and so he was really, really sweaty. The film required a lot of lights, very hot arc lights, for the Technicolor cameras, and wow, did Bert Lahr ever sweat. He swore a lot too—he and Ray Bolger and Jack Haley had been acting a long time, and they were grown men, and they really liked to make a lot of noise, practical jokes and such, and they all hated their costumes and makeup. Once the Cowardly Lion was made up for the day's shoot, he wouldn't be able to eat a thing at the Commissary, just drink chicken soup through a straw.

Ray Bolger, the Scarecrow, wore a lot of makeup too, but he had to wear a kind of specially made rubber bag—with holes cut in it—over his head. The bag was supposed to look like a sack that's called burlap. Someone once told me that they made over a hundred different rubber sacks for Ray to wear, and I believe it. Those sacks didn't last very long, and sometimes they had to be peeled off of Ray's face at the end of the day's shoot. That hurt. But I think Ray and Bert are the most real-looking in the whole movie. In fact, when we were filming, the two of them used to make me laugh so hard that I would get in trouble with the director—I couldn't stop laughing! I would laugh and laugh and then I couldn't do my lines. When I laugh that much, I get short of breath. Does that ever happen to you?

Christmas, there are many, many things I want to tell you. I hate that you have cancer. Your letters seem to say that it's bad—is that true? How long do you have to live?

I want to tell you that I'm not very good at this. Giving advice and all. Dear Dorothy, I mean. I'm kind of a fake. But life, I mean, can be fake too. I don't think I'm very good at life. I kind of live it, but I also don't. I mean, I got married and thought I would have a family, but I couldn't get pregnant, which was probably okay, because my husband was really boring, and maybe not very nice, and we got divorced. I live in LA because I always have—where else would Dorothy live? You're not going to find this Dorothy in Kansas. I have a job that lets me work with young people and teach them about movies, but they don't really care a lot. Or maybe I don't care a lot. Although every once in a while, one of them cares.

But I did meet a new guy. He's cute. Something about him seems weird to me, but that wouldn't be a surprise. I'm not very good at relationships either.

I don't know why I'm telling you all this. I guess I'm sorry for what you won't experience, because you're dying, so you won't get to suffer from all of the stupid decisions people make. But I'm sad you won't get to make those stupid decisions yourself too. Dying is like having a house dropped on you by someone you've never met.

But I also want to cheer you up. The Wizard of Oz is a sappy movie, I know that, and I think you do too. It lets people be sappy and forget that their real lives are kind of bad.

So what to say to cheer you up? I hope dying doesn't hurt a lot. I think that we could write to each other like this, and that I could come visit you. I'm not going to look like Dorothy Gale—but I imagine you know that.

I think being dead won't be so bad. I think it's probably pretty peaceful. Will you write to me soon? Please?

Love,

Dorothy

I sat back from my iPad and put my hand on Phil's leg. He put his hand on top of mine, without looking at me. Nice Phil. Then he went back to his project.

Within a minute, an answer appeared.

Dear Dorothy,

I'm not very good at this either, but I want to be.

I will write to you and write to you. I think you're awesome. I don't really know how to talk to you.

We should have brunch again next week.

Love,

Christmas

I read her letter once, twice. I looked over at Phil. He put down his laptop. The expression on his face: that was the truth.

"You...?"

"I'm sorry," he said. "The first one was real. She...I..."

"You...?"

"I didn't know what to do." He looked away, and then came back, and looked at me. He was Phil, looking at me. "I've...I liked you since the beginning, like over a year. You didn't know, I couldn't...I can't...I don't know. Then we did this together, and it means so much to you, and you were checking all the time, and you seemed like you needed to write to her, and then she didn't write back. And now you like me. So I did, I wrote the rest of the letters. I'm, like...I'm Christmas. I don't know how to talk to you." He put his head down. "I'm not a girl with cancer."

"You," I said. "You wrote those letters. Fuck you."

"I know," Phil said. He looked at me again.

"Phil...this is so fucked up. It's sad. I want so much." I was crying, I didn't think I would be. "We're talking through her. She's dying."

"Yes."

"Hold me."

BLUE THE DOG

"Blue the Dog, stay."

The girl was trying to vomit again, retching, and Blue the Dog was worried, whining with that little huffing noise, his nostrils flaring, his big tail smacking against the leg of the table. The girl had been puking on and off for about an hour, and now, worse, she lay suffering on my porch sofa. I held a cup of spring water to her lips so she could sip, but she wasn't keeping down even a dribble—her body was being hateful, and making not to stop. She couldn't calm her singleness: the toxins must be deep in her cells.

I put a mop bucket nearby, thinking she wouldn't have the strength to get up and step to the railing to vomit on the butterfly bush. The butterfly bush was being so nice. Blue the Dog butted his way past the bucket, though, wedging closer. He wasn't ready for the next moment, or maybe he was owning this. Blue the Dog sat right there staring into her, the way he does, less than a foot away, having found her and chosen her, and now she was his. Blue the Dog is always who he is: six years old, some Lab, some Pit, some Boxer, some other giant breed, block-headed, with one black ear and one white ear and an underbite, a huge mutt, and the best.

The girl would hang her head off the edge of the couch cushion, open-mouthed, spit and moan, the puke and spittle stringy, her head in the bucket, right in front of Blue the Dog. He stared, uncertain, every once in a while stamping his back feet. He hadn't once growled at her. I never saw his dander up around her. Blue the Dog doesn't like children, but he liked this girl.

•

Blue the Dog had come upon her first, in the woods. We had been moving from the birches toward the clearing to the south, a field and a swamp still to go on the way to my beehives, and even though Blue the Dog had been on a scent, he had broken form.

"Something!" Blue the Dog had said to me.

Blue the Dog talks, no matter that I don't really understand.

"Blue the Dog? What is it?"

"Something!"

"Okay, buddy. Go see, Blue the Dog. Release."

Which he had done, because he likes to make his own decisions, cautiously but sure too, all ninety pounds of him low to the ground in a stalking crouch. I had followed—something was there. He had tracked through the scruff and the ferns, the dandelions and the purple clover, run the edge of the meadow in his hunting pose. But then I had lost him. Until he had barked twice, as he was trained to do, come see, come see.

Lying on the ground, she had looked like someone's laundry, just a balled-up heap of clothes. She had been a ball of pain. She had smelled.

"Stay." I had given him a shred of deer jerky from my pocket. "Good boy, Blue the Dog." Then I had tried to wake her up. I had touched her shoulder once, again, and she had moaned, half-conscious, and she had said something I couldn't make out. I had shaken her a tiny bit, but that had scared me, shaking another person seemed wrong. It wasn't in the universe I knew.

I think she might have said "Help." It also could have been "Crap."

I can always tell where I am outside, more so than in. We weren't far. What else was I going to do? I don't keep a phone in the summertime. I'm strong enough: I could haul her home and help her there. So I had knotted my pouch, pulled her up gently, swung her arm around me carefully, let her weight move her forward but supporting her too. She kept bonking into me with her funny little purse, too shiny a thing. Our walk hadn't taken twenty minutes, her leaning on me as we had trudged to my house.

Time, glory, and grief. I had felt the chemicals soaking through her clothes, leaching. Which meant I couldn't let her inside, not that walking cloud of poisons. Thinking smart, I had laid her on the porch instead, where the air would help. If she polluted my rooms we'd both be sick.

I had eased her down slowly onto the cushions, propped her head with a little pillow. She was sweaty, and even though the day was hot, hers was a bad sweat. She had looked gray around the eyes, a light gray around the lips, a bad skin color. She had smelled light gray too, with another color in there, but I hadn't known what. When I had laid her down, I hadn't decided whether to take off her purple hat. I could tell she had no hair, and so the hat was probably important to her. A hat full of ego, I had supposed. All of that being, especially at her age, which I had put at fifteen. No one was ever free, I had thought, with this girl lying on my sofa.

•

Now she was present, toxic on my porch sofa.

Plus there was some of her on me. "Blue the Dog, stay," I said to him, although he wasn't going anywhere. "Keep," I said, a word he might not know.

With Blue the Dog in charge on the porch, I hustled around back, stripped at the outdoor shower, and washed from the rain barrel, scrubbing at my hands and face with birch twigs. After, I chewed a few mint leaves for my digestion and rubbed some lavender into my beard, because I could smell her.

Blue the Dog doesn't mind if I smell like lavender—he kind of likes it, I think, even if he never says. The bees don't care.

When I came back around front, clean and dressed, the girl was deep asleep. Blue the Dog lay on the sofa next to her, stretched out along the length of her, kind of on top of her, together on that narrow couch. I had never seen him behave like this. That's a lot of dog, a heavy log of a dog on top of a girl.

Blue the Dog looked at me; he had all sorts of words in his eyes. He didn't know what to feel.

"Shhh," I said. "Blue the Dog, keep." Maybe "keep" meant lie on top of a girl.

I ate my five o'clock meal, did an hour of sundown poses out back, facing the ridgeline, ending with the presence of the trees in my arms, upright, joining with the branches, and I soared my energy nicely. It was a good day.

When I came around to check on her, the girl was awake once more, leaning up a little, sipping spring water, and petting Blue the Dog, who was still flattened on the couch, even more on top of her. He was seeing her.

"What's his name?"

"Blue the Dog."

"Blue." She scratched between his eyes: he liked that spot, and squinted in pleasure.

"Blue the Dog."

She looked at me with feelings in her eyes too. "Be nice," she said. "Blue the Dog," she said to Blue the Dog, scratching. Then she seemed to panic: "Who are you? Where am I? Who are you? I remember...being sick...*who are you?*"

I waited. It was not unpleasant.

"Who are you?" she asked again. "Did you carry me?" she whispered. "You carried me," she remembered.

Who is anyone?

"I mean, thank you," she said. "For helping. I...I got sick...my name is Christmas."

I think she wanted to shake hands. I felt a little proud, a feeling I don't want. I worked to let my singleness collect before I answered. I used one of my visualizations: be like the thinnest branch of pine, be the needles with the wind tickling. Hear the tickling. Lift up into the wind, into the sky...

"Hello? Mister?"

I didn't realize I had closed my eyes until I opened them, and there she still was.

"Mister," she said again. I didn't know why.

"Blue the Dog's hungry," I said.

"I'm okay," she said. She elbowed herself up a little more, not easy under the weight of Blue the Dog. "Uh-oh," she said. "I'm fine," she told herself.

"I'm Snow Joe," I said.

"What?"

"You asked. Snow Joe. See the truck?"

My pickup, parked in front of the house, has SNOW JOE painted on both doors.

"What?" She craned her head. "That's your name?" She pointed at the truck. "Are those snowflakes?"

"I plow driveways. Truck's got a plow."

"It's July," she said.

"And your name's Christmas."

I stepped by, to go fetch Blue the Dog's dinner. Blue the Dog jumped off of her, which made her grunt, and then she struggled to sit up more fully, moved as though to stand and follow. I could smell her. Sitting up seemed to hurt.

"No." I opened, raised my palm to the source of the conflict, calmly, with power. "You can't come inside."

"What?…Why?"

"My house. I keep a clean zone. You're polluted. Lie there."

Blue the Dog pawed at the screen door, worn from where he paws. He's right-pawed.

I lowered my hand to steady Blue the Dog. "Stay," I told him as I scratched his ear. "I'll bring your food. It's okay. Hold."

This was different, not his usual dinner in the kitchen, but Blue the Dog, he's Blue the Dog. He panted as he lay down by the door and looked at me. I felt he might be getting upset.

"It's okay. Hold."

The girl lay back on the sofa, and sighed. She was only gray around her mouth now.

I think she was relieved. I was. But I didn't know what she was, and I was working with that, too.

"What are you wearing?" the girl asked.

"This? It's a mekumi. It's a breathing robe. I made it."

"Oh," the girl said.

"Look," I said. "Do you want to take a shower? I'll show you. I've got an old shirt and some shorts that could fit. I don't need them. Are you able to stand up?"

"I'm okay," she said. "I feel better."

"You're not okay," I said, pushing open the screen door. "We can't trust your clothes. Just smell. You're reabsorbing."

"Wow," the girl said. "You are crazy."

We did what we did. I mixed his dinner, brought his bowl back outside. Blue the Dog gobbled his squash and venison, slurped spring water. From my cedar closet, I grabbed an old denim shirt and a pair of shorts, snatched a safety pin for the waistband. I couldn't help her with underwear.

I showed her the clothes.

"I don't know," she said, eyeing me, holding up the shirt, deciding. "You're not a creeper, are you? Okay, I guess…" Her nose wrinkled and squeezed a couple of times, like a rabbit kit. "I really stink."

Blue the Dog finished, grabbed his knucklebone, and trotted into the yard to chew in the grass, which he likes to do after his dinner. Sometimes I bring food, join him, and we chew in the grass, lying together pleasantly.

•

We moved in the world. She was steadier: she showered, I waited. When the water stopped running, she could hear me. I asked the stall door, "DO YOU WANT ME TO BURN THOSE?"

"WHAT?"

"YOUR CLOTHES. I'VE GOT A BURN BARREL. IT'S—"

"NO!" I could hear she was upset. "THOSE ARE MY CLOTHES!"

I thought not to reply.

I wondered about this girl. I could hear her presence.

When people get angry at me, I take their anger, and then I don't like that, both of those angers in me.

"WHAT ARE YOUR FEELINGS?" I asked the wooden door.

She wasn't answering.

I waited.

I admired her silence: the question was too big. What were my feelings? I couldn't answer either. My life is learning.

The stall door swung slowly open, and she stepped out, dressed, my stained old shirt more of a blanket than a shirt, even though she was pretty tall, the purple hat back on her head. "Thank you." She handed me my towel. "Here's your towel. You don't have to shout, you know. I'm not deaf."

"Today was nice," I said.

She looked at me. People look at me.

She kicked at the bad clothes on the ground. Her toenails were painted black. "Can I burn them? Really? People do that?" Her voice was little. "I want to. Not the boots, of course. Can I…can I have some socks, Snow Joe?"

●

"It's cancer," she answered, even though I hadn't asked. She was feeding the burning clothes into the burn barrel with the burn stick, a hardwood branch I had seasoned, turning over her ruined shirt to make sure of the flame, purifying.

"No one dies," I said.

She looked at me. "Everyone dies. Me first."

"No," I said. "We're used, we're absorbed and reabsorbed, it's all…it's like one shapeless sponge. The Buddha says, 'Know the outside as false.'"

She poked the fire harder. She was angry—I felt her anger again, and again, I didn't want it. I cannot have anger.

Poke, poke, jab, jab, she made the fire spit as the ashes rose.

I waited.

I was saved by Blue the Dog, as I am. Blue the Dog barked at something in the trees, and looked at me for permission, his eyes full of knowledge.

A dog may yearn.

"Release," I said to him.

Blue the Dog tore off into the garden, whipping around the compost, headed for the pine trees, fixed on a scent or a sound, dog muscles in concert.

The girl and I together watched Blue the Dog run, and what we felt changed to love.

"He's such a big dog," Christmas said. "Can I keep him?"

Was that a real question? It hurt.

"Blue the Dog is Blue the Dog," I said.

"Jay *Kaaaay*," she said. "Dude, I was kidding. It's all right. Snow Joe, it's cool. I was kidding."

I didn't know what we were talking about anymore.

The sun would be going down soon, July a month of hot sun, my favorite next to May and October and November. The girl needed to go home.

"Can I give you a ride? Let's have a cooling beverage and then I'll drive you home."

We were sitting on the other side of the sleeping porch, on the chairs Buster had made me, enjoying sumac tea and the cloudless sky. The seats of the chairs aren't comfortable, so I usually grab a cushion from the outdoor couch, but the girl had thrown up on those cushions. Buster's special chairs were hard. He had made allowances for my height, he had measured me, and we had run through our poses together in the sunshine, as we do, and Buster had done well, so the chairs were tall enough for my legs, as he's a good carpenter, although upholstery wasn't Buster's specialty. He did strike a very good mushroom pose, though, rounding in ways that I couldn't. I had to remind myself not to want what Buster could do, but only what I could do.

I was comfortable as a body in those chairs. A chair is like a car without wheels, I was thinking, a car was a body for thoughts that move, the motion is in me.

"Snow Joe!"

"What?"

"Listen to me!" Christmas pouted. "I was talking."

"Sorry," I said.

"You are such a freakazoid. Yes, I'm ready. I live with my aunt. Does Blue the Dog ride in the truck? My old dog used to get carsick. Can I ride in the back with Blue the Dog? Does he ride on the front seat? Can he come too?"

Driving, we drove. Then we were there. The aunt's house was a house. I've been in houses.

"I'll come back," the girl said. "Can I?"

I didn't say anything.

She gave Blue the Dog a quick hug, grabbed her little girl's purse, then jumped down, out of the truck, and turned back to look at us.

I looked straight ahead, a good place to look, to see all of the imperfections in the windshield. Glass up close is a lesson.

I had emotions.

"Can I come visit Blue the Dog?"

I waited to know how to answer. Christmas stood there waiting. The engine was running.

"Can I?"

I waited. "Okay," I said. "If you help."

"I can help!" Christmas liked that.

"The bees. I will bring in the honey tomorrow. The nectar flow—"

"Tomorrow?"

I looked up at the sky. Tomorrow would be a fine day, even a favorite day, hard work and honey.

"Tomorrow. I'll pick you up at two o'clock."

"In the afternoon."

Something made a noise in the corner of the dashboard, on the girl's side, maybe a trapped Japanese Lady Beetle.

Why did Christmas say, "In the afternoon"?

"Blue the Dog likes you," I said, and I put the truck in reverse, checked my mirrors, and pulled out of her aunt's driveway.

•

Honey helps the mouth make sense. The honeybees work and work, no one works as much, and they are pure. I work to help them survive, to ensure that the brood box has plenty of food for the bees to winter, but they know what they're doing without my help. The bees seal the frames with propolis, protect their eggs, cap their cells. They isolate their anger, which I admire more than anything about the bees—but I cannot keep admiring, since I am trying not to be an admiring man.

One wouldn't guess by looking at me, seeing how tall and awkward I am, but the honeybee is my spirit guide.

To prepare for the honey extraction process, for each full afternoon of hard work the job takes, I need a full morning of singleness. Harvesting the honey requires emotions for which I need to prepare. Bringing in the honey crop from the hives means stealing, after all: to pull the frames, I have to smoke the bees, calm them, distract them, do anything in order to take their food. It's a crime. To take the bees' honey requires that I put my thoughts in a place where injustice can yield to serenity, where I can join with all, and especially where my treatment of the honeybees makes me feel no shame. Although if I say "especially" to myself, I feel special, which is what shame can see in the mirror.

When I first started beekeeping, I would tell myself that I wasn't stealing, we were sharing, but that was a lie, and since I don't lie, I was ashamed. Now, to harvest the honey I acknowledge the lie, live in anticipation of the act. A beekeeper will steal the honey of his bees, no matter how hard they have worked to make that honey. I am embracing my contradictions, and my individual power, as I have learned in my studies. I hunt animals for their meat, fish for fish, kill and eat, I grow and eat plants, I forage, I steal honey, I give Blue the Dog commands, and all of these actions acknowledge the privileges of my humanity. I help the bees prepare to winter, and that's good for them, although I do so for me, too.

I was up at dawn, Blue the Dog asking to go. Out the back door, the sunlight said hello to us both. Honestly, I could never really decide what the sunlight said, but I imagine the sunlight means well in July.

Blue the Dog sleeps in my room on a bed. I stuffed an old duvet with sweet-smelling grasses, pine needles, cedar chips, and white milkweed flowers, all to absorb the poisons he excretes and to soak up what bad dreams he has. As I started to store Blue the Dog's bed, I smelled the padding: the aromatics had taken in all they could, which meant I had to change the bed, or Blue the Dog would be reabsorbing poisons in his sleep. Reabsorption poses the greatest threat to our singleness, the expelled toxins having soaked into our environments, saturated our clothing and furniture and the air we breathe. We have to make sure not to reabsorb.

In my daily practices, I was learning how to keep my life a clean zone, to think of each minute within its circle, as a clean idea, and to keep my days and nights in motion, with silence and purity, rather than be threatened continuously by recycled poisons. Blue the Dog was vital to my education in this polluted world, teaching me always with his great singleness about a clean life through the singleness of his one dog self, in every way uncorrupted. A dog is a dog. Even still, a dog lives in the polluted world too, and this dog's bed needed changing.

Which made me think of the girl's smells, and who she might be in my life. Her age was the same as every girl her age. I had met other teenagers, and they were a lot like Christmas. She did have cancer, though, and her cancer seemed to me real, or the symptoms did, from her throwing up to her colors and her smells. But I knew better than to become attached to sickness: believing in illness is an illness. True, cancer has one of the highest reabsorption rates of all human poisons, and as a result, she would need to keep clean, but she could learn how.

I don't like kids, and I had liked them even less when I had been a kid and had to spend time with other kids. Kids don't think, kids only feel, kids make so much noise, kids pollute, kids break things, kids reabsorb, kids are far from singleness. When I was a kid, kids didn't like me. But I couldn't like or dislike Christmas. In my seeking singleness, I wanted neither liking nor disliking.

Blue the Dog doesn't like kids either, so his behavior yesterday had been even more remarkable. I had never seen him care for a child until yesterday, when he had chosen to care for Christmas.

What is the difference between liking and caring? I don't know.

A dog can smell toxins far beyond the abilities of a human. But a dog doesn't believe in toxins or illness, not like people do. A dog has only the certainty of his senses and his affections. Blue the Dog has no beliefs apart from his knowledge, and this is his genius. And yet, from the very moment he sensed her, he had been certain about Christmas, finding her in the woods, guarding her on the porch, lying on her as she slept, the ninety-pound man-dog acting like a mother dog.

The day would be hot. I liked the day so far, and I would be ready for the bees. In the backyard, I slowed my body into a series of morning poses, in the uncountable time I planned to be in time. From the flat work on my mat, moving into the grass, to the waist-high horizontal shapes I made, to the planes and the lines of reaching verticality, up, to the great embracing of size and scale, and back to the center of non-me, I moved my energy. I felt my energy pool and the surface of the pool shimmer. I came down into myself, drew down my energy into my lower extremities to end my poses with a long squat, a seated form. My hands no longer mattered. My arms and shoulders no longer mattered. My hair, my eyes, my nose, lips, mouth, chin—nothing mattered. Today was a favorite day, because it was the same as all days. Singleness.

Squatting, the poses completed, I shaped my energy into one question: Why choose this girl, Blue the Dog?

It was a moment for my early meal. I was hungry, and I needed to prepare the equipment to bring in the honey. Blue the Dog was somewhere in the woods. As he often did during my morning poses, he had disappeared, only to return muddy or a bit scratched up, and often with a prize from his hunt. I thought of his hunt as his morning poses, in a way, Blue the Dog moving his energy in his body, settling into his singleness too, but doing so kinetically, not in stillness, his singleness in motion, different from mine. A dog and a man moving and not moving, each in singleness. Each in the woods of his life: I liked that idea.

Liking an idea is liking. The idea would be fine not to be liked.

•

Blue the Dog was so happy to see her, he lifted his paw and scratched the air in a greeting, his eyes open wide. He even whined.

"Blue the Dog," I said. "Down. Make room."

The girl got into the truck, sliding next to him and shoving him back. "Move," she said to Blue the Dog. "Hi," she said to me. "I have permission. Aunt Nikki says she knows you, and she called your sister. She says you're actually nice. Aunt Nikki says she loves your honey. You even plowed her driveway once, she said, when her regular guy didn't come…so I'm allowed to hang out, I can help, but I have to be back by nine o'clock. Here," Christmas said, reaching over Blue the Dog's head to hand me a little package in a plastic bag. "Aunt Nikki washed your stuff."

"In what?" I asked. "In the washing machine? With detergent?" I took the bag and threw it out my open window, onto Aunt Nikki's lawn. "No way."

"Snow Joe! Don't do that."

"Toxins," I said. "Not in my truck. And a plastic bag!"

"Wow," she said. "You gotta relax."

"Yes," I said.

I put the truck in reverse. I thought that driving backwards was what Christmas and I seemed to do together, so far. The thought gave me an inside smile.

As I drove through the neighborhood, Blue the Dog pushed his butt hard against my thigh, his head in Christmas' lap. He wiggled, wedged between us, connecting. I drove.

"Blue the Dog," she sort of cooed, making smoochie sounds and scratching both of his ears.

"Blue the Dog says 'thank you.'"

"I see," the girl said. "He talks."

"No," I said. "Yes. Don't see. Listen."

"What's he saying now?"

I didn't answer. Once more, I didn't know what to do with my feelings.

"Crazy," she said. "Blue the Dog says you're nuts."

Christmas and I didn't speak again until we got to my house, where I parked, and then she opened the door. Blue the Dog immediately sprang over her, down into the weedy gravel driveway, before dashing away into the woods.

"Blue the Dog!" she called. "Come back, Blue the Dog!"

"Probably something. He's a dog," I said.

"I know that. But he has to stay with me, he has to…" She didn't finish her sentence. She was distracted, having trouble unbuckling her seatbelt, and she punched her thumb at the release button a couple of times, something else in her actions. But then she got it.

I unbuckled my belt too. My feelings were swirling.

I waited.

"I…I want to help," she said, not getting out yet, the door open. She had feelings too. She tugged hard on her purple hat. "I hate it, I hate it." She punched herself on the thigh. "I'm going to try…" She banged on the dashboard with a fist, twice, and then slid out, slipping down from the truck. "I want to help with the honey. But I get sick," she said, looking back at me. "I'm not due for treatment until August, and I'm still…I get sick. I hate it."

I got out of the cab too, climbed down. I waited to know what to say. Christmas and I looked at each other, across the bank seat, neither of us closing our doors. Our doors were open—the thought gave me another inside smile.

"You need to suit up," I said. Whatever ridiculous thing she was wearing would be covered up: that was good. The bees.

She adjusted her purple hat again. It said "Meg's Team"—I hadn't noticed before.

"Were you in the war or something?" Christmas asked.

"No," I said.

"World War I or something? Did you kill Nazis? You seem like you could."

"I don't like children," I said. "Children say awful things, and they mean them."

"Snow Joe! No need to get nasty." Christmas slammed the door of my truck. "Jay Kaaayy." She might have been giggling over there.

"I'm trying to like you," I said quietly, shutting my door so she didn't hear.

I led the way to the honey shed, where I had laid out the protective gear for Christmas to wear. She could suit up here, and then we would drive to the hives. The smoker and the coolers were already in the truck bed. What else? I took down the bee brush from the pegboard. Of course I had my knife.

"Awesome!" she said, when she saw the suit laid across the workbench.

"Check the drawstrings. Double and tight. Then meet me at the truck."

"We're driving?"

I stood there in the honey shed, made myself stay in myself. How could I cope with her noise, and her childishness? I needed to be clear to do my work, to communicate with the honeybees and settle my energy. They're a strain of Russian bees that can be very aggressive. The bees know my feelings, and they move to the feelings I have, which is one reason they're bees. She would not understand.

I thought I might try another visualization.

"Hey! When someone talks to you, it's not cool to close your eyes."

I opened my eyes.

"That's better," she said. "Look, there goes Blue the Dog."

We drove down the bumpy work road past the pines to the edge of the field, turned and then drove the rockier and even more rutted road by the dry swamp to the beehives at the south edge of the woods. Blue the Dog ran, and on occasion we saw him. At times, when I thought of Blue the Dog, I had a feeling that was a perfect sphere.

I parked by backing in so we could load and unload easily. I began to haul the coolers, but Christmas wanted to keep her gloves on, which made her clumsy. She had worn sneakers for the honeying, okay. I provided her with the overalls, the jacket and gloves, and the Hamman veil, the good one with the built-in flat-brimmed hat. Now she wanted to jump around in the oversized gear, and Blue the Dog had joined us, and she wanted Blue the Dog to jump too, but he wasn't going to do that.

"Blue the Dog, come on! We're on the moon!" Christmas said. And then she stopped suddenly, and stumbled to her knees. "Whoa, I'm dizzy."

"Don't puke in the suit," I said, pulling down an empty, stacking the coolers, still working. Work ends when work's done.

"Oof," she said, and she plunked down into the grass, falling over. "Wuh."

I didn't know what to do. I kept working.

Christmas was gulping under the veil. She had folded her arms across her chest.

Blue the Dog watched her, checking with me, what to do, but watching her the whole time too, vigilant. Blue the Dog wagged his tail a very little.

She rolled into a fetal position. That was wrong. She needed to spread herself, increase her surface contact with the air. The beekeeper suit might be a bad idea, I thought, too enclosed to release her toxins safely.

I waited. She's wasn't throwing up yet.

The coolers were unloaded. I sat on a cooler. For a long time, while she lay in the grass, I watched the treetops in the wind. I was enjoying their waving. The clouds didn't care. Maybe I should do an afternoon pose, I thought, a better kind of waiting.

"Snow Joe? Tell me something nice." Her voice was quiet.

I thought about what to say. I felt a need to answer. "It's my favorite day," I said. Taking the honey was my favorite, I thought. "But any day can be your favorite," I said. "Feel it collect in you."

"How?" she was able to ask. She uncurled a little.

"Singleness," I said—and then I regretted revealing such a word so early. I turned away, to the dog. "Blue the Dog, stay," I told Blue the Dog, because he shouldn't run off once the beehives were open.

"I can't do anything," she said, and then she moaned, and rolled back up into a ball of pain.

She lay in the grass for a while longer. Finally, she uncurled, sat up again. She took a deep breath, made her mouth an O, exhaled, and repeated the action, again, slower. "The nurse taught me some breathing," she managed. "It helps a little."

"I breathe," I said.

She made her mouth another O, but didn't seem to be doing her breathing any more. The girl looked at me. "I'm going to stand up," she said. Then she managed to do so, clumsily, in full beekeeping gear.

We stood there. We were a pair. Blue the Dog was there too, in his different way.

"Okay," she said. She exhaled, another O. "Snow Joe, your head's on backwards," she said. "That's what Grandma Josie used to say about nut jobs like you, for realz." She looked at me. "Hey, what are you gonna wear? You don't have a suit."

"This," I said. "I wear everything. The world." I opened both palms to show how I hold the air and the light. "See?"

"Oh my God," Christmas said.

A smoker is a simple device, with a burn box, a bellows, and a spout. The bees don't like the smoke. The bees react by flying into the hive and eating, although some of them buzz around a lot too, and they can get angry. The trick with the smoker is to keep it lighted, because there's often a need for more smoke when the keeper starts pulling the supers—the racks—from the beehive, and the stealing begins. Christmas would handle the smoker, puff the bellows, and stay suited. Her job would be pretty easy, but essential. My job would be to wedge open the upper supers (the three smaller boxes on top of the big brood box) with the hive tool and cut through the propolis that the bees used to seal the hive tight. Each super contains ten frames. Each super would be rich with beautiful honey, loaded with honey, so much honey stored in the cells. I would slide out each heavy frame, the weight of the bounty almost too much. But Christmas would be able to help. Then I would use the bee brush to scrape the bees off of the frames—gently, with my apologies, remembering to acknowledge their goodness—to free the bees from their food and their homes, and once free, stash the frames full of honey in my coolers.

We would take the coolers back to the house and leave them outside the honey shed. The bees would follow. Once the sun went down, the bees would go back to the hive, to the brood box, and Christmas and I could safely bring the coolers into the honey shed for extraction.

A bee lives with himself.

A couple of problems might be problems. If the cells were uncapped, the honey was either not ready or had gone bad. Uncapped honey ferments, too much water in the mix, the sugar content wrong. But the bees know, and they don't care for uncapped cells. They are clear in their propagation.

Another problem: Christmas could drop something. The frames, loaded with wax and honey, were hard to handle.

Another problem: the bees' anger.

Another problem: me.

I explained most of this to Christmas as I prepared the fuel for the smoker, some pine straw to light as a starter, to be followed by layers of burlap, which would burn heavily and slowly together, the smoke thick. I had always liked waving around the smoker, it felt kind of mysterious and powerful without being harmful. The smoker made me feel like a priest in an old religion, confusing my congregation, but I didn't say that, because I don't talk like that, it's not me.

We were twenty feet from the hives, close enough to watch the unpredictable swoops of the honeybees tracking their scents, diving the air currents, scuttling into and out of the hives. I have trouble telling each bee apart, even after all of these years—though oft times, and especially when the bees were busy in the spring, I would come out here just to watch and try to predict which hive a single bee might be headed for, maybe that one. They're so fascinating, buzzing toward their friends, always a little heavier with their pollen pouches when flying home.

Having the bee as my spirit animal, my fetish, helps me remember that looking happy isn't the same as being happy. A lot of bees buzzing around make great sounds and their bodies are wonderful colors, and they have so many fascinating habits, and different pheromones, and as a human, I think they're kind of merry, but that's just my human ego. The bees have anger. That is how the bees are like me.

Maybe I would incorporate the bees into my afternoon poses, practice a pose to honor them, a new movement in the air, something to include them in my singleness. Because I have long been capable of feeling like the worst kind of garbage, and the bees were also a reminder of who I am—a wanting man raising bees to steal their honey, process their sustenance, and then go to his indoor home and shut the door. A man who sells the bees' honey as his own.

"Can I light the smoker?"

I think she had a fire complex. Children do.

"Fire is a transition."

"Snow Joe. You're so wise."

I looked away from her. She was making fun of me. People make fun of me, so I know.

She actually did look like she was on the moon, swallowed up in my big beekeeper's suit. "You'll need to come out of the suit, between pulls," I said.

"Where?"

"Reabsorption," I said. "You'll need to breathe. You'll need to take breaks. To lie down and open your cells."

"'Course." Christmas picked up the smoking can, stuffed at the bottom with the driest pine straw.

We were almost ready. Blue the Dog was excited: he knew we were going to do something important. Five times he had done this. He whined, and I petted his head, sharing calm energy, me to him.

"Blue the Dog," I said.

I buttoned the sleeves of my work shirt. I glanced at the girl—I would need to light the smoker for her, because that was difficult to do. For a moment, she looked like a real beekeeper. "Do you have any questions?"

"Snow Joe," she said. Her shoulders seemed to sag.

She could become so suddenly different, I thought.

"Snow Joe," she said again, and sniffled. "I…I mean, what do you mean? You know a lot. I mean…" She was upset. "What do you mean, 'Do I have any questions'? Like how did I get cancer? I mean…did I catch it? How did it happen? I didn't want to ask the doctors. I want to know, but I…" She lowered her head, the suit making a crinkling sound, her gloves too. "I mean, they think I'm just a stupid little kid. I mean, the question's stupid, I know."

I didn't have an answer.

"Maybe everyone has cancer," Christmas said, "but only some people get it. All I have is questions," she said more quietly.

I waited.

We waited together.

"What about animals?" I said.

She looked at me. "Blue the Dog?"

"Blue the Dog. Even the bees," I said.

Christmas sniffed. She looked up. "Or the trees—even the trees," she swept her hand toward the woods. "What about your truck?" I waited. "No, not your truck," Christmas said in a funny voice, her little girl's voice. "That's just a joke."

It was almost time.

We looked at the truck. We couldn't think the same thoughts together, I knew that, but it was good to remember.

"Ready?" I finally asked.

"Yeah," she said. She cinched the Hamman veil, adjusted.

"Now I have a question," I said.

"Shoot," she said.

"What are you doing here?"

"Freako. You know."

"Why are you here?"

"Aunt Nikki said I could. I'm here to take care of you."

I didn't know that answer.

I must have stared at her.

Her answer wasn't the answer. Of course, to seek an answer is to believe that apart from singleness, an answer is to be found.

I heard a red-winged blackbird, I think.

Silence was impossible. There was no silence in me.

I could feel now how we waited differently. That was the most important idea in the moment: we waited differently.

"Blue the Dog found me. He told me," the girl said at last.

"My dog?" I said. "Blue the Dog? He talked to you?"

There are the teachings and there is the life. There are the lessons that matter. What should I do with my feelings? I was standing there with Blue the Dog, a girl, the bees who don't know us, and all of my feelings.

I had worked so hard, and now this. I would need to start my work again, try less, find a longer pose, a pose for life. What had I been waiting for? I had been so wrong.

"Of course he talked to me," Christmas said, doing a little shifting sideways, adjusting her skinny body in the wide beekeeping suit. "He's Blue the Dog. He told me to come take care of you."

"Thank you," I said to the girl. "Thank you," I turned to Blue the Dog.

"Oh, Snow Joe," Christmas said. "You're nuts."

We waited there together, a singleness new to me.

Maybe waiting is the question and the answer, I thought.

But no, wrong again, that was wrong too.

Time is the question and the answer.

GLITTER

At approximately 2:30 p.m. on July 27, a brutally hot Tuesday afternoon, I stepped out of the Saxon Hills Post Office into the worst sunlight ever for a hangover, reached for my sunglasses, stumbled, tripped, and stopped myself from falling. I kind of caught my hand on the railing. I stood there a moment, rubbing my wrist, and for some freaky-do reason looked around slowly. Something wasn't right. I put on my sunglasses—better. I thought about the delicioso possibilities of an iced Venti skim latte and a chocolate chip yogurt muffin. I had not yet eaten. A muffin would be perfect. I turned to my left, toward Starbucks, standing in an uninteresting place on a boring afternoon, and although I was as sane as I would ever be, I saw a ghost. I was only twenty-six years old, and everything I had ever known was changed. A ghost made my life different forever.

How did I know it was a ghost? No doubt, Dudley. A girl who sees a ghost that's different from the rest of the world knows: the ghost is a ghost. That's how.

For sure, that same girl would also have a variety of responses to this bonkers situation. To begin, there are no ghosts—so what was I supposed to think? I was of sound mind, henceforth and yadda, yadda, yadda. I was scared. This was new.

Plus the ghost was rude, a rude ghost. Are all ghosts rude? I mean, if I were a ghost, I would be rude, too—and that thought made me realize another important point. The ghost knew me personally.

But really, I hate rude people, so I hate rude ghosts: there's no reason to be rude. I called out, "Hey, you!" but the ghost walked or floated away, whatever it was doing to move, and never turned around. Then the ghost disappeared around the corner by the First Commerce Bank.

While the ghost had facial features, I hadn't recognized the ghost. My Nana had died over a year ago, but the ghost hadn't looked like Nana. Or maybe my dead Nana had become a different person, now that she was a ghost, even though I had no clue why that would happen. What if ghosts became their original people, who they were meant to be when they were alive—and did that mean Nana was the wrong person when she was alive? That would account for Nana's being so bitchy all the time, and especially to my mom, but it also didn't make any sense. I mean, who's to say a person's the wrong person? The whole thing seemed way too complicated, like a philosophy question some guy asks you in line at the movies when you only want to see the movie. He up and says something that's a puzzle about life—I mean, come on, everyone standing there knows why the guy's asking you.

Seeing a ghost's a biggie. Just seeing a ghost once was enough to make me decide to stop going to church, right there, for good, no more of that. I had never liked church. I only went to church because of Mom and her friends, and my family's position in town, but I had never believed in Jesus, although he did have an A-1 PR and marketing team. No more church for this ghost girl.

Of course I wanted the ghost to be mine. The ghost had something personal to tell me, just for me. A girl knows. The ghost had a message that was too hard to communicate directly—the ghost hadn't stopped to chat—and the message for sure was for me, Evie Starkweather Louis, daughter of Bertrand Ellison Louis and Nancy Robinson Starkweather Louis of Saxon Hills, Maryland, living in a town with streets named after my grandparents on my mother's side. I am not unrecognizable: the ghost could so easily know what I look like, and who I am. I am one-sixteenth Navajo, "a bubbly socialite"— according to the local paper—a willing volunteer in various charities, and trying to make a difference because I can. Just a month ago, I was named to the Board of the Boys and Girls Club. I'm single, attractive, with good bone structure, my cheekbones memorable. Anyone who sees me remembers. I work as an event planner extraordinaire, in public relations, a job I like some days. More secretly, because a girl needs secrets, I am the online administrator of an anonymous group of friends who communicate in a chat room and trade pictures and stuff, people with whom I share a fetish. Because I am not only Evie Starkweather Louis of Saxon Hills, Maryland, but also Evie Glitter, glitterevie@gmail.com.

The ghost was gone and there I was, and it occurred to me for a moment that maybe the ghost was me—that I was dead. But no, that didn't make any sense either, since I still had a hangover.

Ghost and Evie, relationship status: It's Complicated.

Should I change my life? Give me a reason to change my life. I mean, really, what would I change? I like men, and I am past kissing girls because it's cool. Quitting church doesn't count—it wouldn't change my life, just get Mom all huffy. My older brother had quit years ago, and my family were show-pony Presbyterians. They didn't care anymore, not really, so I only needed an excuse to quit.

I couldn't think of anything to change that would matter enough to a ghost. So, as a result, pretty much right there, like ten seconds later, I made a promise: no matter how terrifying or dangerous, I was going to see the ghost again. I would find the ghost, speak to the ghost, and learn why I, who don't believe in ghosts, had seen a ghost. Why me, why here, why now, and why especially just four days before the first annual GlitterFest in Saxon Hills, Maryland, organized by me, Evie Glitter, which I had planned to be my coming out as Evie Glitter. Was the ghost here to ruin everything? If the ghost and the ghost people were here to ruin everything, why didn't they just send my mother?

Were there ghost people too? Could be a whole bunch of them, why not. One ghost, two ghosts, whatever. But a girl's first ghost is her most important, even I knew that.

I decided. On that hot July day—uncomfortable in the humidity despite my woven cotton summer hat and new Ray-Bans, in my pinstriped yellow linen suit from Tremonte, the one with the little bow on the back of the boat collar, wearing cute black flats—I made up my mind to haunt this ghost until I learned its secrets. The ghost probably knew all about me already, so it was only fair.

I imagine it's unusual at twenty-six to have an experience you don't believe is possible, and as a result to get a new secret to keep—different from my fetish life in Glitter. I had just seen a real live ghost, not a fake ghost, and that was important too, even more reason to keep the ghost secret. There's so much fake stuff. Of course there had to be fake ghosts in the world too, because there are knockoffs of everything, and so many people are fakes. But my ghost wasn't one of those.

The idea of a real ghost, one I had to find, my own ghost—well, I have to confess I was a little jazzed. Maybe the ghost's job was to make me *interested*. I mean, I was interested, and Glitter was dope, but there's always more.

Have you ever found yourself in the middle of a Supertramp song, like "Bloody Well Right," at a bar in OC? Drinks with pink umbrellas, on Thursday night girls get in for free, your skin's got that tight and prickly feeling from laying out all day, the boys are sweet and sweaty, and the words of the song are being hollered drunkenly by everyone at your table, "Right, you're bloody well right. You know you got a right to say!" Binky Magruder's there in her perfect tan, cutoffs, and bikini top. Little cousin Belle, who's never had sex. The Maymores' adopted daughter Rose. The girl from your sorority, the one who wants to set you up with her boring brother, the guy at Deloitte in DC. Some locals from the Surf Club. The Cross twins must have just left. The bartender's hot in a ponytail way, but he won't be tomorrow, and luckily, you figured that out already. You don't need that kind of sex tonight. The saxophone in the song feels like having another shot of tequila. I love when the moment is all for me, even with each of those other people hogging it, when the music gets life right and the bar's smelly in the best worst way.

Seeing the ghost felt like that, as though the saxophone solo in the Supertramp song, the sexy horn solo, was just for me, the sexiest me. Of course, it was possible that the ghost was someone else's, since the ghost had not paid total attention to me, or even that the ghost was shareable. Other people in other bars are always singing "Bloody Well Right" all up and down the Maryland shore, in bars everywhere in the country, for sure, and believing the Supertramp saxophone solo was theirs alone, too. But for whatever reason, I was pretty sure that ghost had to be mine.

A girl sees her own boutique ghost for a reason.

•

Everyone should have a gay brother. Mine's named Charles.

"What about hiring a private investigator?" he asked.

"To find a ghost?"

We were in Charles's office at First Commerce. He had taken off his suit jacket. He had on a pale pink shirt with a white spread collar,

French cuffs with blue and silver cufflinks in a diamond-in-a-circle pattern, and a simple navy-blue tie tied with a Pratt knot, along with a shiny pair of tasseled loafers. I had finished my muffin and I was feeling better from the 450 calories.

"Guess not," he agreed. "Take your feet off my desk."

"You don't believe me." I gave a little kick in the air before sitting properly.

"Well…" Charles rolled his eyes. "Why don't you ever bring me anything?" Charles aimed his pout at my latte.

"You're not taking me seriously."

"Buns," he said, his childhood nickname for me, "you're insane."

"Don't say that! I saw it!"

"Fine." He stood up to look from his tinted window down at the post office. His office is on the second floor, a corner office with a good view of the plaza. "You saw a ghost right there. Right there?" He pointed vaguely, wagging his finger. "What are you going to do about it?"

I stood up, so we both were standing. He stands, I stand: that's how business is. I went to school too. "I'm going to find it, and you're going to help."

"No."

"Please?"

"No…" He turned away from the big window. There were piles of papers and folders on his messy desk, and even some on the floor—everywhere, really—but his clothes were always perfect. "You've already got me doing everything for your Glitter thing. And I'm not even allowed to tell."

"You're such a queen," I said. "All you do is whine, like that's your goal in life. I want a different gay brother," I said.

Charles smiled at me, came around to my side of his desk, put one hand on my shoulder and with the other snatched my latte and chugged what was left, slurping just to bother me. He has a great smile. "You're going to give Mom a stroke, you know. A gay son and now a Glitter daughter. I love it."

"We're their children," I said.

"Oh, Buns," Charles said softly. "It's okay. She'll live—she always does. And you'll find your ghost."

•

I was off this week, taking five of my vacation days as I handled the run-up to GlitterFest. Mr. Wozinski, who wanted everyone to call him Stan, even though no one would, had been very supportive. The vice president of the firm where I worked, E & F Consulting, Mr. Wozinski had allowed me to bring my laptop into the office to do GlitterFest work at my desk. He had ignored my commandeering of secretarial help, my use of the conference room Smart Board, and all of that copying, way over budget. Charity work was good for E & F, Mr. Wozinski had said, but of course he knew who my family was, or why else was he being super nice? Sometimes it was a pain to be a Louis in Saxon Hills, and sometimes it was worth the hassle. I often didn't like it.

GlitterFest was only scheduled for one day, Saturday—so soon!—and I still had a crap ton to do. But I just couldn't go back to the office. Instead, I went to sit by my favorite fountain in Memorial Park, where I like to go to eat my lunch salad and feed the birds the walnuts I push to the side. Walnuts make my lips itch.

The benches are crude and they need to be repainted, but the fountain's pretty, the water bubbling out of the raised bowl and the mouths of the concrete fish and down into the pool, and I can stare into the falling water and feel like there's a connection, the drops a little like my life in Glitter. Or maybe I'm one of the drops, I haven't decided.

Charles hadn't been any help. Should I sit on the PO steps in the sun, to see if the ghost came back? If I were a ghost, why would I go to the Saxon Hills Post Office? I had decided the ghost was a girl. My ghost had already been to the PO, and she was coming out of the PO, which told me her PO business was done. I don't know a thing about ghosts or their lives, as in, to whom would a ghost send a real letter? Or a ghost letter? Had she needed to mail a letter to a ghost in Ghostville? Why not simply send a ghost email with a ghost attachment, like the rest of us?

She hadn't looked like Beetlejuice, a classic movie I love. She wasn't a cartoon. She had nothing to do with my Nana. I had been able to see through her, even though she seemed solid from thirty feet away. There were some rainbow colors to her edges, but not like a full-on rainbow you see in the sky, just a lot of colors. Not the rainbow flag. Not colors in order. She had sort of flowed, I think, but that might have been a memory I had of a cartoon from when I was a kid. Cartoons and memories are hard to tell apart.

I had only seen her face in profile, but her chin was strong—definitely strong enough to make me self-conscious, if that were my chin. She might have had hair, but I wasn't sure. I hadn't seen what she was wearing, and I always see what people are wearing. That was a shocker. How could I not notice what a ghost was wearing? Not noticing her outfit was another reminder that this had to be important.

There was just too much to do before Saturday, and now I had a ghost. I didn't know how to find her. I took out my phone, answered a couple of texts quickly—to one of the promoter/band managers for GlitterFest, who handled a band called Wagawagawaga, I replied "Srsly? Its 4 charity." The jerk had asked again for ten more gate passes. I wanted to say, hey, have you seen my ghost?

Why in the middle of the afternoon on a Tuesday, ghost chick? What the hell? Like, I could see you right there. You were right there—you showed up, you walked into my life, right there.

I answered a few more texts. In my business career, so far, I had already become a person who has to tell everyone no. Over the long term, before I turned thirty, being so negative was going to make me unhappy. I'm a positive kind of person. I need a yes kind of job. After GlitterFest, I would speak to Mr. Wozinski about letting me have a job that wasn't such a downer.

For Saturday, thanks to Charles, the use license was a go, as were the event permit and the insurance. The tent company would do the install late on Friday afternoon on Ball Field #2 at Findlay Park. The Saxon Hills Parks and Rec guy seemed happy with my planning, but I think he has the hots for me. He was texting me a lot of emojis. I hadn't told him yet that I hate hipster beards, and emojis are so yesterday. Of course, he might shave, maybe that would help. I could get a man to shave, I'm that kind of girl, and as we like to say in Glitter, you never know what's under there.

The two stages were rented and ready to be built. The GlitterMart was roped off in Parking Lot #4, the numbered parking spaces useful for assigning vendor spots. The off-duty cops were lined up to work security. The cleanup crew was arranged—through another board member of the Boys and Girls Club, who knew someone who knew someone whose mother knew someone who had a little company. The cleanup crew would be Mexicans, in Saxon Hills, because that's how companies in Saxon Hills handle illegals. Connections were always useful, of course, it's the world, and we had gotten a lot of goods and services lined up. The T-shirts were printed and being shipped. I had made an appointment at my mom's hairdresser for Friday at one. The concessionaire who had the Parks and Rec contract had texted me this morning to say that in addition to their usual, they would agree to serve garden burgers after all. That guy had been a pain in my patootie. I mean, how can garden burgers be a problem? I didn't even try to mention quinoa.

The bands were set. Four local acts: Wagawagawaga (lots of dope percussion, with bongos too), Tom Thumb (their front man was a rapper like seventy feet tall), Holden and the Cauliflowers (kids in art school), the Child-Bearing Hips (a roots band). The tribute band was booked, You Too, to bring in a different kind of crowd, although I thought their lead singer looked more like Adele than Bono. After the tribute band played, we would finish with the headliner, who would do a two-hour set beginning at eight o'clock, a girl band called Chicksburgh that had been at SXSW this year and were rumored to be opening for The Razors on their next tour. Just last week, one of the Chicksburgh guitarists had Instagrammed a Coachella logo, vaguebooking like a year ahead, or just creating demand for more vaguebooking, because that's PR.

Before Chicksburgh hit their first chord, I would make my speech.

I texted Charles: "c my ghost?"

He texted back: "cray cray."

For the past three years, I have lived a life in Glitter. We're a society, a passion, a lifestyle, a community: we're a guerilla fetish dedicated to innocence. Those of us who live in Glitter—who meet in our chat room, and in our one public venue, a bar called The Glitter Dome in Charlottesville, Virginia, and who run the online GlitterMart—all wear glitter. We paint our bodies and then go to work, to class, to therapy, even to church on Sunday with Bertrand Ellison Louis and Nancy Robinson Starkweather Louis of Saxon Hills, Maryland. We keep our secret, the fabulous sparkles of our kink, under our clothes or our uniforms. We tell no one. Someone's pumping gas at the gas station, or locking up people at the police house—that's not the word, I mean the police station—and they're in Glitter, and no one would know. We go in Glitter to Nana's funeral.

I have come out to Charles, and I tried to tell a boyfriend once, right after college, because I wanted him to spray me and then let me spray him. I knew it would get me hot. I liked him too much, I learned. He thought that living in Glitter was the same as Glitter Boobs, those chicks that go topless to festivals and glue on nipple tassels and then use body spray. That's just half-naked: we're a secret, underneath. Now I don't say his name anymore, that would be bad juju.

These days, if I'm out drinking and I'm in Glitter, I won't have sex with anyone. In the chat room, some people say that living in Glitter is like taking the pledge, but that's not how I roll. If I'm going to have sex with someone, I only do my nails in Glitter, and some eye shadow, and maybe on my neck and the top of my boobs. So it only looks like makeup. That way, no one knows about me, except for other people who live in Glitter.

But there's another big push inside the movement, which began in the chat room about a year ago, to come out, and to live in Glitter in public. People want people to know. I mean, there are Furries. We're harmless too: we're a fetish dedicated to innocence. If I could be in Glitter at work, full time, underneath my new Mike and Suz blue linen pantsuit, that would rock.

Hence, the First Annual GlitterFest. I am throwing myself an enormous coming out party, with six bands playing on two facing stages at an all-day, substance-free festival in my hometown, for a $50 cover charge, cheap for a music palooza, the proceeds going to the Boys and Girls Club of Saxon Hills. Online, I invited everyone in Glitter to attend. There will be the first ever in-person GlitterMart, with vendors selling everything imaginable in Glitter. Only those in Glitter know that the day will be for us. Otherwise, GlitterFest has been billed as a family fun party for charity. Of course, no one else has to come out.

GlitterFest attendees will be sprayed with glitter at the gate. We're using a PABA-free spray with great stick-on factor that's water-soluble and will last four hours, provided *gratis* by Glitter Gems, a company started by Joan Glitter, glitterjoan@gmail.com. She knows what she's doing, that Joan Glitter. She's a baller. Festivalgoers can be resprayed at any time—we're thinking they'll want to, once they see. At the beginning of the Chicksburgh set, for the finale, we're going to light up the whole crowd with black lights.

I haven't written my speech, but I did invite my parents.

●

I stayed in the park for a long time, fielding the increasingly irritating inquiries, ones I couldn't ignore or could give a quick no to, my phone on vibrate. After a while, I just closed my eyes and tried, tried, tried to take notes in my head, to think of something to say in my speech. I have always been an awful public speaker: I get shaky nervous, and for some reason, in those situations, I become convinced my hair looks terrible. All I can think is that it's totally flyaway, so I keep tucking my hair behind my ears, and then I start mumbling, and that's it, I'm a shit show. Although the hair thing's better than flop sweat—that would be the worst!—it's still a thing. In the Public Speaking portion of Advanced Marketing Tools in college, the prof made me wear mittens.

The title of my speech would be "What Glitter Means to Me." Or not. I had the title, so far. But maybe a different title.

There were a lot of messages from the Wagawagawaga manager: he could go wagawaga himself. Priorities. Mine were two: a speech and a ghost.

After a while, I had to give up, the weather too sweaty even to sit by the cool fountain. I could smell me, and that's not good. Luckily, the forecast for Saturday was great. My condo, only four blocks south in one of the new Riverview Towers, might be a better place to think. I decided to go home, hit the treadmill in the fitness center, juice up a very-merry-berry recovery drink, take a bath upstairs, redo my Glitter, and see who would be around tonight. I said goodbye to the fountain, then caught myself making a little hand gesture, a finger how-di-do wave to the concrete fish, and thought that was weird, I don't do that, Evie, what the hell.

That made me do a little swish turn, like my ghost had, going away. I don't do that either. See what a ghost does to a girl?

I had another idea. I texted Charles: "mojito."

He texted back: "work."

●

Here's what an event planner extraordinaire does: she uses her networking talents, her party skills, her social media obsessions, her bossiness, and her improvisational ballsiness to make sure other people live their lives joyfully. That's what I adore about my job, and how it's just so perfect for who I am—although a lot of people don't want fun, and they get in the way of fun progress. That's what I call it, fun progress.

What throws me, though, is that I try to treat myself the same way, with the same kind of mad skills I apply to my job, and other people's fun progress, and I can't. Why can't I live my life how I decide, how I treat everyone else? It's the worst. I'm like a doctor who's always sick.

The walk home was fine, but a sign in the lobby said the fitness center was closed due to an air conditioning problem. Someone had graffitied HOT POCKET! on the sign. People who aren't funny shouldn't try.

There was no point to a recovery drink. Upstairs in my condo, I found some fresh-enough salad in the refrigerator—possibly belonging to my roommate, Candace, who has a little bit of a big weight problem and hates when I eat her food, she gets so precious. Like, come on, it's a salad. I squirted the greens with lemon juice. The sink was full. I would do the dishes tonight, if I came home early.

I checked my phone. There were four messages from the same manager guy—Señor Wagawagawaga, I had taken to calling him in my head. He was not my favorite person on my thinking list.

Fine, I would listen to the last one: "Hey, Evie, it's Carson again. I know it's bad, but the band's just not feeling it. I wish you'd call me back. Sorry. Good luck on Saturday. Next time. Ciao."

O-M-God. Here's what an event coordinator extraordinaire does when one of her bands flakes: she throws a glass salad bowl against the wall of her condo, and she explodes like the bowl. There are a lot of little shards to her, and she can shatter into everything she feels. No one can pick up all of those pieces of glass. She screams. What she screams probably doesn't make any sense, because the sounds are glass too.

•

Girl needed to change her feels. I racked a shot of vodka, took an Iced Mint Lemonade bubble bath, thank you, Sephora, got in Glitter, put on my backup sweats and a Reds baseball hat with the sticker still on the brim, and called no one back. Then I took the bottle of vodka and went downstairs to the River Walk, to drink and cry and hope to see the prep school crew team have their practice on the river, trailed by their cute coach in a motorboat. The coach sometimes waved to me with his free hand, the other on his megaphone. I took my phone, too, because that's who I am, but I put it on Airplane Mode. It was like going to the movies.

My spiritual life was on Airplane Mode, I thought. I'm not sure why I was crying, although it could be crying in advance, future nerves, because I do that too. I can tell some of the time what I'm worried will happen later, based on what kind of crying I'm doing.

When the sun went down at last, maybe forty-five minutes later, I was hammered. I was sitting with my feet dangling over the wall, kicking, my self-pity and I in the reflection of the water, poor Evie, the current passing me by, just like my life. I saw that two nearby streetlights on the River Walk were out, and it occurred to me to move to a brighter area for safety purposes. I was pretty sure I had my pepper spray, but I didn't want anyone to see me look.

My ghost sat next to me.

"You're not real," I said to the ghost. "Fuck you."

The ghost didn't answer. In the darkness, she was hunter green, a different color from in the sunlight. She stared straight ahead. She had on those sneakers that don't need laces, they looked like Damn Daniel knockoffs, but otherwise, I couldn't call her outfit an outfit, even though she wasn't naked. Up close, she was sort of transparent.

"Why are you here?"

The ghost didn't answer.

"You're my ghost," I said. "I love you."

The ghost didn't answer.

"Don't fuck with me. I need GlitterFest," I said. I was crying. "I need another band. Fuck you. If this is your fault, fuck you."

I pulled up the hem of my sweatshirt to wipe my face, and dry my tears, and it took no more time than that, and the ghost disappeared.

"Come back!" I yelled. "Fuck you! Fix this!"

•

After that, I went out. I was home late—and I was sick in the Uber. Candace had been staying at her boyfriend Robby's a lot, so I'm not sure what time I crashed. I didn't black out: I would have known if I had blacked out.

Lately, I was a little done with what I was doing. Too much of it. In case of ghost, break glass.

Wednesday, I didn't feel bad, so I worked my phone and spent two hours in the office, mad texting to try to find a band, hung out in front of the post office trolling for my ghost, went to the river the same time of day, when the sun went down, but no Asti Spumoni, no fashion disaster from the spirit world. Wednesday night, I partied with Binky and Rose, but I didn't really drink. Late, late, we went for a swim in the Cross twins' pool, even though they were out of town, and I wore my monokini. I hoped the twins would be back for GlitterFest.

Thursday, I spent a bit of the morning crying in my bed. I couldn't say why. Not too long, maybe a half hour. I texted Charles to come over, but he had a meeting. Future nerves, maybe.

Thursday afternoon, I felt better. I did an hour on the elliptical, showered, sprayed, and went out in Glitter to meet with one of the board members of the Boys and Girls Club, someone who wanted to talk through the GlitterFest schedule. She was just high-strung, I could handle her.

Thursday night, my luck changed, and I got a text from a promoter for a band called the Sad Huns, out of DC. They had a single, and they had just uploaded a preview video of an unplugged performance onto their site. They had a zillion hits. I texted back, the guy called me, sent me the link and password, asked that I watch the video and then call him back. I don't know how he got my text, or who had told him about GlitterFest, but he was totally doing it, the Sad Huns were available.

The song was called "You Make Me Old," and I loved it, and I never say that. Two guitars, a drummer in motorcycle goggles banging on a single snare, two singers in beehive hairdos, one of the girls on tambourine like it was the eighties and the tambourine was just invented. It was a ballad about a dumped chick wanting revenge, and one of the singers sounded a little like Bebe Rexha—I had seen the Black Cards in college—but you could tell they had their own sound, the bass was thunder, even unplugged, and the rhythms were tight. I loved that they weren't Auto-Tuned. "I never wanted to rescue your ass, but to be in the middle of the champagne glass." They passed the audition. I downloaded the song to share on the Glitter site, called the guy back, talked through what they needed. Turns out he was the drummer.

I ordered in on Thursday night. I had a gross mini-pizza I shouldn't have had, and I worked on my speech. At least I had the self-control to throw out the last slice. If my ghost had something to say to me, she could ring the bell downstairs, and I would buzz her in, yo. Or not. If my ghost had future nerves, that was just too bad for her.

Friday, I was up early, on site. The Parks and Rec hipster dude was there with a couple of trays of coffees for everyone and some disgusting Bavarian cream donuts, like how I would die someday. I signed for the T-shirts, the dude dealt with the bandstand guys, we took delivery of the HO Portable Toilets, the FedEx boxes of gate passes on their strings arrived (so cool), and he began to register the vendors, although I would assign who went where. The morning wasn't too hot, the humidity lower than my cat's IQ for a change. Perfect. Glitter likes low humidity.

Have you ever hung out in college with the girls on your hall after a really brutal Valentine's Day? You go on a date with that guy from Sig Ep, but he's a disaster, he was for sure on steroids, and you come home early and then you have to drink peach schnapps alone until your roomies return, and they are just as bad, and Sam's dress is torn, she can't even talk, but she says she wasn't assaulted. Down the hall, Olive from Alabama cranks a Kelly Clarkson song, "Already Gone," and you hate that song, but you find yourself with your best roomies belting out the lyrics together, swaying together, something like ten women on your hall: "I want you to know that it doesn't matter where we take this road, someone's gotta go." Those BFFs include Binky, for whom you will always be grateful, and who insists on meeting for lunch after your 1 p.m. hairdresser appointment today, the day before GlitterFest, because she is a true BFF and she knows otherwise you won't eat. Feeding a BFF is a BFF's job.

But college was pretty much before you lived your life in Glitter. The "before" of the before/after experiences, even those party days, seems so blank now, the life of someone else. Pictures in your head aren't real, they're just a funeral for what you've done already. Pictures with no pizzazz, no glitter, dead pictures.

In Glitter, I was going to live free.

●

Friday was the worst day because it wasn't Saturday yet, but the organizing and prep went okay. Deliveries were made, stages were built, the endless sound checks were stupid and went fine, the talent was occasionally nice. The managers were assholes, all except for Brat, the drummer from the Sad Huns, a cutie pie. Swooping sideways across his forehead was a lock of dyed black hair, a little emo curl (the rest of his flat top was blond), and I wanted to touch it. When I was sitting under the tent we were using as an office, he came up to me from behind and put his hand on my shoulder, to ask me a question, and I knew it was him just by his touch. I wanted to trip him and roll on top of him and squish him good. Yum, I said to Evie in my head, a boy.

On Friday night, for security, we left on a couple of the portable banks of lights—not the full field towers, but some smaller racks of arc lights, running off a generator—and dimmed the power. Around midnight, the ball field looked underwater, the rented tent like a town that drowned. Do ghosts drown? Ghosts don't breathe, so probably not. But maybe a ghost is made out of stuff like clothing, and their skin feels like silk, only human too, and their bodies get soggy and heavy enough to sink when they're really wet. I was thinking a lot, walking around in the world on Friday. I was trying to determine what a ghost could be.

I still had to finish my speech—well, I still had to write it. There were only some notes on a couple of scraps of paper in my purse, not a speech. Just like me, all of those scraps, nothing together.

I thought I might get some inspiration from staying in the park once everyone left. I had taken a break by going to Jingo Juice for a Jingo Mango Smoothie, and that had been a good idea, I could go for hours on a smoothie.

My ghost apparently likes when I hydrate—I think it's cute, she gets concerned, and she wants to make sure I'm not skipping meals— because when I sat in Row 2 of the portable chairs facing Stage 1, slurping my most excellent Jingo Mango Smoothie, my ghost sat next to me. Finally.

I tried to pretend it was all normal. I stared at the stage—that was where I would give my speech, up there, facing this way. I would stand at the microphone, looking out at my parents and all of the festivalgoers, and everyone I cared about in Saxon Hills. After three years of living in Glitter—no, wait, it was four years, my math was wrong—I would come out. My hair looked good, and I was deter-mined to be ready.

I kind of peeked at my ghost, to check her hair, but she was too transparent for me to get a good take.

"I know why you're here," I said to the ghost.

She said nothing.

"You're my old life, before Glitter."

She was not a talking ghost, I decided.

"Sip?" I turned to and offered her my smoothie. "Jingo Mango."

This ghost wanted nothing.

"Okay, don't answer. But here's my theory. You're here because I brought you here, to put my old life down…to like bury it, or leave it behind. You're here because I invented you, and I need you to rest in peace. So I can come out, right?"

The ghost didn't answer.

"Do you exist?"

The ghost didn't answer.

"I want you to say something!"

She didn't flinch.

"Is this all there is?" I don't know why I asked that.

No answer.

"Nuts to you, girl," I said. "You're not helping. I don't understand what you're here to show me."

The ghost said nothing.

"Fine," I said. "But I'm going to post your picture." I had my phone out and I clicked and swiped. Of course not, I knew that wouldn't work, ghosts don't show in pictures, but what the hell.

She was the same as any ghost: aim a camera at her, and presto, gone goes the ghost.

I'm the same as any ghost, too, I thought, an idea I knew was right but I didn't really understand.

Sitting in Row 2, picturing myself up there tomorrow, I wrote my speech. Who knows what time it was when I finally fell asleep in the chair, and then I woke up on the cold ground, stretched out and curled up, my hoodie a half pillow. It was like being on an airplane going nowhere, just flying back to where it started, returning to the hangar. That's what living in my hometown is like—it's like sleeping on the ground. But no one came to haunt me, or to kill me with a horrible cronut, or to ask me for something I couldn't do. No bad ghost made me sit up, grabbing at my heart attack, I can't breathe, I can't breathe, showing me all of the horrible mutilations happening to my body every day I got older, only more intense, all at once.

When I finally woke up on Saturday morning, I had Glitter on my tongue, which felt weird. I had been dreaming after all. Maybe I needed to live my body in Glitter on the inside, too, and that's what I had tried to do in the dream. A girl could die eating Glitter.

There wasn't a lot of time. I rushed home, showered, shaved my pits and legs, sprayed fully, got dressed: panties, little pleated skirt, bra and cami, pink Chuck high-tops. I put on heavy black mascara, did my eyeliner and eye shadow in Glitter Gem's own Rainbow #4. I did the winged eyeliner, like Lana del Rey. I did my lips in Glitter gloss. Then I sprayed again.

In the pocket of the skirt, I slid my folded-up speech. My speech was ready, the words waiting, like me, to come out. The gate passes were in my trunk, the cashier's checks were in my purse. I grabbed a Nalgene from the kitchen of the condo and looked around—what else? Maybe I wouldn't live here anymore. The difference between being dead and a life in Glitter and being a ghost could be as easy as moving out of your condo.

My ghost and I should sell real estate, I thought. She would make people want to move, and I'd sell them their next place.

•

By the time I returned to Findlay Park, even before I could turn onto the access road, there were cars, oh my God, so many cars had arrived, bumper to bumper. There were three or four cars done fully in Glitter, too. There were so many people, I felt like I would never be able to hug them all, to say thank you. I pulled off the road and onto the grass, parked, and texted the bro beard Parks and Rec guy, and he walked out to my car, to help carry the boxes (it was girly, I know, but

I had a latte in my other hand). Here I had been worrying about five hundred people—our break-even—and hundreds were there already, four hours before the show, maybe even a thousand people!

The dude with the beard found me. "You look amazing," he said. "It's so early! Look!"

I wished, for the first time, that I remembered his name. Ray? Troy? "Thank you. Stuff's in the trunk, please."

"Isn't this unbelievable? Evie, you're the best!"

Joan from Glitter Gems had it going on already. She was setting up four spray booths just inside the entrance. Nose plugs, earplugs, close your mouth, step into the stall, and *tsit-tsit-tsit-tsit*, with a kind of airbrush, head to toe, the festivalgoers would be sprayed in the brilliant colors of Glitter. Joan was serious and totally in charge of her artists.

"Evie" was all she said, nodding.

"Joan."

Being cool with each other, me and Joan.

Inside the park, on the fields, there was music. A band was playing on Stage 2. It was the Sad Huns. When he saw me, Brat stopped, rose from behind his drum kit, and the tune fell apart. He slid up his motorcycle goggles onto his forehead. "Hey, like, Evie. Wow. We kinda…we wanna jam. I hope it's okay. There were people here, and people…I mean…people like it." He was being so polite. "Okay?"

"It's cool," I said.

The Parks and Rec hipster nodded.

"I want to be Glittered!" said one of the singers.

"Oh, yeah," Brat added. "We brought a friend. This is Anders Fly. You know."

I looked at a guy I hadn't noticed, a guitarist standing by an up-stage monitor. "Anders Fly? *The* Anders Fly? From the High Mighties? *That* Anders?!"

"What it is," Anders said. He had on a turban, parachute pants, a tuxedo jacket, and no shirt. He hit his wa-wa, hello.

"Oh, awesome!" the hipster whispered to me. "Anders Fly."

"What it is!" I squeaked back at Anders.

"We need more security," the hipster said really quickly. "Evie, this is awesome. That's Anders Fly. I mean, that's…God! He's a god! Dude! Evie! I'm on it!" He handed me my walkie-talkie, pressed TALK on his, and said in a deep voice, "Evie Glitter," even though we were standing next to each other. Then he kind of skipped away, toward the admin office.

What was happening? I felt my heart go bumpity.

I don't know what I remember. Memory's just a part of it all, anyway, and it's not real either, it's just what happened already and won't again. When I think back to the day, it's like trying to remember something from when I was a two-year-old, before my first memory, and I know I can't know, but I know. I was there, it all happened, but it's not real anymore, because what's happened isn't real. A ghost had to be a memory, because a ghost isn't alive now, so a ghost was there. So a ghost isn't real? I was so turned around.

What will happen, now that's the show.

So many people came that the SHPD called the SHFD, and at three o'clock, the hour when GlitterFest was supposed to begin, the police began to turn away disappointed latecomers. We closed the incoming lane of access road 1055 to Findlay at 3:30. We got a couple of ambulances to come park by the tent, just in case someone had a GlitterFit or a GlitterMeltdown. The head count was around 4,500, although we ran out of the printed gate passes early, so I'm only guessing based on estimated gate receipts.

Charles brought my parents. Luckily, I remembered to comp them.

I think I ate a garden burger, at one point, and if I did, it was awful.

So many friends in Glitter, so many colors and sparkles, but also so many people who had no idea—there was dear dumb Binky, and I showed her, and I helped her get sprayed, and I sat her down in the grass later, and we talked and talked, but who knows. I liked her big hat; it was from Remarkable Relix.

She had found glitter around me, she said, like in her passenger seat after driving me to the quarry last year. She had thought it might be just from my shoes or my bra, although she admitted she hoped I had a thing. A thing is so interesting, she said. I want a thing too, Binky said.

I told her I loved her. She told me the Cross twins were still at Hilton Head.

I realized when I walked away that I don't love Binky. She can be a real bitch. That's okay. Or I did love her—because if I felt love, that was love, so maybe I did love her after all, BFF ♥ 4evs.

GlitterMart must have had fifty vendors in the parking lot, all of these people who had spent hours coating their things in Glitter, who had bought cases of water bottles and done them in Glitter or had just made T-shirts. I couldn't get through the aisles, there were too many shoppers. I saw a computer and computer printer in Glitter, book covers, golf club covers, a toaster, and every pet outfit ever. Dogs in Glitter and an iguana in a Glitter cage. I tried not to stare. I didn't think the iguana was me.

A couple of the bands sucked, especially You Too, but I expected them to suck. During "I Still Haven't Found What I'm Looking For," the guy pretending to be Flea went to do a kind of split and dropped his bass and it broke. That was loud. Some of the crowd—okay, a lot of people—cheered.

There was a run on the Official GlitterFest T-shirts, and then we had no more. The margin on those was $14 per. That was my bad, not having ordered too many and dumped the extras online later. The kids' sizes sold first.

The weather was unbelievably great, that day where one cloud hangs out really far away and watches. All of that Glitter in the sun. I couldn't wait for the Chicksburgh set, and for the black lights.

I wasn't that cloud either. Something was different with me, though, because I was checking myself in everything, Evie Glitter in every mirror.

The hipster guy from Parks and Rec hugged me like thirty times. I think he used the walkie-talkie to find out where I was so he could show up and look all surprised and then hug me. He was getting cuter.

I met Glitter Del, who owned the Glitter Dome in Charlottesville, and he introduced himself and invited me to come hang out. He was a Latino guy in his fifties, with a poufy 'do. He was pushing Glitter Alice in her wheelchair, which was totally pimped out in Glitter. Of course, I Instagrammed.

I made sure to avoid my family. Charles had agreed to keep them occupied. I spied on them for a little while from behind a tower of amps, as they looked around and pretended to be happy. My mom was like a skittish mare. My dad was all proper, even in a pretty chill purple polo, collar unpopped for once. He pops his collar and it's the worst. But they looked so normal and out of place, I got scared again. Was that me? I was like that too. I was a ghost, an iguana, my mom. I was none of the above.

My parents of course had not been sprayed, not Bertrand Ellison Louis and Nancy Robinson Starkweather Louis of Saxon Hills, Maryland.

Just after eight, the sun going down, I turned off my walkie-talkie and waited in line for the women's bathroom behind Ball Field #4 to be sick. I had ten minutes before my speech. All of the stalls were occupied, the veggie burgers working.

When the far stall finally finished, and I rushed in and locked the door, I was hyperventilating.

When I began to vomit, so did the person in the stall next to me.

Vomiting always takes so long, and it makes my hair tingle, for some weird reason, or maybe it's my scalp. I hate, hate, hate throwing up. When I was done, I tried to catch my breath and stop gulping.

The person in the stall next to me was also done.

I knew something, I thought. I knew who she was, and I said so. "Hey," I said through the stall, to the person next to me. "Are you my ghost?"

There was a long silence.

"Did you hear me? Are you my ghost?"

Again, nothing.

"What are you doing here?" I asked. "I have to know."

Her foot moved. She had on big black boots that had been sprayed in Glitter. That was a new look for my ghost, a little mall rat for me, but okay.

"I..." She coughed.

"What?" I interrupted her. She had never talked. I sat down on the closed lid of the toilet. This was it.

"I came for the show," she said in a whisper.

"I knew it!" I cried out, and banged my palm on the wall of the stall. Suddenly, there was applause outside, a vamp from the band. "Oh, shit, that's me." I gathered my stuff, jammed things into my purse again. "Thank you. Oh my God. I'm on. Wish me luck, oh my God. Thank you."

I threw open the stall door, ran to the sink, splashed my face, rinsed my mouth, washed my hands, and came back to the mirror. I popped a peppermint from a box of Bix, a square Bix Mint, favorite mints of the Queen of the Netherlands. I pinched the tops of my cheeks.

"I'm going," I said to the ghost in the stall behind me. "Feel better."

I stopped for another second, to look good in the mirror. Then I was running and it was the best feeling ever.

CHRISTMAS IN JULY

I moved back to Saxon Hills, Maryland, to live, never thinking that my thirteen-year-old niece and goddaughter would move in with me to die.

I had spent childhood summers here at my grandfather's cabin on Upper Lake Fanning, just ten miles north of town, so I knew Saxon Hills, or thought I did. Saxon Hills—where I had swum and canoed, had my first French kiss, gotten my first period, and touched my first naked boy—looked familiar enough, when I needed a place to run two years ago. I believed my memories could protect me.

No matter that the cabin had burned to the ground, or that some of my firsts were unforgettable for the wrong reasons, or that in Saxon Hills I had once stood at the side of the road and watched a deer get hit by a truck, a memory that had become a vision that had become a symbol and then a prediction. As I was in the midst of what was clearly a breakdown, moving back to Saxon Hills seemed an opportunity to hide in an idealized past rather than have my face rubbed in an awful present. At the time, I had only those two choices, or so I convinced myself. Renting a house here cost one-fifth of what I was paying for a duplex on Long Island, my credentials suited the job for which I was being recruited, and the people of Saxon Hills looked to be puttering along happily as though it were still 1985, when I was seven years old and not yet hostage to my own life. That Saxon Hills appeared safely unappealing made the decision to move here appealing. Boring looked happy.

I used to be Nikki Danzig, a Maryland girl by birth and circumstance and a New Yorker in spirit and temperament—go-getter, dynamo, a woman accustomed to being in charge. The more I battled and won, the better I got at my job, the more inclined I became privately toward certain eccentricities and terrors, a divide that ultimately became a chasm. I was thirty-five and childless. I have always been far too relentless and scared to be a parent, and men in general had started to become too male for me, so I was also thirty-five and single. In Saxon Hills, I met with no aggression to match my own or to amplify my phobias; I was allowed to ebb at whatever ease I wanted, to take the edge off of my needs.

Until, after two years here, at the end of June, I agreed to drive to DC to pick up Beatrice—my late brother Otto's kid, Otto the Favorite, Otto the Success, dead Otto—and bring her here, and thus I began to participate fully in the lie that became my niece's palliative care, each day lying more as her condition worsened. Lies of omission, lies in every glance, lies at each meal. Beatrice was told she would be okay, the biggest lie of all, first told by her wide-eyed, dipshit, junkie mother, and never corrected by me.

Beatrice wasn't stupid, she was a Danzig after all, so she knew plenty, including the fact that she was sick, and anyone could see that her mother didn't want her. Whom did Beatrice want? There wasn't a choice, only a booby prize. Once her good dad was gone and her bad mom had been checked into rehab, Beatrice got me. The thirteen-year-old kid raised in the gentility of Adams Morgan, dying of cancer, was sent to stay with a terrified aunt she didn't know in a tiny western Maryland town where nothing happens. A thirteen-year-old who would no longer answer to either Beatrice or Bea, who insisted that we call her Christmas—a willful adolescent gesture I pretended to mind because I thought a mother should. Secretly, I admired her bravado. Christmas was the right name for my kind of kid.

Growing up, I was so bad at being a girl, I had never known what girls were. I told Christmas this much, or tried to tell her. I spoke to her a lot, for me, when she was in my house, even when it felt as though I were speaking at her. When I'm silent, I'm listening—but I couldn't tell if she was. On the drive here, and over the course of those first lopsided days we lived together, I talked to her as an adult— which in retrospect might have been the wrong approach. Christmas was precocious, sassy, capricious, smart, and mean; in short, she was thirteen years old, a combustible mix of an ever-changing seven- and nineteen-year-old. I think I overlooked the little girl hidden in her and only saw the petulant young woman, whom I treated as an antagonist. Christmas deserved to have a childhood, even and maybe especially at the end.

Shortly after moving in with me, Christmas began to roam, to disappear all day, and then overnight, and then for a couple of days at a time, and always she came back sicker. She looked to be returning to the wild, but how wild could Saxon Hills get? It seemed pretty safe out there—even if it terrified me. What was the worst that could happen that I hadn't imagined already? It was as though she had saved her money, and decided to backpack across Europe—that's what I told myself at first—only she hadn't any money and Saxon Hills isn't France.

Later, I began to understand that a biological imperative had taken over, that her body was making a decision. Like an animal, Christmas was finding a safe place to curl up and die. She was wounded, scratching at the grass to make herself a hidey-hole. I do the same. My body makes decisions too. I rationalized: she was making her own Make-a-Wish ending. So I kept tabs on her, Saxon Hills being a small town, and me the assistant town planner, and I did nothing to deter her expeditions. I wanted her to do whatever she wanted; she'd never had the chance, I reasoned. But in truth, of course, her wandering took the burden of her future death from me.

The Internet has made stories like Christmas' ordinary, those human interest profiles once saved for the last three minutes of the Nightly News, stories introduced with "and finally..." the lead-in a sure sign of impending sentimentality. Now the Nightly News has become all headlines; now we coo to Yahoo instead of to each other in the family room, rage against the pixilated president, close our eyes before we open them and click again. I admit I don't mind, as I'm better at feelings when I'm alone. But it's sad that the true story of the thirteen-year-old Christmas has become a roll-over, her death inaudible, the mouse sliding past.

Much of my time since Christmas' death has been spent in these kinds of spiraling thoughts, spinning like a wobbly top through the universe—a spinning top without a table on which to spin, just spinning every which way, no surface and no friction. I have more than a passing acquaintance with death, which should have included Christmas, but never quite believing in her as a person, not having chosen, has screwed up my sense of the universe's order. Or maybe that's one of the lies she taught me.

That my grandparents died seemed inevitable, an act of Nature; that my brother died seemed tragic, a decent, well-loved man plucked too young from his affairs; that Christmas died seemed a travesty, a cosmic joke, all the more so as a result of how she died, which became a challenge to our safe lives in Saxon Hills, Maryland.

I will tell her story. I will get it right. I promised myself that I would get it right—there are still too many unknowns surrounding what exactly happened, and what she did. The police have one version, the Internet another. But I am a person who asks questions.

Questions are more than my inclination; they are also my profession. Where shall we build that road? Who benefits from a new public park? How will we evaluate bids for waste removal? How can we keep the water clean? What should the land use policy be on the other side of the river? Although only an assistant, I have my eye on the top job: I am a town planner. I understand laws, rule, bylaws, easements, allowances, dispensations, rights-of-way, codicils, and partnerships; I can negotiate, file, post, project, demure, attach, deliberate, manage. Professionally, I'm sensible. I understand the civilizing powers that keep the chaos at bay.

Privately, substitute the word "life" for "town" and you'll see how incompetent I have been, never better than an assistant life planner. Christmas knew: she saw who I was.

Everyone wants something. The dangerous people let you think they want something, but they want something else. The innocent people tell you what they want, because they only want what they want. Too often, the most innocent people don't know what they want, they can't see it, there's only a blur. My ignorance of the difference between what I want and what I need has the power to incapacitate me.

As Christmas showed me, I am bad at love, possibly even incapable. Maybe I can be better at understanding her death.

•

Many of the facts are known. On a Sunday afternoon, on the last day of July, Christmas went wandering. She apparently wanted to pet the puppies at Pet Land, the ones the Saxon Hills Humane Society brings to place in the arms of sympathetic shoppers to encourage adoption, but she got the day wrong, the puppies are only there on Saturdays, not Sundays. The clerk at Pet Land remembered Christmas: a tall, sick teenager in combat boots, plaid shirt and skirt, and a purple hat. She was trailing glitter, too—like a little dying star. She left. She stopped at a hardware store and bought a cold Coke from a cooler. It was hot, the end of July was ridiculously hot this year, and she was getting sicker every day. That Sunday, the heat had risen dramatically—ten degrees hotter than the previous day. Christmas walked more than two miles in over ninety degree heat toward the downtown business district of Saxon Hills.

Downtown, she met someone she knew—perhaps they arranged to meet, that part's unclear—a young woman named Sarah Wasserman, who was acting bizarrely, according to multiple witnesses. Wasserman had run into a Greek diner off the square and then run out again; she appeared to be fleeing someone, "her head on a swivel," one report noted, but whoever scared her wasn't in view. Wasserman had lain down in the grass at one point, and might have been crying. A dog walker saw the two girls together on a bench in Memorial Park. A mother with two toddlers splashing in the Memorial Park fountain saw them, too. A trio of Sunday joggers saw too—three sweaty men, jiggling in their silly Spandex, as I imagine them now. No police officers. No crazy aunt named Nikki to protect her.

What Sarah Wasserman and Christmas animatedly discussed for more than an hour on that park bench, we don't know. At 4:45 p.m. on the last day in July, Sarah Wasserman and Christmas rose from their park bench, walked together to the corner of West Starkweather and Third, and began to cross in the crosswalk, the WALK sign in their favor. A white, late-model Kia—that's what the police report says, "a white, late-model Kia," because the investigating officers obviously watch too much TV, every Kia's a late model—ran the light and swerved toward them, perhaps even at them. Numerous witnesses agree the driver seemed enraged, his face livid.

In an upstairs window of a nearby building, a young man was standing on the balcony, out for a smoke. He claimed the driver sped up before impact, "like he meant it," the young man, Thomas Perry, repeated on the news. There were four passengers in the vehicle, three wedged in the backseat.

Christmas and Sarah Wasserman struggled. Were they pulling one another this way or that? Was something else happening?

Contact. The bumper, the hood, the roof of the car, and then her body rolled off sideways, her head hit the curb…

The driver of the car never stopped.

A number of witnesses recalled especially the faces of the people in the backseat as the car accelerated out of the intersection. Thomas Perry reported that the three passengers twisted around to look through the back window. The three passengers and the driver were easily identified later by witnesses, although one of the backseat passengers was made to identify the front seat passenger. The politics of murder.

Thomas Perry didn't say more on the news, but I can see them in my mind's eye, the three passengers and their open, empty faces. When human sympathy leaves us, we have such an empty look—I think we can see those people, they're on TV all of the time.

●

The day of Christmas' death was a bright, hot day. I was home, working on the Comprehensive Plan, as enjoined by the State of Maryland under Article 66B. The Saxon Hills town planner, my boss Greg Rossi, had assigned me the water and sewer assessment—in truth, he was pretty much willing to have me write the whole damn plan while he read bestsellers and took two-hour lunches at Santiago's—and I had colonized my dining room table with blueprints and spreadsheets. I liked to work this way, even though the air conditioning in my rented house was set on High and only capable of Low.

I was wearing shorts and a tank top but still sweating. I remember thinking, when the police rang the bell, came inside, stood everywhere, stood next to me, were too close to me, I couldn't move, they were everywhere, that the dripped sweat on the spreadsheets looked like bird shit. Memory's a bitch, Aunt Nikki.

Of course, Christmas became in my dreams the deer of my childhood, getting hit by a truck. I had been that deer for so long, and now it was Christmas.

•

"Christmas was a smart girl who wanted to be a fashion designer."

"Christmas was tall for her age."

"Christmas had seen a lot of hurt."

"Christmas' best grades were in math."

"Everyone who met her thought she was at least sixteen."

"Christmas was going to start a babysitting business."

"Christmas wouldn't eat fish."

"Christmas hated her mother."

"When she was killed, Christmas was still covered in glitter from the music festival the day before, which she must have sneaked into (because she didn't have fifty dollars, the cost of the ticket, that's for sure)."

"Christmas' taste in music was..."

"Christmas liked to..."

"Christmas' favorite movie was..."

"Christmas' favorite memory of her father was..."

"Christmas used to..."

So many of those pronouncements fail to find an object. Who was she? The paint was still wet, at thirteen. I have heard the news reports, I make myself talk with the occasional person who met her, the authorities have shared some information with me, and I simply don't understand. I feel like I'm trying to look at a picture of a girl in a locked museum, the lights are off and I'm standing in the bushes, at the window, and all I can see of the figure is a thin sheen of the moon in the reflected glass. The moon can be so bright, so far away and bright.

Because I was not her mother, and didn't claim to be, and she and I only lived together for five weeks, I barely glimpsed who she was. She never trusted me enough to share.

Not that I blame her: I don't trust myself either.

I suspect that one of her skills, what Christmas was capable of, perhaps as a result of the object lesson provided by her lying, meth-head mother, might have been an ability to figure out whom to trust, who among the grown-ups would let her down. Is this a skill a child learns when the child has to fend for herself too early? It's a kind of street smarts—although that's a joke about town planners, that we have street smarts. Could she smell bad people, get up her dander like a wild animal who knows?

Don't get me started on Nature versus Nurture.

I let her die too soon. What I suspect about myself: when I got Christmas, I had already made her death into a done deal, and that led me to ignore who she was as a living girl. She was Otto's daughter, Otto was dead, there was Otto in Christmas, and I couldn't stand that Otto was dead. Or I was protecting myself, because she was a temporary person, only alive for a little while longer.

There is another version of the story, one in which I don't blame myself so much. There may not be ways to forgive oneself, but I can see how Christmas was only Christmas, in pain, returning to the wild, doing what she needed to do, and I (accidentally, blindly) let her. I was here for her, and once or twice, she came to me. Maybe that was all the wild girl could handle, in terms of intimacy.

•

Every night, I sleep in the closet of the spare bedroom upstairs. It's a tight space, not a walk-in, with a small shelf above the clothing bar. I have removed the hangers—I would hate getting up to pee in the middle of the night and banging my head on the hangers, or hearing their ringing in my dreams. I wheeled an old desk chair into the closet, removed the ant traps from the floor, and I laid out my cotton blanket as though readying a bed. Each night, I yank the string to the bare bulb overhead, settle into the chair, the darkness mine, and there I am. The closet smells faintly of potpourri, or maybe some old woman's perfumed rayon blouses hung there too long. Old lady smells. But I try not to let anyone else's body into my closet—no hands, no feet, no shirts or shoes, no one reaching in—when I go to sleep. Sometimes I think that the closet smells like popcorn.

Well into my teens, I tried to sleep in regular beds. In my twenties, I didn't, and some of my sexual behavior (in retrospect) seems to have been a mild kink related to other people's bedrooms. Then other people's bodies became a problem.

Now, in my thirties, I've tried again. For too long, the worst part of the first month in Saxon Hills, I tried to sleep in the queen bed in the master bedroom downstairs. That was obviously the right bed, I would tell myself; be gone, fears. I was working on the whole being, brain first. Cognitive behavioral restructuring.

I walled off one side of the real bed with pillows wrapped in a blanket, to make the space tighter and safe. Even still, too frequently in the night I would forget, and think that the lump was a lover—there were hands, feet, breathing—and I would hyperventilate until I remembered no one could be there.

Walled off and wedged, the pillows my protection, I nonetheless felt the bed a sacrificial platform on which I was laid exposed. It's been a new thought, and not good. But I kept up the pretense. As though I could simply live normally, I would set a glass of water on my night table, a boring biography of a politician to fall asleep to, a pair of cheaters, a flashlight, and my alarm clock, the dial covered with a sock. No need for a girly gun under the pillow; violence has never been my forte.

Now, again, I sleep in the smallest space I can make mine. I am not a survivor: that's what I tell myself when I go to sleep in my chair in the closet. Who needs to be a survivor? I just need some goddamn sleep.

Christmas asked me right away about my closet. "That closet thing. What's with that?"

"I...I sleep there," I answered. "None of your business. I have to."

We were at the grocery store together, having driven all day the day before, an awful day, hauling her stuff to Saxon Hills in a garbage bag in the trunk of my car, our new relationship at a ceasefire only when she jammed her stupid earbuds in her ears and we both could be silent. Now, day two, she was already refusing to say what she wanted for dinner, so I was pissed.

"That's screwed up," she said. She put two big bottles of pop in the cart, no eye contact.

"Okay, it's screwed up."

"That's fucked up. You need help."

I tried to laugh. "But you're okay? You're just so sane, aren't you, Beatrice?"

She slammed a bag of Oreos too hard into the cart, breaking the cookies for sure, the bag popping. "I'm Christmas."

"So we're doing my problems, not yours?" I asked. I reached into the cart and took out the Oreos, I wasn't buying those.

Christmas was quiet for a short time as I wheeled our cart through the canned vegetables aisle, through soups. I was so bad at this. I couldn't help calling her Beatrice, to make a useless point.

We arrived at checkout. There was a line of shoppers, a pimply cashier.

"I hate you," Christmas finally said softly, her meanest words almost always delivered in a whisper. "Fucking bitch."

She elbowed past me, around a young mother and child, and out the store's automatic door into the searing weather, waves of heat visibly undulating from the asphalt and the cars in the parking lot.

Christmas on fire, I thought.

Only weeks later did it occur to me that her nausea had probably been severe, that shopping for groceries couldn't have been fun. She had thrown up that morning, even, and I had dragged her to the grocery store.

I was always pissed at her, those first few weeks. Yes, she treated me like shit—as though I were her reprobate mother and not her well-intentioned godmother. But I think I was mostly furious at her for dying, for being the daughter of my beloved dead brother, who died, he died, he was dead, and for bringing her own imminent death, along with the pressure of love, into my quiet house. Christmas and I were both under pressure to love each other, and neither of us was thrilled. We were both Danzigs, full of Danzig emotions. We might love each other some day, but neither of us asked for this.

If Christmas had any nightmares, I never knew. I was too clenched in my blanket, deep in my safety chair, desperately trying to sleep, wanting to be safe, and I had given her my bedroom on the first floor, so we were a world apart. For me to sleep, no one else could be there.

She did say "Thank you" when I showed her to her room.

In our five weeks together, she said many nastier things to me, usually reserved for the moment she went out the front door. I suspect she often waited for me to come home from work, and then she would leave while saying something awful to make a point; sometimes, though, she would simply be gone when I returned, to make the same point differently. Either way, she was never there. She would never text me back.

How to tell a thirteen-year-old who has lost her hair to chemo that I stopped dyeing my hair Clairol Red Hot Red in sympathy?

We went shopping for clothes. Under ordinary circumstances, I find the West House Mall terrifying, my agoraphobia fully activated, set off by the indoor shopping experience. The atria were hung with lights and banners and cartoon characters, colors and neon everywhere, right on top of me, the wheelchair ramps and pop-up kiosks and mall walkers, the incessant voice-overs, the music a horror show. The pumped-in smells, the swirly patterns in the heinous carpeting—it all was designed for the person I am least like. I knew, too, that I would again never find my car out there in the parking lot. We would never get home. But I had offered to buy her clothes, and Christmas insisted on the mall. At least that once, she had agreed to accept some credit card love.

She was trying on a bathing suit in one of those generic stores. They all have the same names—Forever, Unlimited, Eternal, Future, Endless, Boundless. They all sell costume jewelry bound to break, the plastic beads spilling on the checkered linoleum, rolling into oblivion. I'd be the one on my hands and knees trying to pick up those beads; that's what the store sells me.

Christmas was never going to be someone else, I realized, as she rang back the little blue curtain to model for me the hideous one-piece. There was no promise.

Wow, I was in a foul mood, I realized.

"Great," I said. "Let's buy it." My phone buzzed, a text from Rossi. "Hold on, hold on," I said.

"Great how?" She turned around to flaunt her nonexistent ass, elbows in, palms out.

I texted Rossi back. "Great color," I said. "It's flattering."

"You're not even looking," she said. "You're on your phone."

"I was looking...hold on." Rossi needed to reply: it was important.

"No!" Christmas said. "Aunt Nikki..." She scowled at herself in the triple mirrors. "It's the worst. I'm gray."

"Well..." I thought I might put my hand on her shoulder.

Christmas looked ready to cry. "Aunt Nikki..."

"It's bad," I admitted. I looked at her more carefully, checking how she took it. "Color matching is going to be a challenge," I said, half a joke. We made eye contact as I stealthily turned off my phone.

Then I spun around again to face the store, more demons to come, including my own. My back was to her: I closed my eyes to gird myself. "Let's try somewhere else. Come on, girl. Nothing here goes with cancer."

Finally, Christmas laughed.

•

Before Christmas was gone twelve hours, the news broke, and with shame and blame and horror, Saxon Hills joined the twenty-first century. An anonymous caller had led the police to the hit-and-run vehicle, a stolen car hidden in a garage at a house in the woods north of Saxon Hills, just past the abandoned quarry. For an unidentified reason related to the information in the original phone call, Homeland Security had been alerted. By the middle of the night, the house had been raided by multiple federal and local agencies, resulting in the arrests of sixteen people on the premises, and later, four more people living in Saxon Hills, a long list of felony charges, including various acts of domestic terrorism, and a serious and self-satisfied press conference. More warrants were issued for people in other homes in other areas. The conspiracy was national.

Automatic weapons, homemade explosive devices, and plans to attack the local middle school as well as the First Church of the Holy Spirit, a local black church with seven hundred parishioners, had been discovered upstairs in the house, which the anchorwoman on the news described as the outpost of a cult that had become a terrorist cell. The terrorists had a "war room," the newswoman said. The cult's leader, a man known as Jebediah Farley, among other aliases, was subsequently arrested attempting to board a Greyhound bus at the Eleventh Street depot in Pittsburgh.

Among the detainees was nineteen-year-old Sarah Wasserman, of no fixed address, the woman who had struggled with Christmas in the crosswalk.

Had anyone pushed anyone into the path of the Kia? Was the driver of the Kia hunting, running down Sarah or Christmas? Had Sarah killed Christmas?

Or, maybe, had Christmas saved Sarah?

•

I go through periods of managed anxiety, and at times, when I feel better, I come off my meds, usually just after their effects on my life become intolerable. Ritual and repetition are my recourse. I keep my sunglasses, my sunscreen, my keys, my wallet, my lip balm, an extra scarf, my antibacterial gel, my pepper spray, my dental floss, my travel toothbrush and mini paste, and my mascara all in the exact same place in the hallway every day, below a row of ready purses hung on hooks. The purses might be color-coded on their hooks, but that would be admitting too much.

That was a little joke.

As soon as I'm in the door, I empty whatever purse I'm carrying. I place each item in its spot on the tabletop built into the umbrella-

cum-shoe stand. My entrance is complete, arranged. Only then can I face my house, having performed my welcome home devotions, and revel for the rest of the evening in the stillness of domestic life alone.

Christmas learned this about me right away, and on occasion she would surreptitiously move an item, even just an inch or two, askew. Mean, mean, mean.

One evening, early on, I tried to speak to her about it. "You know—"

"Here it comes."

"Christmas. Don't be like that."

We had dragged two folding chairs into the backyard and were sitting there until the fireflies came out. Or I was—I didn't really know what she was doing.

"My stuff. In the front hall."

Christmas started to laugh.

"What if I fucked with your garbage bag?"

She stopped laughing. "You wouldn't."

"You should unpack. What if I threw out your bear purse? That's all I'm saying. You live here."

I used the wrong word. I said "live."

"This ain't living, Aunt Nikki." Christmas made a series of sounds, her beatbox, and then rapped: "*Pah, pu, pu, pu.* That's all yo sayin', but I'm not stayin'."

●

A news reporter tried to find Christmas' mom, but I wasn't going to help. I called a few cousins and let them know I would be okay alone. My parents were devastated—their son had died, and now their only granddaughter, although they knew about the cancer, of course—and yet they debated making the trip from their Michigan cabin. My father's diabetes was under control, although he found long drives un-comfortable and the next day worse. Having arrived home at their cabin just a month ago, after helping me close the apartment in DC, then stopping to visit friends in Ohio, they clearly didn't want to leave, or face Saxon Hills ever again. I wanted them here, but I couldn't ask, so I promised them a memorial service at the cabin, where we could be together again, and I'd bring Christmas' ashes.

My parents and I took turns being shell-shocked on the phone, unable to speak for long periods of time. During those endless si-lences on speakerphone, never-ending absences filled with the purest emptiness of grief, I could only stare at the phone too, that thing in my hand.

Thankfully, the news media weren't particularly interested in me, probably because I wasn't listed anywhere as her guardian, "godmoth-er" our unofficial title with her junkie mom still alive. I kept my front door closed, and the human interest story of the dead girl with the ter-rorist conspiracy who was killed by a hit-and-run played better without me. That Christmas had martyred herself—even though "we'll never know" was the popular tagline—seemed to be a favorite take.

I have another notion. I think Christmas' death was stolen from us. Let's say she saved Sarah Wasserman, that they were friends and Christmas pushed Sarah to safety. Who knows—we weren't given the opportunity to be there. But if that's how it happened, I still don't see her death as very Christian. She didn't die for anyone's sins, despite what the news likes to imply. If anything, if she saved Sarah, Christmas owes me an apology. She took her dying from me, kept me from helping her. It's like that Internet meme: one job. She took my one job.

Sometimes, I think of her like a girl in a fairy tale. Go do some-thing in the woods, they always tell the girl in the fairy tale, and you'll come back a hero with a prince for a husband. It's nice to think of her this way—that she was in the fairy tale, but she never got out of the woods. Besides, she was in my life so little, she felt a little made up.

I am a town planner, and I know enough about demographics to understand the phenomenon of the cluster. Poorly insulated high-tension wires stretch over a neighborhood and the incidences of leukemia increase, the children miss more school, dental bills soar. Toxic landfills, downriver runoff to bespoil the drinking water, buried electronics, acid rain in a concentrated weather pattern, just a morsel of noxious metabolites in industrial emissions...we know too well what these insults to the environment entail for our public health and concentrated morbidity. Even a conspiracy theorist can be right; even a dismantled EPA could offer up the science.

In truth, Christmas was a cluster unto herself. This one young person drew to herself the violence of human behavior and bad fortune. No, I don't think she was merely unlucky. But I also don't know what to do with my newfound belief, or this pseudoscience (which I know cannot be true, which seems to me an intuition I will never corroborate). Not a girl in a fairy tale, not a martyr, not unlucky— who was she? What do I do now?

It's true my grieving seems to have layers and pockets, grief within grief, mourning both Otto and Christmas, their deaths collapsed in my heart into one event. I didn't know Christmas, and so it's Otto I miss, but saying so makes everything worse.

Here's a question: did she know she was so close to dying?

Here's another question: did she know what Sarah Wasserman was up to, what the cult was planning?

Here's another question: do my compulsions make my behaviors excusable?

One more: Christmas became her illness, her emotions victim to her sickness. Shouldn't a person be forgiven her body?

●

One evening toward the end, I came home from work to find Christmas had ordered a pizza (my money, my earlier suggestion) and that she had eaten all but half of one remaining slice, leaving me no dinner. Her behavior seemed the most willful yet, looking Aunt Nikki right in the eye.

We fought about the pizza and other things, I don't recall what, and I ordered another pizza, just because, and she stomped out of the house.

Later, I went to sleep in my chair in my closet. I tried clutching a memory and then wrapping it carefully, folded in a piece of paper, and letting the gift float away on the tide. The tide wasn't really my thing, I like the mountains more than the ocean. I tried letting the piece of paper float away in a little river, or a creek or something; carried downstream, too, I let the memory float. That seemed to be helping.

I heard a scream. Christmas was home—something was wrong. There were terrible sounds.

I found her in the hallway with her back to the bedroom door. She was panting and wide-eyed. She was clutching her purple hat.

"Aunt Nikki!" she stage-whispered. "They're in there!"

"What?"

We opened the door to see two furious raccoons. They hissed and spit and we gasped. We slammed the door.

She had left open her bedroom window, and a slice of rubbery pizza on a plate on her bed. She had come home quietly—or not, I was in my closet—to find two raccoons on her bed, sharing the pizza and squabbling. The raccoons had been furious and aggressive, snarling at her, and once the light was turned on, they forgot which way they had gotten in. They squealed and chittered and spit and ran around, and now they were ready to bite us to death.

"I think they're lost," I said.

Christmas began to giggle.

"Oh, don't laugh," I warned her. I began to laugh too.

"Jesus," Christmas said. "I'm screwed," Christmas said. "That was the slice I saved you." She began to laugh and laugh. "I was going to put it in your briefcase. *Not.*"

It was funny, beyond funny. We both were in hysterics.

Ultimately, I cut off the circuit breaker, thinking that in the darkness, the raccoons would find their exit window. They could eat the pizza or take it with them, to go.

I gave Christmas a pair of safety goggles I found in the tool drawer, who knows who had left them. She pulled down her purple hat. I considered wearing a colander, but that was too sitcom—instead, I put on my bike helmet. We had on winter gloves, she wore a hoodie and I had a big scarf wrapped around my neck and shoulders like a saint's chainmail. We were armed with pots and wooden spoons (mine a spatula-spoon), banging our absurdities in the hallway to scare the raccoons away. It worked. They either finished or took the pizza; the plate was empty.

Scaring them off was the best moment. We were together. We cried tears of hysterical delight. Banging on our pots and hollering in the darkness, wedged against her bedroom wall and drumming on our pots and yelling, we were touching, our shoulders, our hips, and we leaned into one another.

●

Men play games I don't like. My boss, Greg Rossi, is a prime example: he can dick around when directness is required. Unfortunately, the day after the news broke, he and I needed to be in contact a lot, texting and talking on the phone, to figure out what to do about the Comprehensive Plan and the imminent deadline, as I was too much a wreck to know if or when I could continue. At least he expressed sympathy. But when he texted me to say "Answer your door," I wasn't happy.

Rossi's a sweaty white guy with a classic comb-over. He's a familiar sort from an old Saxon Hills Italian family. He's going to retire soon, he keeps saying—that's what I was promised, I would be the inside candidate for the town planner job and a significant raise. But no one can afford to retire today.

There he stood on my doorstep, along with two older black people, a man and a woman. All three of them had their hands full, bearing gifts.

"Hi, Nikki. I'm just dropping off," said Greg. He lifted his hands to show me a dish covered with foil. "It's Carol's lasagna. Maybe you have the Assessment?" His voice rose with the question. "I thought I might take it? Can I have it?"

"Hello, dear, may we come in?" The woman had sparkly eyes. She was also carrying a covered dish.

"Miss Danzig," the other man said. "We've brought dinner." He too had a foil-covered food container, which made me abandon all hope of cake, my weakness. "We are so sorry for your loss. I am the Reverend Dr. Henry Hines, of the First Church of the Holy Spirit, and this is my outreach coordinator, Mrs. Emily Johnson. Excuse us. Could we lay these down? They're heavy. May we have a word?"

"Nikki?"

"Miss Danzig?"

I guess I hadn't spoken yet. "Sorry, yes, of course. Come in. Hello."

For Rossi to leave quickly, I had to liberate my dining room table, stack the water and sewer eval pages without anyone seeing my hands shake. Hide my life, maybe.

I showed my visitors the kitchen, to lay down their burdens, but then Greg disappeared for a moment—oh no, where was he?—only to arrive once more at the front door, come back inside bearing an ugly old orange Igloo cooler marked with masking tape and pen: ICED TEA. He nodded at me as he walked by. He looked scared.

Me too.

"You keep a lovely home," Mrs. Johnson said as she came from the kitchen, a potholder in each hand. "Dr. Hines?" She looked around for her associate.

The Reverend Dr. Hines followed her out through the kitchen's swinging door. "Mrs. Johnson," he said. "Miss Danzig." He strode into the living room, swept his hand toward the couch. "Let's sit."

These three people were everywhere. That preacher was too big for my house, I thought.

"Nikki?" Rossi had to say again.

"Yes," I said. "Please. Sorry." I gave him the papers I had been clutching.

"Okay!" Rossi said. "If this is the Assessment, I'm outta your hair."

I had never seen Greg Rossi move so fast, waving over his shoulder as he fled. Man moves that fast, he won't ever retire.

"Here." Mrs. Johnson had somehow poured me a glass of iced tea. She patted the sofa next to her. Hines had already fallen into an armchair. I sat, sipped the tea. Too sweet.

Rossi better not have touched any of my stuff on the hall table.

"Miss Danzig, I can see that you're not sociably inclined at the moment. We won't keep you."

He was deep in my green Ikea chair. I used to like that chair. Once upon a time, that was my chair.

He took another big gulp of his iced tea. "Let us get to the reason we've gathered together. Your niece's death is an awful matter, but she has gone to be with the Lord Jesus Christ Our Savior."

"I'm not a Christian," I mustered.

"Yes," he said. "We know. It's why we're here."

"Don't," I said, and moved to stand up—but Mrs. Johnson put her hand out calmly, wait, everything's fine.

"We would like to hold a Unity Rally in town," Mrs. Johnson said, lowering her hand. "It's not a funeral. It's non-denominational. Miss Danzig—"

"She can't have a service in our church," the Reverend Dr. Hines interjected. "We can't do that."

Get out, I wanted to cry.

"Those cult people, they were going to slaughter the lambs," he added. "Innocents. My flock…"

"Miss Danzig," Mrs. Johnson began again. "It will be for everyone. No one has to be a Christian. The mayor wants to say a word or two. It will start the healing of Saxon Hills."

"Christmas…" I began to say, and then I realized the rally had already been planned—this was a courtesy call.

"Yes," the reverend said gravely.

"With your blessing, we hope," Mrs. Johnson said. Now her hands were folded so nicely in her lap. "Maybe you will join us? The Unity Rally has the town's go-ahead. Christmas…well, she touched so many of us."

"She did?"

I didn't know what to do with that. It sat there like another casserole.

"I don't know," I said. "I won't have to speak?"

"Of course not." Dr. Hines laughed. "I can talk enough for the Devil's army!"

"Miss Danzig," Mrs. Johnson said softly. "I'll be with you the whole time. Would you like that? Arm in arm, I won't let you go. We'll soldier on. Miss Danzig, my nephew met your Christmas once. He liked her so. We're all family here." She smiled. "It's what we do in Saxon Hills."

I was trying to believe her smile. That's what I focused on, believing what I could see.

•

There is a band shell downtown, and a goodly expanse of lawn for summer Pops concerts. Green spaces are my specialty, and as such, I actually liked this part of the Saxon Hills downtown area, its peacefulness at the edge of Memorial Park, the creek, the footbridge, the slight slant of the broad lawn in front of the open structure to allow for sightlines and proper drainage, the tile done right. Walking towns—I like that shift in urban design. But we were too close to the famous intersection. Everything was too close to everything else, even outside.

A rainbow flag had been hung from the front of the band shell, with the word TOGETHER in script in the bow of the rainbow.

I liked the banner. That was a surprise.

Amplifiers had been set up on either side of the microphone on stage, and row upon row of folding chairs waited at attention, the town maintenance crews still unloading the chairs when I walked through at 5 p.m. I knew those guys, or maybe just their boss. The first three rows of seats in the right and left orchestra areas were taped off, as were the first couple of rows in the center, another twenty seats for dignitaries. I thought I would be seated in the taped-off section in the center—so maybe the other sections were for the choirs? Surely there would be singing.

I didn't know what had made me leave my house to scope out the venue, but here I was, two hours early. I had decided that if they used Christmas' picture on a poster, or on flyers, I would object. Or I could draw a moustache on her—or give her gray hair to match her skin tone.

I was crazy with grief. I knew it. Days of grief, grief for Otto, weeks of grieving with her alive, and now, another grief. Standing there, unable to be anywhere else.

I didn't want to be there, and there I was, hours early.

"Hey," a voice behind me spoke. "I'm Sam."

I turned to see a young couple, in their early twenties, holding hands, looking at the empty stage. He was much taller than she.

"This is Liana."

"Hi," she said.

"We knew her, you know," Sam said. He laughed to himself. "I caught her shoplifting."

I didn't want them to know me. I said nothing.

"I've gotta go to work," Sam said. "We thought we'd stop by."

"Me too," I was able to say.

"Shame," said Liana.

"Shame," said Sam. "She was a cool kid."

I don't know what I did, or where I walked, except I avoided West Starkweather. I bought a bottle of water, I sat somewhere for a while. I had heels on, a mistake: blisters for sure, although a good long walk might have let me miss the whole rally. There were already people in the seats, and on blankets behind where the rows of chairs ended, up the hill, when I returned. There was music playing.

It was too early again. I couldn't go sit in the front row, I wouldn't.

I turned around again, walked away again, walked around a block, past the post office, over by the CVS, past a shuttered family grocery, the family longtime Saxon Hillers, a portent of the town's future, the big box stores coming in, the working poor sure to struggle. I checked the time on my phone.

I was being Christmas, I realized. Walking and skipping out and ducking out and showing up and walking and walking. Never texting Aunt Nikki, never answering a question directly, a simple, polite question such as *How are you?*

I was a deer looking for a truck.

There was a choir in robes in the front of the stage, the sections each being handed their repertoire in a black folder by a director, her collar up but not priestly, and some high school kids were monkeying around with the microphone, one of them wearing a technician's headset.

"Miss Danzig…"

I turned. "Hi." I would speak brightly.

"I'm glad you're joining us," said Mrs. Johnson. "You look so nice." I nodded.

She took my elbow. "There's someone who wants to meet you. Would that be okay?"

No. I started to shake my head.

"Miss Danzig, only for a minute. See all of those men? She's with them."

I looked where Mrs. Johnson was pointing. There were a lot of older men filing in, they kept coming, maybe forty, fifty, a phalanx of men in colored T-shirts, different teams from something, many with their wives or girlfriends, some with kids too.

"Who are they?"

"Nikki Danzig, Meg O'Daly…"

I hadn't felt like I was walking, but I had walked.

"Miss Danzig, I'm Meg O'Daly, I knew your niece. She was a fine girl. She had such thoughts, such an individual. How do you do? I'm so sorry for your loss…" She kept on talking. "I brought my boys," she said, indicating all of the men and their wives and girl-friends. "She was special to me, and my boys are here…"

"Thank you," I said.

She seemed to run out of words suddenly. "Senior softball," she added.

"Thank you."

Here it was, and here I was, and life was happening to me. Christmas' life was ending in us. How someone else's life ends in us—I hadn't considered that idea before, only that a person died a person.

There was the Reverend Dr. Hines, there were two rows of police officers, Rossi was there, the Hmong family from the carwash, the school board would probably be somewhere, the town council. Maybe someone really knew her.

Just as the choir started to sing the National Anthem, and the crowd stood to join the singing, my body chose otherwise. I closed my eyes. They wouldn't see me, standing in the front row, leaning on Mrs. Johnson, they wouldn't know. If I can't see them, they can't see me, my body decided.

In my head, I opened a door to my upstairs closet, safe. Saxon Hills could hold us now. In my head, there were two chairs ready, two blankets and two pillows. The bare bulb with the string pull. There was music playing around me, drums and horns and earnest words in the mid-summer heat, but no one could come in, I only had two chairs, one each.

There was Christmas, with me. We would keep our eyes closed together and see.

She was covered in glitter, as she had been when I had gone to identify her body.

Her body. I held her body in my arms. A little girl's body.

The music was louder. I shook against it. They couldn't have her.

In my head, I reached up, found the light string, and gave it a good yank.

ACKNOWLEDGMENTS

I am grateful for the support and the expertise of many people, without whom this book would have been a disaster:

Sandra Beasley, The University of Tampa, Tampa, FL

Ben Benshoof, Town of Huntersville Parks & Rec, Huntersville, NC

Jonathan Berkey, Davidson College, Davidson, NC

Keyne Cheshire, Davidson College, Davidson, NC

Matt Churchill, Robinson, Bradshaw & Hinson, P.A., Charlotte, NC

Lincoln Davidson, Davidson College, Davidson, NC

John Hamman, Montgomery College, Montgomery County, MD

Tristan Kirvin, Communications and Events Manager, The Corportion of Yaddo, Saratoga Springs, NY

Susan Leet, Registrar, Bailey Middle School, Davidson, NC

Patrick Lynch, Store Manager, Ace Hardware, Cornelius, NC

Officer Scott Misenheimer, Police Department, Town of Davidson, Davidson, NC

Bjorn Ordoubadian, Davidson College, Davidson, NC

Felicia van Bork, Parker/van Bork Incorporated, Davidson, NC

And to the woolly, adorable beasts of Dzanc Books, Michelle Dotter, Guy Intoci, and Michael Seidlinger, *mille grazie.* Thanks too to the American Academy in Rome, Davidson College, the Corporation of Yaddo, and the Virginia Center for the Creative Arts.